MOUNTAIN RESCUE

SANDRA OWENS

carina
press

**carina
press®**

Recycling programs
for this product may
not exist in your area.

ISBN-13: 978-1-335-40185-4

Mountain Rescue

Copyright © 2021 by Sandra Owens

Carina Press
22 Adelaide St. West, 41st Floor
Toronto, Ontario M5H 4E3, Canada
www.CarinaPress.com

Printed in U.S.A.

This book is dedicated to every reader
who has said, "Just one more chapter!"
(I think that covers all the book lovers in the world.)

MOUNTAIN RESCUE

Chapter One

The passengers on the red-eye from Salt Lake City to Atlanta were asleep. All but Dallas Manning. He didn't trust his nightmares. They were persistent fuckers, rarely allowing him to sleep through the night. The three weeks he'd been home at his family's ranch in Montana, his screams had disturbed his family's sleep, too. He wasn't about to chance scaring the hell out of a plane full of strangers.

Unable to take another day of his family alternating between smothering him and tiptoeing around him, he'd jumped on his friend's invitation to come to Asheville, North Carolina. Not that he blamed his family for their worry. He was damn lucky to be alive after enjoying a two-week stay at Hotel Hell on Earth as a guest of the Taliban. He snorted. *Enjoying*. Yeah, right. But he'd survived the torture, the starvation, and the mind games.

His body was a bit messed up, and he'd have permanent scars, but he'd held strong, never giving his captors more than his name, rank, service number, and birthdate. If his SEAL team hadn't found him when they did, he didn't doubt for a minute that he'd be dead by now. His captors, frustrated and angry that he wasn't spilling his secrets, had been growing more creative by the day in their efforts to make him talk. The bastards' last gift to him was the damn nightmares. After the first one his family witnessed, they'd treated him differently.

He couldn't take their pity, their need to baby him, never mind that he was the youngest. He was a damn SEAL, not a baby needing coddling. He loved his family, would willingly die for them, but his former teammate's invitation felt like a lifeline.

Jack Daniels had started a foundation, Operation K-9 Brothers, training service dogs for their military brothers and sisters suffering from PTSD. Another former teammate was also working there with Jack. If anyone could understand what Dallas had gone through and what he was dealing with now, it would be his SEAL brothers. One thing he could count on, neither man would try to baby him.

In Atlanta, he changed planes, cramming his body into the seat of the commuter plane that would take him to Asheville. Fortunately, the last leg of his trip only lasted an hour. He had difficulty being in small places thanks to the two weeks he'd spent in a cell where he could stand in the middle and reach all four walls. After deplaning and getting his suitcase, he headed for the short-term parking lot and found the Jeep where Jack had said it would be. When he had refused Jack's offer to pick him up, since he was arriving in the middle of the night, Jack had insisted on loaning him one of Operation K-9 Brothers' vehicles.

After tossing his suitcase and carry-on in the back, he got in the Jeep, then reached under the seat for the envelope with the keys and address to the cabin. Jack had invited him to stay with him and his new wife, but

Dallas needed a place of his own, where he could get away from people when he needed to.

Turned out Operation K-9 Brothers owned a cabin, and Jack had said he could stay there. He programed the cabin address in the GPS, adjusted the seat and mirrors, then headed out.

Thirty-five minutes later, he pulled to a stop in front of a small log house. He couldn't see much of it in the dark, but he didn't care what it or the surrounding area looked like. It was a place to crash and hide out for a while.

Inside, he dropped his suitcase, found a light switch, and glanced around. The place had an open floor plan, living room, dining room, and kitchen. It wasn't as rustic as he was expecting, and he was kind of disappointed. A stone fireplace on one wall with floor-to-ceiling windows along both sides were the best part of the place. The furniture was sturdy and basic. Brown leather couch, two leather recliners, TV, and coffee table in the living room, and a dinette with four chairs next to the kitchen. Deciding to unpack in the morning, he left the suitcase, and taking his carry on, headed down the hall.

The first room he came to was a bathroom, and he made a pit stop, then checked out the next one. The bedroom had twin beds, a dresser, one chair, and a TV mounted on the wall. He continued on to see if there was a room with a bigger bed.

He'd taken two steps into the next room and was reaching for a light switch when something came at him. Instinctively, he dropped his carry-on and put a hand up, wrapping his fingers around what felt like the rough bark of a tree branch. He pulled it to him, bringing his attacker with it, and found himself with an arm full of enraged wildcat in possession of a woman's body.

She went for his eyes, and he grabbed her wrists, gentling his hold so that he didn't bruise her. When she tried to knee him, he flipped her around and wrapped his arms around her, her back to his chest.

"I'm rather fond of that part of me, sugar."

Robert's people had found her, and this was the day she was going to die. Rachel Denning refused to make it easy on Robert Hargrove's man, though. She stomped on his foot, but because she was barefoot and he wore boots, that was about as effective as slapping his face with a feather.

A fight scene from a previous movie where the villain had her in a similar hold flashed through her mind. In the scene, she'd gotten away by slamming the back of her head into his nose.

The problem with that scenario was that this man was a good head taller than her, so no way she could reach his nose. His chin, maybe, but it was worth a try, better than doing nothing. She leaned her head forward, then slammed it back as hard as she could, taking satisfaction when he grunted. Unfortunately, the stunt worked better in the movie.

"Easy, wildcat. I'm not going to hurt you."

Yeah, right, and unicorns existed. "Let go of me." He wouldn't, she knew asking was futile, but it was all she had. He was stronger than she was and had her in a hold she couldn't escape.

Keeping one arm around her, he reached for the light switch, and she blinked against the sudden brightness. Then he lifted her right off her feet as if she weighed less than a bag of potatoes, carried her to the bed, and dropped her. Facedown on the rumpled cover, she waited for the blow…or whatever he planned to do to her. Oh, God, what if he raped her?

No, she wasn't going to wait around to find out what he planned to do. She flipped to her back, searching for a weapon. When she'd arrived at the cabin, she'd gone out and found a tree branch, wanting something handy to protect herself if she had to. She should have brought the whole damn tree in.

She had a knife from the kitchen under her pillow. She hadn't started with that because she'd thought she would have a better chance with the branch. Her plan had been simple. Bash him upside the head and when he was out cold, disappear.

If she could get to the knife, maybe she could hurt him enough to escape. Keeping her attention on the man, she inched her hand toward the pillow. His gaze followed her hand before shifting back to her.

"You got a weapon under there? Go ahead. See if you can get to it before I have you in my arms again. Been a while since I've had this much fun." His smirk faded as his eyes held hers. "I meant what I said. I'm not going to hurt you." He chuckled. "Even though you did try to bash me in the head."

Something wasn't right. The man wasn't acting like a killer. The men who worked for Robert were as cruel as he was. They didn't tease, and if they called her anything besides her name, it would be bitch. They especially didn't smile as if they really were having fun. If he was one of Robert's men, he would just kill her and be done with it.

Now that she could study this man, he…well, he was gorgeous in a rough bad-boy kind of way. A trimmed beard, more like a few days of scruff really, covered his face. A fresh scar ran from the corner of his right eye and down his cheek before disappearing into his beard. She almost cringed at seeing how close he'd come to losing an eye.

No, she wasn't giving him her sympathy, not when he was here to hurt her. Yet his eyes weren't mean or cold. The only thing she could see in them was curiosity as he stared back at her. They were pretty eyes. Hazel, the kind that would change with the color of shirt he wore or his emotions. Dark brown hair in need of a haircut scraped across the neck of his T-shirt. Then there was a body worth drooling over.

Stop it, Rachel. Stop noticing how hot he is. She was totally stupid for letting her mind wander when there was danger in the room. Because, while he was a feast for the eyes, she had no doubt the man could be dangerous when he wanted. Still, he wasn't emitting dangerous vibes, and that confused her because if Robert had sent him, she should be dead by now.

"What do you want from me?"

His gaze slid over her body, those hazel eyes heating. "I have some ideas if you're interested in hearing them."

She had the distinct feeling that he was amused. Not at all how a man Robert would have sent would be acting. Also, that heated stare reminded her that she was wearing nothing but an almost transparent white T-shirt and purple panties. She grabbed the corner of the quilt and pulled it over her. Certain it would take at least a week for Robert to find her, and she planned to be long gone by then, she'd worn her favorite sleep shirt to bed. She should have slept fully dressed, and she wouldn't make that mistake again.

He laughed. "Too late." He pointed to his head. "Pretty in purple is already imprinted in here."

Best to ignore that comment. "Did Robert send you?"

"Who's Robert?"

It was weird, but she wasn't feeling threatened by him anymore…well, still a little, but not like when he'd first walked into the room in the dark. It was her first night here, and used to the night noises of LA, she'd been unsettled by the silence. It hadn't bothered her when she'd stayed here while attending Nichole and Jack's wedding, but she hadn't been someone's target then. This time, every creak the cabin made shot her nerves through the roof.

When she'd heard footsteps coming down the hallway, she'd thought her heart was going to stop. She hadn't known how Robert had found her so fast, but she wasn't going to go easy. That was what she'd thought, anyway, but in seconds, the man had shown her how unprepared and helpless she'd been.

His answer penetrated her mind. "Robert. The man who sent you."

"I don't know a Robert, and no one sent me."

"Who are you?"

He lifted his brows. "Who are you, and what are you doing in Jack's cabin?"

"You know Jack?"

"The question is, do you?" He glanced around. "You needed a place to stay…" Shrewd eyes landed back on her. "Maybe a place to hide out from this Robert person, so you broke in?"

"I did not break in," she said, affronted. Well, she kind of had, but not in the way he was insinuating. "Tell me something about Jack that proves you know him."

"Easy. He has a dog, Dakota. Jack was his team's dog handler until he and Dakota were hurt by a road-side bomb."

That was true. She supposed Robert could have found that out, but there would be no reason to pass that particular information on to his men. She still wasn't going to turn her back on this man, but she no longer believed he was here to hurt her.

"Now, back to you. If I call Jack and ask if he knows…what did you say your name was again?"

"Nice try, cowboy." There was that amusement again. Why? Because she'd called him a cowboy? He did make her think of one with those cowboy boots and that belt buckle with a bucking horse on it.

"I'll tell you mine if you tell me yours."

"That's fair, I guess, but only first names. I'm Rachel."

He tipped an imaginary hat. "Dallas at your service, Miss Rachel."

Jeez, the man even had a sexy cowboy name. "Okay, Dallas, if Robert didn't send you, why are you here?" *And please don't say you're planning to stay.*

"Same game. I'll tell you why if you reciprocate." Dallas sighed when she pressed her lips together, clearly having no intention of sharing.

He didn't know what to make of the woman. She was obviously afraid of this Robert person. An abusive boyfriend maybe, and that didn't sit well. She'd also obviously broken into Jack's cabin, but he wouldn't kick her out in the middle of the night or report her to Jack…at least, not yet. Tomorrow, he'd figure out what to do about her.

What he didn't appreciate was that the image of her

in those purple panties and a T-shirt so thin that he could see the outline of her nipples was imprinted in his mind. Long legs, honey-blond hair, and golden-brown eyes the color of Macallan—his favorite whiskey—did nothing to dim the desire that had shot through him as his gaze had roamed over her.

The intent had been to unnerve her, but the joke was on him. Purple might be his new favorite color, and that pissed him off. He didn't need an irresistible wildcat in his life, not now. He eyed the king bed she'd claimed, then sighed and turned to leave. It appeared it was going to be a twin for him.

"Where are you going?" she said.

"To the other room, unless you want to invite me to get in that nice big king with you."

She snorted. "Dream on."

"Was afraid you'd say that." He should have brought his cowboy hat on this trip so he could tip it to her. She had no clue she'd nailed it calling him cowboy. He tipped a nonexistent one. "Good night, wildcat."

"Wait. You didn't say why you're here."

"Visiting a friend for a while." He'd give her that much. "You?"

"You aren't going to call Jack, are you?"

So she was going to ignore his question. "Not tonight. I don't make any promises for tomorrow. Depends on what bullshit story you give me."

"You can't stay here."

He laughed. The woman really was amusing. "You're a funny girl." He stepped over the tree branch, picked up his carry-on, and closed the door behind him, pausing long enough to hear the click of the lock on her bedroom door. "Good girl," he murmured. He retrieved his suitcase—not that he didn't trust her, but why take a chance—and headed for the other bedroom, where he'd probably spend most of the night staring at the ceiling in a bed that was too short for him.

Who was Rachel, and how much danger was she in? The last thing he needed was a female in distress. Yet, he'd felt more alive while sparring with her than he'd felt since the day he'd been captured.

Not good that females in distress were his kryptonite.

The next morning, after a sleepless night—no surprise there—Dallas sat in a rocking chair on the porch and watched the sunrise. He liked that the cabin was isolated, surrounded by woods on three sides, with a clear view of the valley below from the front. No nosy neighbors wondering who he was or wanting to chat, a definite plus to his mind.

The Blue Ridge Mountains were the complete opposite of the mountains in Montana. Jack had stocked the kitchen, and as Dallas drank his coffee, he debated which he preferred, the beautiful, lush green and gentle slopes of the mountains here, or the rugged and desolate beauty of the ones at home.

From mountain comparisons, his mind turned to the woman in the king bed he coveted…the bed, not the woman. *Uh-huh. Keep telling yourself that.* He'd half expected Rachel to take off after she thought he would be asleep, but she was still here. Thanks to his captors, he'd gotten good at sensing the presence of others even when he couldn't see them. That skillset was apparently still active.

Little did she know if she'd tried to skip out on him, he would have been on her tail, something he would have cursed himself nine ways to Sunday for. But he would have done it anyway. He knew what it was like to be afraid, and she was one scared wildcat in need of protection, in spite of the bravado she tried to wrap around herself.

Also, she made him feel alive. For a man who was dead inside, that was as enticing as sugar water to a hummingbird. Would she tell him the truth today, or had she spent the night thinking up a bullshit story? He was looking forward to finding out.

He was on his second cup of coffee when his mystery woman walked out. She went straight to the railing without even a glance at him. "Morning."

"Oh." She faced him, leaning back on the railing. "You're still here?"

"As you can see. Wasn't sure you would be, though."

She looked away, shielding her eyes, but not before he saw the fear in them.

"You don't have any other place to go, do you?"

Determination was in those whiskey-colored eyes when her gaze returned to him. "I was here first. You find some other place to go."

"Give me one good reason I shouldn't tell Jack he has a squatter."

"How do you know Jack?"

He chuckled. "You're good at that, avoiding answering questions. Here's the deal. I'll answer a question for each one you do." He set the rocking chair in motion, sipped the last of his coffee, and waited her out. Not like he didn't have all the time in the world. Besides, she was keeping him entertained.

A full minute passed, then she sighed. "You're right, I don't have any other place to go. Not at the moment."

It was a start, but there was a whole lot of additional intel he intended to get out of her. "Okay, my turn. Jack and I were on the same SEAL team." Her eyes widened at that. *Surprised you, huh, wildcat?* "Who's Robert? An abusive boyfriend you're running from?"

"No. You could stay with Jack."

"Hurts my feelings how hard you're trying to get rid of me. Answer the rest of the question."

"You said one for one. I answered the second one."

"A technicality, but go ahead. Ask me something else." He liked that she was making him work for that intel he needed. She was no pushover, this one.

"Should I be afraid of you?"

Now, that was a question he wasn't expecting. "No, ma'am. My mama would skin my hide if I ever hurt a woman. What's the story on this abusive boyfriend of yours? Is he looking for you?"

"You're devious. You keep asking two questions."

He swallowed a smile. "My apology. Choose one." The last thing he'd expected from this trip was all the smiling his mouth wanted to do around this woman.

"Robert isn't my boyfriend." She crossed her arms, which resulted in pushing her breasts up, and being a man who happened to love breasts, his eyes fell to her chest before he could stop the rascally things.

"Eyes on mine, cowboy."

Heat flamed in his cheeks at being called out. He didn't mean to disrespect her. It was what men did with a woman who interested them, and however inconvenient, she definitely interested him. She had on jeans and the same thin white T-shirt from last night but had added a gray hoodie. Still no bra, and no complaint from him on that.

"Are you a cowboy?"

"I guess I can claim the title. Grew up on a working ranch. Rode some bucking broncs when I was young and reckless."

Her gaze fell to his stomach. "Is that a championship belt buckle?"

"Yep. Don't know if you've noticed, but you're two questions ahead of me now. If Robert isn't your boyfriend, then what is he to you and why are you afraid of him?"

"I'm tired of this game." She turned her back to him and stared at the mountains.

"No problem. I'll ask Jack if it's okay if you hang out here for a while."

She spun around. "No, please don't."

He thought that would get her attention. She didn't need to know that he'd already decided to keep her existence here a secret, at least until he found out why she was hiding and how much danger she was in. It concerned him that her trouble wasn't a boyfriend. Asshole boyfriends were easy to deal with. "Then give me a reason not to."

"You're a jerk, you know that?" She glared at him, and he was glad she didn't have that tree branch in her hands.

He swallowed another smile. Damn if he didn't like that fire in her eyes. "I've been called worse." Recently, in fact. His captors had had a long list of insulting names they'd thrown at him.

"Fine. Here's your reason. Jack's wife, Nichole, is my best friend. I didn't break in." She pulled a key out of her pocket and held it up. "I stayed here for their wedding because her house was full of family. I forgot to give it back, and when I needed someplace to go, I came here."

That didn't make any sense. "If Nichole's your best friend and you're in trouble, why wouldn't you turn to them for help? Believe me, Jack's capable of protecting you. He's not a man to mess with."

"That's exactly why. He'd want to get involved, and I'm not about to put the man Nichole loves on the radar of a man who's a ruthless son of a bitch. Robert wouldn't see much difference between killing Jack and stepping on a bug."

Dallas was seldom at a loss for words, but she'd left him speechless. What the hell had she gotten herself involved in? While he was scrambling for a response because he suddenly had a shit ton of questions, she walked past him back into the cabin, then popped her head back out.

"If you care about your friend, you won't tell him and Nichole I'm here." Then she was gone again.

He thought about the little she'd revealed and decided she was under his protection, Ruthless Robert be damned. After giving her time to cool down, he went inside to see if he could sweet-talk a wildcat into making him breakfast.

Chapter Two

Rachel wanted to scream at the infuriating man and crawl onto his lap at the same time. He was or had been a SEAL like Jack and would have the skills to protect her, and a part of her wanted to let him. If ever she needed someone at her back, it was now, with Robert looking for her.

But no. She wouldn't let anyone risk their life for her. Not Jack, who was Nichole's everything, or this man who called her wildcat. She'd never tell him how much she liked his calling her that, as if he got she wasn't a woman he could tame.

Her regret was that she hadn't listened to her instincts when she'd met Robert. The man had made her uneasy from the start, but his wife was a sweetheart, so she'd ignored the alarm bells going off in her head.

Robert would find her. With his money and resources, it was only a matter of time. She had to be ready for him, both mentally and physically. Because her job required it, she was in good shape from daily workouts, and she needed to continue to keep it that way. Unfortunately, she didn't have her trainer or a gym handy, so she'd have to improvise.

She exchanged her jeans for running shorts, added

a sports bra under her T-shirt, and slipped on a pair of track shoes. After a good run, she'd find a grocery store. The refrigerator and pantry were stocked, but not with the things she wanted. She'd wondered why there was so much food when she'd arrived the day before. Now she knew the reason for the steaks, hamburgers, and the like. All man food. Cowboy food to be more accurate.

Speaking of cowboys, why did he have to be so hot? It was distracting, and she couldn't afford to be distracted. She'd make another attempt to get him to stay with Jack. If he didn't want to do that, he could rent his own cabin.

"Heading out?" he asked when she walked into the living room.

"Going for a run."

"Stand by for a minute. I'll change and go with you. When we get back, maybe you could make us some breakfast." He palmed his hands together, as if in prayer.

Was he for real? "I'm not your mother, your girlfriend, your wife, or your chef. Make your own damn breakfast." Lord help her. Even his smirk was sexy.

"Retract your claws, wildcat. It was worth a try." He winked, then headed down the hall, presumably to change. "Wait for me," he called over his shoulder.

Nope, not waiting. She needed to put distance between her and the cowboy. Outside, she glanced around and headed for a trail going up the mountain. Ten minutes later, pounding footsteps sounded behind her. She glanced back to make sure it was Dallas and not one of Robert's men. Seeing it was the man she'd spent half the night thinking about, she picked up her speed. She was used to running on a track, not up a mountain, and already her leg muscles were protesting.

"Learned something new today," he said, coming up next to her.

Don't bite. Don't bite. Don't bite. Curiosity got the best of her, though, when he didn't say anything more. "What's that?"

"Wildcats aren't so good at following instructions." He glanced at her, and she could see the amusement in his eyes. "Guess that's typical of a cat, huh?"

Deciding not to encourage him, she didn't answer. He seemed content to let her stew in peace for a while as his stride matched hers. The infuriating man wasn't even breathing hard, while she was doing her best to hide her struggle for air.

It was spring in the mountains and although the air was cool, sweat rolled down her face and back. The only sign that he was expending any energy was the light sheen across his forehead and cheeks, but that was it, and that was even with him wearing sweats and a long-sleeve T-shirt. Who covered up like that to run unless it was freezing?

"Aren't you hot?" She had on her sports bra, and if a man she both wanted gone and wanted to climb like a tree wasn't in her personal space, she'd take off her shirt. Of course, he'd like that and have something witty to say that would make her want to laugh.

"I'm good."

Something in his voice caught her attention, his sharp tone warning her off asking more questions. That made her all the more curious as to why his choice of running clothes was off-limits.

How was it that a man she'd tried to whack upside the head with a tree branch made her feel safe mere hours later? She wouldn't involve him in her problems, but why couldn't she have met him when she wasn't hunted by a man who wanted to kill her?

"You have a job you need to worry about?" he said.

She stopped, bent over, put her hands on her knees, and inhaled air into her lungs. She'd passed the point of talking and trying to breathe at the same time.

"Here. Drink."

A bottle of water was pushed under her nose, and that made her feel brainless. She should have thought of bringing water, but she was used to her trainer thinking of those kind of things. "Thanks." She grabbed the bottle and guzzled it.

"Easy there."

"Hey!" she said when he snatched it away from her.

"I'll give it back but drink it slowly. You barfing will make me barf, too."

She laughed, damn him. He was right, so she took a few more slow sips, then handed him the bottle. "Sorry. I wasn't thinking. My trainer usually takes care of me."

"Trainer for what?" He took a sip from the water bottle, then capped the lid.

"For me. I have to stay in shape for my job."

"And just what is your job?"

"I'm a stunt double."

"Like in the movies?"

She rolled her eyes. "Yes, like in the movies."

"You just get more fascinating by the minute."

Oh, no. She didn't want to be fascinating to him, and she didn't like that calculating gleam in his eyes. "Nothing special about me."

"Uh-huh." He grinned as if entirely pleased with himself. "It's your lucky day. I'll be your trainer."

"What? No." She needed to get rid of him, not spend more time with him.

"No one trains to stay in shape harder than a SEAL, making me the perfect choice for a stand-in," he said, ignoring her. "I'll work up a regimen when we get back. How many hours do you usually train?"

"Did you miss me saying no?" Gah. The man and his adorable grins. She wondered if she could run fast enough to get to the cabin in time to lock him out.

Dallas chuckled when Rachel shot him a dirty look before taking off back down the mountain. He was going to have to thank Jack for inviting him to visit. He followed, enjoying the view…of her amazing ass. It seemed a wildcat was the perfect distraction from his demons. Not that he could tell Jack there was a wildcat in residence at the cabin. Eventually he would, or better yet, talk Rachel into revealing herself to her friends.

He still had to find out who Robert was and why the man was after her, and he would. Until then, he was in the dark about what kind of trouble she was in, and lack of intel didn't make for successful missions. Because Rachel was his mission now. It had been a stroke of brilliance to offer to train her. That would keep her close, and whether she knew it or not, whether she wanted it or not, he had her six.

"So, about that breakfast," he said simply to rile her up once they were inside the cabin.

"Have at it. I need a shower, then I'm making a run to the grocery store."

"Speaking of, how'd you get here? You have a car somewhere?"

"In the garage, out of sight."

"Okay, good." They had some serious talking to do

about what kind of trail she'd left to get here. Since he intended to go to the store with her—again, like it or not—he grabbed an apple on his way to the shower. Afraid she might try to skip out on him, he made quick work of getting clean and dressing.

"Who are you, and what did you do with Rachel?" he said when she appeared.

"Good disguise, huh?"

"That would be an affirmative." If he hadn't been sure there was only one woman in residence, he wouldn't have known it was her. She had on a spiky black wig, red-framed glasses, a half dozen earrings in each ear, and cherry red lipstick. Her jeans were ripped, and that red sweater was about a size too small. "I'm especially impressed with how much your breasts grew since the last time I saw you."

She peered down at her chest. "Being a man, of course that's the first thing you'd notice."

"Not gonna deny it."

The last person that Robert guy would notice if—or when—he narrowed down her location and managed to get a hold of security camera footage would be a brassy woman intentionally calling attention to herself. If he or any of his men were in the area, showing a photo of her, no one would be able to say they saw her.

"Clever to hide in plain sight."

She smiled as if his compliment pleased her. "I stunt doubled in a movie where the star did it to hide from the bad guys. She walked right past two of them without being recognized. Seemed like a good idea."

"What about when you traveled here from… LA, was it? Did you wear a disguise?" He hoped so.

"Yes, from LA I made myself up to look like a college student. Strawberry hair down to my waist, a nose ring, eyebrow ring, and an Ole Miss sweatshirt. Even pretended to work on my thesis while waiting to board and on the plane. Did some whining in a Southern accent to those around me about running out of time to get it done before it was due."

Damn. He already thought she was something else. He didn't need more reasons to be captivated, but how could he not be by a beautiful, clever, and yes, a snarly wildcat? He liked her brain, her face, her body, and even those claws that came out when she was fired up, and he really did like firing her up.

"Why are you smiling?"

"Didn't know I was." But, yeah, she made him smile, and she had no idea how astounding that was. Another reason to like her. "You use any credit cards once you left LA?"

She looked at him as if he was stupid. "No, I did not. I'm not dumb, you know. I went to the bank and withdrew money before leaving. I paid cash for my airline ticket, flew as far as Atlanta, then searched the classifieds for a clunker I could buy from a private individual. I haven't put the title in my name. The only thing that worried me was not having insurance, so I changed my appearance to that of an old woman and drove here like an old woman would…slowly and carefully."

Too bad she hadn't been with him when he'd been captured. She would've had them free before they had to spend one night in Hotel Hell. "Okay, one more test. Phone?"

She didn't even ask what he meant. "Not sure where it is. I deleted all my contacts, quit all my apps, then found a pickup truck full of junk in the bed. Hid my phone under a pile of garbage. If Robert's trying to track it, it's still roaming around LA or for all I know, on its way to Nebraska. I bought a burner."

Oh, she was pleased with herself all right, as well she should be. He could see it in her eyes and the sly smile on her face. "Marry me."

She blinked. "Excuse me?"

He was teasing her. Well, he was pretty sure he was. "I don't know. When a man meets a beautiful woman as smart as him, he'd be a fool not to claim her." He was kidding. Probably.

"As smart? How about smarter? And that's something most men can't handle."

"I'm not most men. You ready to go?"

"You don't have to come. I'm perfectly capable of going to the grocery store by myself."

"I'm sure you are, but it's actually better if I do. We'll look like a couple. Your Robert won't be looking for a couple."

She sighed as if hating he was right. "Fine. I passed one on the main highway on the way in yesterday."

"I'm driving."

"You're such a man."

"Glad you noticed." He thought she muttered, "How could I not?" He chuckled as he followed her to the Jeep. She was good medicine. Not once when he was with her did he have to drag his mind out of dark places.

"This is the same Jeep that Jack gave me to use when I was here for their wedding." She opened the glove box. "Aha!" She pulled out a package of Starburst candy. "My weakness. Want one?"

"Sure." He hadn't had one of these since he was a kid. She unwrapped one, then handed it to him.

"If you're such good friends with Jack, why weren't you at their wedding?" she said after popping one into her mouth.

Because he'd been a guest of Hotel Hell, but he wasn't going there with her. "Unfortunately, our team was deployed at the time, so none of us were able to make it. We all put money in a pot for Jack's bachelor party with orders to Noah to get him drunk. You met Noah there?"

"He was the best man. Nice guy. Nichole told me that he's living here now with Peyton. Have you met her?"

"No, but I guess I will while I'm here." He lowered his arm to the console and rested his hand on the shift knob.

Rachel grabbed his wrist. "Is that a paracord bracelet?"

"You know what a paracord is?" Most people didn't. It was the first thing he'd bought when he'd returned home, and he'd never be without it now.

"It's a survival bracelet. You can do all kinds of things with it, like make a fire, catch fish, cut through zip ties, make a weapon, and I don't remember what else. Plus, it makes a cool bracelet. I want one."

"When we get married, we can exchange paracord bracelets instead of rings." He didn't know why he kept on with the marriage jokes. Although he'd only known her for a day, it was long enough to know that if he'd met her before he'd been tortured to within an inch of his life, he'd be pursuing the hell out of her.

Chapter Three

Rachel shook her finger at him. "When we get married, you better be giving me a paracord bracelet with a big, fat diamond on it."

"Whatever my bride wants. A happy wife, a happy life, right?" He winked at her.

"Damn straight." She wished she'd met Dallas at any other time in her life, not when she was hiding from a man who meant to kill her. She didn't have the time or energy for a romance, no matter how much she'd like to explore that amazing body.

It was surprising how safe and comfortable she was with him even though she didn't really know him. She clicked off a mental list of what she did know. He was a friend of Jack's, so that was an excellent recommendation. He was or had been a SEAL. She still didn't know which, but from what she knew of SEALs—which really wasn't much—she had the impression they were honorable.

Then there was the cowboy side of him, and she really, really liked that side. Talk about fascinating… she was already fantasizing about the SEAL cowboy who'd invaded her life. If she ever saw him mounted on a horse—she pictured a big black stallion—cowboy hat on his head, she was one hundred percent sure she'd make a fool of herself.

There was that sexy smirk when he was goading her, and she knew he did it on purpose to rile her. Annoying man. Another thing on the list, he was protective. He might tease her about purple panties and oversized breasts, but she knew down to her toes that he wouldn't take what wasn't offered. He would protect her from himself and anyone else who threatened her.

Did she want to offer? That was the question, wasn't it? If ever in her life she needed a distraction, this was it. At the same time, the last thing she needed was to be distracted.

"You're thinking hot and heavy over there."

Ha! If he only knew the things she'd like to do to him, that she'd love for him to do to her. What she'd really like was to know everything about him, like how did he get that recent scar on his face. "What's your story, cowboy?"

And, just like that, he shut down. She'd never seen anyone blank their face so fast and so perfectly. That could only mean he had a story, but what was it to make him put up a sky-high wall in the blink of an eye?

The one thing he didn't know about her that she rarely shared because it tended to freak people out was that she was an empath. She'd learned early in her life that people equated being an empath with some kind of magic, and that was far from the truth. All it meant was that she sensed, even sometimes felt, others' emotions.

Whether happy, excited, sad, scared…she picked up on their feelings. That was all, though. Some people thought she could read minds, and that was far from the truth. Her grandmother was an empath, so Rachel assumed she'd inherited it from the woman who'd raised her. She hadn't thought about it since meeting Dallas, but now it hit her. She couldn't feel his emotions. Like any other person, she could read his emotions by his facial expressions, but she couldn't feel them. What did that mean?

"We're here," Dallas said as he pulled into a space at the grocery store.

She guessed his story would have to wait, if she could ever get it out of him. After he parked, she met him at the back of the Jeep. He wrapped an arm around her shoulders, and she glanced at him. "Is that necessary?"

"We're a couple, remember? There are cameras all over the place, so look like you're enjoying it."

Oh, she was. Entirely too much. He smelled yummy, like bay rum soap and expensive aftershave. He'd said he wasn't like most men, and he was right about that. Most of the leading men she'd met were good-looking and had great bodies because it was their job to stay in shape. And most had egos to match all those attributes.

Not one of them could hold a candle to Dallas, though, in the looks and body department. As for an ego, in the short time she'd been around him, she hadn't seen one. Yes, he was cocky and confident, but not once had he acted like an entitled jerk. That kind of surprised her. If anyone was programed to have an ego, it would be a SEAL who was also a cowboy, yet this one was nice. Imagine that.

"Do we need a cart?" he asked.

"A small one should do it. First stop, fruit and veggies."

"Are you a veg?"

"I eat meat, I just try to limit how much."

His phone buzzed. "Jack," he said as he answered the call. "Hey, brother. What's up?"

She shook her head, silently begging him not to tell Jack she was here, and got one of his smirks.

"I'm at the grocery store. Thanks for stocking the kitchen, by the way. Just needed a few other things. Gotta tell you, I'm surprised at how much I like Asheville. The views around here are pretty mind-blowing." He looked at her fake chest as he said that, laughter brightening his eyes.

She stomped on his foot, and he outright laughed.

"No, just laughing because there's a potato that looks like breasts."

She laugh-snorted, then slapped a hand over her mouth. The blasted man was having way too much fun.

"Text me K-9's address, and I'll head there after I grab some lunch."

Rachel breathed a sigh of relief. He wasn't going to rat her out.

"By the way, you ever have any problems with wild-cats nosing around the cabin?"

She'd breathed that sigh too soon. She glared at him when he grinned.

"Thought I heard one growling at me. I'll keep an eye out and let you know if I spot it."

He was both having fun with her and giving her a warning.

"What part of I don't want Jack involved in my problem don't you get?" she said when he finished his call. "I don't care that you think otherwise, it's my decision, so stop even hinting that I'm here." Annoyed with him, she slammed a head of cabbage into the cart.

"Who likes cabbage?"

She stared at the green head. She hated cabbage, had only grabbed the closest thing she could slam to make a point, but not a chance she was going to admit it. "You're an ass." Angry with him, she stormed off.

"Rachel."

It was the first time he'd said her name when talking to her. As much as she liked him calling her wildcat, hearing her name on his lips did crazy things to her, like stopping her stomping exit so fast she almost fell on her face. Good Lord, she was a stunt double. She could perform all kinds of feats—well, they were mostly well-choreographed tricks—but apparently she couldn't perform the simple task of walking away from a cowboy.

"Rachel," he said again so intimately that shivers traveled down her spine. She'd had boyfriends, one who she thought was *the one* until he'd cheated on her. Not one had ever made her shiver just by saying her name.

She was in trouble with this man, and that's a wrap, folks.

Dallas had only intended to rile up a wildcat because he really liked that he could. He didn't want to be an ass in those whiskey eyes. Apparently, he was.

He stepped closer. "You can't know how good you are for me. You can't know how much…" He pressed his lips together.

Why had all that spilled out of his mouth? He'd almost told her that he wanted her. That he'd been afraid he'd never feel desire for a woman again. That she made him feel like the man he was before his capture. When he'd wrapped his arm around her shoulders for the cameras, he hadn't flinched at touching her. What would she think if she knew that he couldn't stand to be touched now, even by his own family…except for her?

And that was something he was having trouble wrapping his mind around. Why her?

"How much what?"

"Nothing. I won't tell Jack you're here, but you need to."

"I told you why I don't want him to know."

He'd let it go for now, but this discussion wasn't over. "What else do you need?"

They finished their shopping and headed back to the cabin. The atmosphere was chillier in the Jeep on the return trip, and he didn't like her shutting him out. He got why she thought she was right in keeping Jack out of whatever it was she was dealing with, but she was wrong. With his and Jack's special talents, this Robert dude wouldn't be able to get near her even with all the money and mysterious resources she claimed he had.

He'd promised her he wouldn't tell Jack she was here, but maybe there was a way around that. One possibility, he could give Jack a hint that he should make a surprise visit to the cabin. Something to think about.

"I want you to find someplace else to stay," she said, breaking her silence as he stopped in front of the cabin.

"No can do, sugar." He glanced at her, almost smiling at the mulish expression on her face.

"Stop calling me sugar."

"Why?"

She huffed an annoyed breath. "Because that's probably what you call all your women, and I'm not one of them."

His smile was getting harder to hold in. "I've never called another woman sugar in my life, and that's the truth." He only did it with her because it lit that blaze in her eyes that he got a kick out of seeing. That he got a kick out of anything was a miracle, and how was he supposed to give that up?

"I don't believe you."

He leaned over the console. "I might be a lot of things, but one thing I'm not is a liar. If I say I never called another woman sugar, that means I've never called another woman sugar." He stared hard into her amber eyes, daring her to call him a liar again.

"Okay, I'll take your word for it." Surprising him, she touched the scar on his face, tracing it down to where it disappeared into his beard. "How did this happen?"

He closed his eyes, savoring the slide of her finger over his skin. He asked himself the question he'd asked earlier. Why her? Why did he want her touch when he couldn't handle anyone else touching him? Even his mother, whom he loved dearly.

"You came so close to losing an eye. What happened, Dallas?"

Hell fucking happened. He'd only shared all that had been done to him in his debriefing while he was in the hospital, and only because he'd had no choice. Once was enough to last a lifetime.

Her mouth was so close and the warmth from her touch was a balm to his soul. Instead of answering a question he had no intention of ever answering, he touched his lips to hers. He hadn't meant to kiss her, but here he was, doing just that, and in a moment of clarity, he asked himself what the hell he was doing. In the second before he could pull away, and he really did mean to, her lips softened against his, and she flattened her palm over his cheek, right where the scar was, and he was lost. In her. The cold that lived inside him now soaked up her heat. Her scent wrapped around him, and he'd never smell vanilla again without thinking of her.

"Wildcat," he murmured against her mouth.

She pushed him away. "What are we doing?"

"I don't know." And that was the honest to God's truth. He sat back in his seat. "My apologies. It won't happen again." And wasn't that just sad? "We need to get your groceries in."

She got out of the car as if the seat was on fire. He'd thought she was as into that kiss as he'd been. Apparently not. He would have been better off never knowing how good she tasted because one taste of her wasn't enough.

"Who knows you're here?" he asked after they were inside, while she was putting her groceries away and he was doing his best not to look at her lips.

"My grandmother knows exactly where I am, and a detective, but he only knows I'm in North Carolina somewhere."

That was an interesting combination. "Why a detective?"

"Huh?" She stared at the head of cabbage in her hand as if she didn't know what to do with it.

"Want me to see if Jack stuck any corned beef in the freezer? You could make us corned beef and cabbage for dinner." He'd been pretty sure at the grocery store that she didn't want the cabbage, now he was positive.

She glanced up at him, eyes narrowed. "I'm not—"

"My mother, wife, girlfriend, or chef. Yeah, yeah. Got it. Doesn't mean you get away without doing your share of cooking in our relationship. I mean, I'm an enlightened guy and all, but I do expect my woman to do her fair share." Wait for it…and there it was. Flames in those whiskey eyes.

"We. Do. Not." She poked him in the chest on that last word. "Have a relationship. Not even in your wildest dreams."

His dreams sure as hell would be a vast improvement if they were of her. He'd riled her up enough. Any more and he'd be going too far with the teasing. Time for a peace offering. He went to the refrigerator and peered at the contents. "How does an omelet sound for lunch? I make a mean one."

When she didn't answer, he glanced back at her. She was staring at him as if trying to solve a calculus problem. "What?"

She shook her head. "I can't figure you out."

"I'm just a simple man. Nothing to figure out."

"Uh-huh. If that was true, I should be able to feel you."

"Feel me? Sugar, you're free to feel me anytime you want." *But you're the only one.* He didn't think she'd meant that literally, so another puzzle to solve.

"That's not… Forget it."

"Hey, you want that omelet or not?" he called as she walked away. She didn't answer, and he heard her bedroom door close. "Guess not."

He made a sandwich instead, and after eating, knocked on her door. "I'm heading over to Jack's. You want to come?"

She opened her door. "No, and don't be telling Jack I'm here."

"Copy that. You going to be here when I get back, or are you planning a disappearing act?" He really didn't want to have to track her down, but he would if he had to. No way he could sit back and do nothing knowing she was alone and fearing for her life.

"I'll be here."

Seeing the truth in her eyes, he managed to nod a second before she closed the door in his face. He chuckled as he headed for the Jeep. He was curious to see what Operation K-9 Brothers was about.

"This isn't anything like what I envisioned," Dallas said after a tour of the place. Funny thing…he hadn't frozen when Jack and Noah gave him man-hugs on arrival. He'd known it would be different with his SEAL brothers, but he felt guilty that he'd turned to a rigid board when his mother had wrapped her arms around him the minute he'd arrived home.

Noah nodded. "Yeah, I was pretty impressed myself on first seeing it."

The place was beyond what Dallas had imagined. He'd expected something along the lines of an animal shelter, a building and some cages. Truth be told, he hadn't been looking forward to seeing that part of Jack's operation. After experiencing Hotel Hell, he would have wanted to open the doors and free anything—animal or human—confined to a cage.

Instead, the dogs here were housed in individual kennels, part concrete flooring with a roof, and part an open grassy area. They had plenty of room to move around, their water bowls were clean and full, and they had food in their bellies. They even had beds that appeared to be more comfortable than the paper-thin pallet he'd been given. Best of all, they looked happy.

There was a large fenced-in area where several dogs

were playing with each other, and the building housing the puppies had even been climate-controlled.

A few yards away, a woman missing an arm leaned over and praised a dog. A man stood a few feet away, and Dallas wondered if they were together. How did all this work, anyway? "Is that dog hers?"

Jack nodded. "Yeah. Rebecca took Cricket home with her for the first time last week. She's back for a little follow-up training."

"Tomorrow we'll take you on a tour of Operation Warriors Center," Jack said. "I think you'll be impressed with our plans for that. But today let's go meet your dog."

"My dog?" He backed up a step. "I don't want a dog." He was barely able to take care of himself.

"Good luck with refusing. Didn't work for me." Noah gave a sharp whistle, and a dog raced toward them, skidding to a stop in front of Noah. "Meet Lucky."

"What is it?" It looked like a collie mixed with... who knew what? The dog had one brown eye and one blue eye, and he stared up at Noah with total adoration in those odd eyes.

Noah laughed as he leaned over and gave the dog's chin a scratch. "Pretty certain it's a dog, but I've never been sure."

The last time he'd seen Noah had been when he'd shipped out after failing to find a bomb and the bomb maker hiding in a room he'd thought he'd cleared. The man who'd left to return home had been devastated by his mistake. He'd withdrawn into himself and his eyes had been haunted. The haunted look was gone, and he was back to the Noah before that ill-fated mission. Dallas wasn't buying for a minute that a dog was responsible for Noah putting his demons to rest.

"I'm going to head over to the site," Noah said. "The building inspector will be there in an hour."

Jack nodded. "You're not expecting any problems, right?"

"No. Everything's good." Noah gave Dallas's shoulder a slap. "Don't bother fighting against the dog. Won't do you any good. How about we get together for dinner tonight?"

"We could throw some steaks on the grill at my place," Jack said.

"Can I take a raincheck? I'm jetlagged from flying all night and just want to crash." He'd actually like to get together, do some catching up, but he had a wildcat to tend to. Besides, he couldn't call her to let her know he'd be late returning. He'd neglected to get the number of her burner phone, which he'd correct tonight.

"No problem," Jack said. "Let's do it tomorrow night."

"Sounds good." He didn't like the thought of leaving Rachel alone at night, but it would be suspicious if he didn't agree.

"Let's go introduce you to Bella."

"I don't want a dog," he said as he walked alongside Jack after Noah left. There were dogs all over the ranch, working dogs and pet dogs like his mother's shorkie, Oliver. The schnauzer Yorkie mix was a cute little thing, totally devoted to Dallas's mother. Dogs were okay. The cattle dogs played an important role at the ranch, and he liked seeing his mother's laughter when Oliver acted silly. But horses were his jam, not dogs.

"You're used to being around animals." Jack opened

the door to a large metal building, and they walked past kennels, coming to a stop at the last one. "This is Bella. I'm hoping you can help me out with her while you're here."

Dallas eyed the black dog quivering in the corner, looking like it wanted to disappear into the wall. He knew the feeling. "What is she?" She was hiding her face and curled in such a tight ball that he couldn't tell what breed she was.

"Labrador retriever. Animal Control took her away from the owner. She's been terribly abused."

"And I'm supposed to do what with her?"

"See if you can get through to her. No one else has been able to."

"Why is she even here? She doesn't look like she'd be much of a service dog. More like she needs her own therapy animal."

"We've tried that, too. Even the puppies scare the shit out of her."

Dallas narrowed his eyes at his friend. "You didn't answer my question. Why do you have her?" He was getting an uneasy feeling, and when Jack glanced away, it confirmed his suspicion. "You think a dog can straighten out my head? A damaged one like me? The hell, Jack?"

"I think dogs can do a lot of things, and yes, healing is one of them." Jack stared straight into his eyes. "But I didn't get her specifically for you. I was looking for possible candidates when I came across her. The shelter had her scheduled for euthanasia because she's so damaged mentally, and I saw a brief spark of hope when I stopped in front of her kennel before she decided a panic attack was in order."

"I repeat. What am I supposed to do with her?"

"Hopefully save her life. Spend a few minutes with her, and if you're not willing to work with her, we'll put her out of her misery."

"Fuck you," Dallas yelled as his friend walked away. What? Two damaged souls save each other? This was a setup, no other way about it, and it seriously pissed him off that the animal's future was in his hands.

Bella had whimpered when he'd yelled, and he cursed himself for scaring an abused dog half to death. He studied the dog that might have endured as much torture as he had. She wouldn't meet his gaze, and that bothered the hell out of him. A Labrador should be proud, friendly, and a little full of herself. This dog wanted to die and have any future tortures over and done with.

He'd lost count of the number of times he'd wanted to die while cruel men had devised new ways to torture him. Maybe he and Bella did have something in common, but still… Damn Jack for this.

"So, Bella, if you were an abused horse, I'd know what to do with you." He kept his voice soft as he slipped inside her kennel and lowered his ass to the opposite corner from her. "Well, about Jack. I love the man. He's my brother. Not in blood, but still. He's also a devious son of a bitch, otherwise I wouldn't be sitting here on a hard concrete floor talking to you."

The dog whimpered again, and the mournful sound wasn't unlike some he'd made more times than he liked while a guest at Hotel Hell. "You don't like me talking to you? Okay, I'll just sit here and make sure no one hurts you again. That work for you?"

He got the impression she wished she could climb

into her own skin and fade from sight. He needed her to know one more thing before he stopped talking. "I get it, Bella girl. Been where you are myself." He made a decision. This dog wasn't going to die. He might not be able to save himself, but he'd damn well save her.

Chapter Four

Rachel ran up the trail until the muscles in her legs burned and she was close to crawling back to the cabin. Dallas had barely broken a sweat on their run this morning, and no way was she going to beg for mercy if he decided to go farther up next time.

Why was she even thinking about running with him again? So she wouldn't think about that kiss, that was why. That incredible kiss! There hadn't even been any tongue, yet it was the best kiss she'd ever had. How she'd managed to put a stop to it, she didn't know. It couldn't happen again. She'd used up all her willpower where a certain Montana cowboy was concerned.

He needed to find someplace else to stay because he was distracting, and that was something she couldn't afford. Back at the cabin, she showered, then put on body armor—loose jeans, socks, and a sweatshirt, pleased that she felt and looked far from sexy.

Armored up, she wondered if she had time to call her grandmother before Dallas returned. As she walked down the hallway, she glanced in his room and frowned. There was no way his six-plus feet fit on that twin bed.

Twenty minutes later, after trading rooms with him, she called herself a fool for her soft heart. Hadn't she just decided he needed to stay someplace else? She was especially a fool for giving up the bigger room's attached bathroom. She got her things put away and then called her grandmother.

"You manage to lasso a hot cowboy yet?" she said when June answered.

"Ya-hoo! This place is crawling with pretty boys."

Rachel laughed. "That's what I wanted to hear." From the time Rachel could talk, her grandmother had insisted that she call her June. No granny names for her fun-loving grandmother.

June had buried three husbands, had cried from a broken heart over each one, and after the last one, she'd announced she was done burying men she loved. "From now on, I'm just going to have me some fun," she'd said.

"You should have come with me to Wyoming. We would've fixed you right up with one of these pretty boys."

"You know why I didn't." When Rachel had become a target of Robert's rage, she'd needed to hide until the police found and arrested him. Fearing that he would use her grandmother to find her, she'd convinced June to take an extended vacation and had laughed when June decided on a dude ranch. June had wanted Rachel to come with her, but Rachel wanted as much distance between herself and June as possible. Wyoming and North Carolina worked.

"Honey pie, I worry about you."

She closed her eyes against the sting of tears. Her grandmother had always called her honey pie, and hearing the endearment made her want to crawl onto her grandmother's lap where she'd always felt protected.

"I'm safe." For now, anyway. "You're going to like this. I managed to find my own cowboy."

"Do tell."

"Actually, he's a SEAL cowboy." The only person she told everything she thought, felt, or did was to June, even things she might not tell her best friend. The woman who'd raised her when her mother died giving birth to her never judged her. How could she? June was wilder than Rachel ever thought to be.

"A seal shifter? Send me a picture, honey pie, right now. Two of them, the man and one of him in his seal form."

Rachel laughed. This was why she loved her grandmother to death. June would totally believe Rachel had snagged a seal shifter. "He's a Navy SEAL, not a seal seal."

"Well, that's disappointing."

"Only you would be disappointed that my SEAL wasn't actually a seal shifter."

"You could never disappoint me, Rachel."

"I love you, June." June never called her Rachel except when it mattered, and never disappointing her grandmother mattered very much.

"Love you more, honey pie."

Tires driving over gravel sounded, and Rachel jogged to the window, letting out a relieved breath when she saw a Jeep instead of a car she'd never seen before. "Gotta go. There's a cowboy driving up."

"Since arriving here, my new motto is save a horse, ride a—"

"I get the picture. Please, stay there where you're safe until I tell you it's okay to come home. Promise me."

June's third husband had left her a fortune, and she

could afford to flirt with hot cowboys to her heart's content, and if it took every penny of that fortune to keep her grandmother alive and kicking, it would be money well spent.

"Why in tarnation would I want to leave all these pretty boys, so stop your worrying about me. You just worry about yourself. Please stay safe."

"I will, I promise." She prayed that was true.

She disconnected, then tried to decide where to be and what to be doing when Dallas came in. The man confused her. He was bossy. He was sometimes funny. He was annoying. He was...okay, she hated to admit it, but he was cowboy hot, and she liked him.

"No kisses, no jumping his bones when he walks in." And now he had her talking to herself. She decided hiding in her room was the best thing to do. Maybe he'd go away.

Dallas walked into a quiet cabin. Where was Rachel? He didn't like how eager he was to see her. He walked down the hallway, puzzled at seeing his bedroom door was closed and the bigger bedroom door was open. He hadn't closed his door when he'd left.

He passed the closed door and stopped at the threshold of Rachel's room. Why was his duffel bag on the bed? And there was his suitcase on the floor at the foot of the bed. He walked through the room to the attached bathroom. Nothing of hers was on the counter. Backtracking, he checked the closet. It was empty.

His first reaction was to panic. Had she left? He returned to the hallway and knocked on the second bedroom door. "Rachel? You in there?" He knew she was, he could feel her. She mumbled something he couldn't understand, but which he translated as *go away*. He'd do that for a while.

It was nice of her to exchange their rooms since half his legs hung over the end of the twin bed, but he felt bad about running her out of the better room. To thank her, he'd make dinner.

After showering the dog smell off, he headed for the kitchen to see what his options were. All the Manning children knew how to cook, their mother had made sure of it. She'd spent one-on-one kitchen time with each of them, and he'd grumbled about it each time it was his turn because that was what kids were supposed to do. Secretly, he'd enjoyed every aspect of it—alone time with his mother, meal planning, the preparation, and a sense of satisfaction when the result was good food.

Rachel had said she ate meat on occasion, but he didn't know if that included red meat. He decided on baked chicken, potatoes au gratin, and the asparagus she'd bought at the store.

While the chicken defrosted in the microwave, he peeled and sliced the potatoes. As he prepared dinner, his thoughts turned to Bella. The dog was so traumatized that he wasn't sure she was savable. During the hour he'd sat in that kennel, softly talking to her, she'd stayed curled up in a ball, her face buried under her tail, her body quivering.

She reminded him too much of himself during his last days of captivity. He hadn't been sure he was savable either. He'd somehow managed to put on a good front with his family even though he was dead inside.

Yet…thanks to a prickly wildcat, he'd had glimpses of the man he'd been before the day his team had been ambushed. If there was hope for him—and he really wanted that to be true—was it fair to count Bella out?

He wasn't happy with Jack putting Bella's life in his hands, and although he was sure his devious friend thought pairing a wounded dog with a wounded warrior was clever, he didn't have to like it. He also couldn't turn his back on Bella, so he supposed Operation Save Bella was on.

Rachel still hadn't made an appearance, and he hoped that making dinner for her would earn him points. She still hadn't answered some of his questions, and if he was going to protect her, he needed to know who Robert was and why he was a threat.

In the meantime, he could do a little research. While the chicken and potatoes baked, he retrieved his laptop. Since he didn't know her last name, he did a search on a stuntwoman named Rachel. He whistled when he saw the number of hits.

The oven timer dinged, and he glanced at his watch, surprised to see how much time had passed while he'd fallen down the rabbit hole learning about the public Rachel Denning. When she'd said she was a stuntwoman, he'd imagined that she'd done a few minor movies.

Wrong! She was a highly respected stuntwoman and had doubled for some of the biggest names in the business. "Pretty impressive, Rachel Denning," he murmured. He found a list of all her movies and copied and pasted it in his computer notes. When he couldn't sleep tonight, he'd watch one or two.

He closed the laptop, and after returning it to his room, he took the chicken out to let it sit while he sautéed the asparagus. As he finished getting dinner ready, his thoughts were on Rachel. What kind of trouble was she in? Who was this Robert she was afraid of and why? Did she have a boyfriend? He assumed she wasn't married, because no man worth his salt would leave his wife unprotected when someone was out to harm her.

Before the night was over, he'd have her story, even if he had to threaten to tell Jack she was hiding out in his cabin to get her to talk. It was important intel, and if he was to be successful in protecting her, he needed to know what they were facing.

He carved the chicken, plated their dinner, then went to her bedroom door and knocked. "Rachel, dinner's ready." When he didn't get a response, he knocked again. "Rachel?" Was she asleep?

The door opened, and he sucked in a breath at seeing a sleep-tousled Rachel Denning. Were those heavy-lidded whiskey eyes and mussed hair how she would look after making love? He wanted to know. Maybe he wasn't dead inside after all.

"What?"

He grinned. There she was, his prickly wildcat. "Dinner's ready."

"Not hungry."

"Sure you are." He put his foot against the door when she tried to close it. "Besides, you can't refuse me. I toiled in the kitchen all afternoon just for you."

"Did you now?" She huffed an annoyed breath. "Fine, give me five minutes."

"Make it three. It won't be any good cold."

He figured she'd take five minutes or more just to prove a point, but two minutes and fifty seconds later, she appeared. She was wearing black leggings and a purple off-the-shoulder top and had brushed her hair.

Too bad that. He liked the messy look on her. He also liked—a whole lot—how her eyes roamed over him.

"Hungry?"

"Huh?" Her gaze shot up to his.

"I asked if you're hungry." Hell, yeah. She was hungry, and food had nothing to do with it. He filed that insight away for later use. He swept his hand out to the table. "Let's eat."

She stared at the plates on the table. "What's all this?"

"That would be what's commonly referred to as dinner."

"You cooked all this?"

He liked that he'd surprised her. "Yes, ma'am. I wanted to show my appreciation for trading beds with me." He pulled out a chair. "Have a seat and dig in."

"This is really good," she said after eating a few bites. "You bought all this at a restaurant and want me to believe you cooked it."

"You wound me." He slapped a hand over his heart. "Such little faith you have in me." She rolled her eyes, making him chuckle. "I promise I cooked this amazing meal."

"I'm impressed."

He ate the rest of his dinner while trying to think of other ways to impress her.

"Since you cooked, I'll clean up," she said when they finished.

"We'll clean up together. It'll go faster that way." The cabin didn't have a dishwasher, but he didn't mind. They worked well together, her washing the dishes, and him drying and putting them away. While she wiped down the counter, he made a pot of coffee.

She glanced around the kitchen. "All done."

"Good. Let's sit on the deck and have a cup of coffee." And then the interrogation would begin.

"Um…"

"It's a beautiful night. You might want to grab a sweater." He poured coffee into two cups. "Two sugars and enough cream to turn the coffee caramel color, right?" She lifted startled eyes to his, and he swallowed a smile. *Surprised you again, eh?*

"Ah, yeah, but—"

"I'll take these out to the deck while you grab your sweater." Not giving her a chance to answer, he walked out.

Would she come out or hide in her room again? If she decided to hide, he'd have to force her to come talk to him, and he didn't want to do that. For her own safety, he would if he had to. The glass door slid open a few minutes later, and relieved, he settled back in his chair.

"Lots of stars out tonight," he said, handing her one of the cups when she sat in the chair next to him.

She looked up at the sky. "Amazing. We don't get to see stars like this in LA. Too many lights."

"As amazing as this is, you should come to Montana sometime to stargaze. It's truly remarkable." They sat in silence for a few minutes, her gaze on the sky, and his on her.

What was it about this woman that so fascinated him? She was pretty, yes. But so were plenty of other women. Her well-toned body—which he'd very much like to explore—put all kinds of dirty thoughts into his head. But he'd known women with great bodies. It wasn't that. Whatever it was, it went beyond the physical.

Maybe it was because she was the only woman who'd tried to bash him in the head with a tree branch.

"You're chuckling. Why?"

What would she say if he told her that his chuckling was a fucking miracle? "I was thinking about how close I came to death by tree branch."

"Not going to apologize for that. You could have been one of Robert's men."

He'd never want or expect her to apologize for trying to protect herself, but she'd just given him the perfect opening for what they needed to talk about. "Tell me about this Robert person. Who is he and why are you afraid of him?"

"You're not going to stay out of this, are you?"

"No, Rachel Denning, I'm not." He couldn't see her face clearly, but he heard her gasp.

"How did you find out my last name?"

"The internet is a marvelous invention. I thought it'd be harder, but a search of Rachel stuntwoman and voilà, I instantly had a long list of hits. Color me impressed with your credentials." He let a full minute pass, waiting for her to answer his question, then he sighed. Apparently, he was going to have to threaten her with telling Jack she was here.

"I'll make a deal with you. You tell me how you got that scar, and I'll tell you who Robert is."

Now she was playing dirty, and as much as he did not want to talk about it, he had to admire her tactics. "That's an ugly story, sugar."

Chapter Five

"So is mine." Rachel glanced over at Dallas, wishing he wasn't so intent on pushing his way into her troubles. She'd been doing her best to put distance between them, going so far as to actually hide in her room when the Jeep came up the driveway.

It wasn't only that she didn't want him putting himself at risk, but he was just too tempting. He wasn't like any man she'd dated, no doubt why he fascinated her as much as he did. She'd rubbed elbows with some of the hottest men on the planet—famous and rich ones—had been hit on by several and had briefly dated one. Not a single one of those men had bewitched her the way this one did. Not one of them had spiked her blood the way he had because of a kiss.

Then he'd gone and made her dinner. Damn him, anyway. She didn't want to tell him about Robert, didn't want him risking his life for her, and especially didn't want to like him in a *I wonder how his hands would feel on my skin* kind of way.

Maybe his allure was only because she couldn't sense his emotions, something that had never happened before. She could always feel people's feelings, even when she didn't want to. The first time she really wanted to, the man was closed to her. Weird that.

He'd made it clear that he wasn't going to go away, though, and she really did want to know how he'd gotten that recent scar, so that was the deal—you show me yours, and I'll show you mine. She hoped he refused since that would give her an out.

"My team was ambushed, and I was taken prisoner. My captors weren't happy with me when I declined to answer their questions."

Dear God, he'd been tortured? "Oh." That was such a stupid response, but she didn't know what to say. What else had been done to him? Was that why she couldn't read him? Because he'd learned to shut down to survive?

His laugh was harsh. "Yeah, oh."

"Wait. That was you on the news a few weeks ago?" She hadn't been paying much attention to the news but had glanced up from the book she was reading when a segment came on about a SEAL who'd been rescued. The news camera had been at a distance, filming the man as he deplaned. She remembered thinking the man was walking as if he was in a lot of pain. Now she wished she'd paid more attention to the story. How long had he been a prisoner?

"That was me. I should have never been on the news, but a nurse in the German hospital ratted me out to her boyfriend, who happened to be a reporter, who tipped off his network about a SEAL who'd been rescued. So, who's Robert?"

Talk about whiplash. She had more questions, lots of them, but sensed he'd said as much as he was willing to. Guess it was her turn. "I don't want you playing hero, Dallas. The police are involved, and they can deal with Robert." If they ever found him.

"That's good, but obviously, since you're hiding, you're afraid. I have no intention of going looking for the man, but what if he does show up here? I need to know what we're dealing with."

"You could go stay with Jack and Nichole or find another cabin."

"Negative."

She blew out an exasperated breath. "Fine. Robert killed his wife, and I'm the only witness."

"Whoa. Wasn't expecting that." He pulled his chair around so that he was facing her. "Tell me everything."

"Okay, but for the record, I'm not happy about this."

"You'll get over it."

To stall, she finished her coffee. When she couldn't think of anything else to delay her story, she said, "His name's Robert Hargrove. His public story is that he made all his money, and he has lots of it, in the tech industry. Two years ago, I met his wife at my yoga class. Her name was Henrietta, but everyone called her Henri. She was one of the sweetest people I've ever known. We became friends." Tears burned her eyes, and she stared down at the hand Dallas put over hers.

"Hey, take a minute. You want another cup of coffee or a beer?"

"Definitely a beer."

"Back in a sec."

He was giving her time to get her emotions under control. "You're a sweet man, cowboy," she whispered to the night.

When he returned, he handed her a beer and a roll of

toilet paper. Puzzled, she glanced at him. "Um, what's this for?"

"I couldn't find any tissues, so next best thing."

Definitely a sweet man. "Oh, thanks."

"You okay to finish?"

"I want to get this over with." She waited for him to sit. "So, I'd see Henri at yoga, and one or two times a month, we'd meet for lunch, sometimes at her house… I guess I should say mansion. I met Robert when I went to Henri's for lunch. From the first, I didn't like him." How could she explain the malicious vibes she felt coming from the man without telling Dallas she was an empath?

"What about him didn't you like?"

"It's hard to explain. He was…solicitous, I guess that's the right word, with Henri, but I didn't see love in his eyes when he looked at her. He was polite to me, at first anyway, but there was just something cold and arrogant about him."

"Did he ever hit on you?"

"Not in the beginning. We maybe had lunch at Henri's three or four times the first year we were friends, and I didn't see much of him. I was thankful for that. But one time, near the end, Henri was sick when I arrived for our lunch. I wanted to see her for a few minutes, maybe see if she needed anything. Robert wouldn't let me, said she was too sick. He stated he was having lunch with me. Didn't ask, more like gave a command. He put his hand on my lower back and tried to steer me toward the pool deck where Henri and I always ate." She shuddered at the memory of having that hand touch her.

"What did you do?"

"I told him I wasn't feeling so good either, that maybe I'd caught whatever Henri had. He laughed, and Dallas, that laugh sounded so evil. He said, 'I doubt that,' and I don't know why, but I just knew he'd done something to make her sick. Either that, or maybe he'd given her a black eye or something like that, and that was why he wouldn't let me see her.

"I headed for the front door, and two of his men were standing in front of it, blocking it so I couldn't leave. Robert sneered, and I knew he was sending me a message, telling me he was in control. Once he seemed satisfied his message was received, he nodded at his men, and they moved away from the door."

"Did he always have men with him when you saw him?"

"Yeah, there were always two. Lots of wealthy people around LA have bodyguards, so I didn't really think much about it. It's almost a status symbol to have one or two. You know, hey, look at me, I'm so rich I need a bodyguard."

"Tell me you never went to Henri's house again."

"Except for that last time, never. After that, I always insisted that she meet me somewhere for lunch. When I first met Henri, she was a vibrant, happy woman. The last few months, my sweet, happy friend changed into someone afraid of her own shadow. I didn't know what to do. I wanted to help her, but at the same time, I didn't want to get in the middle of anything going on between her and Robert. I was afraid of the man."

"Always go with your gut feelings."

"And I tried to, even going so far as to try to distance myself from Henri, and I felt really guilty about that. After I'd claimed the movie I was working on was running over schedule as an excuse to not meet her a few times, she called, begging me to come to her house. She said Robert was out of town, and that she was leaving him, and she needed my help."

"And you couldn't say no."

He hadn't made it a question. "Would you have if your friend needed you?"

"No. What happened?"

"I went. Robert wasn't there, and while I helped her pack, she told me the truth about Robert Hargrove. She claimed that she'd learned he was an illegal arms dealer. She said that was where his money really came from, along with some other stuff he was involved in. She didn't say what specifically."

"Did he know she'd found that out about him?"

"She said not, and I believe her. Otherwise, Robert would have had his men watching her, and they weren't there that day. All I wanted as soon as she told me everything was to get the two of us the hell out of there. We didn't make it." The tears were stinging her eyes again, and she tore off some of the toilet paper.

"He came home?"

She nodded. "I... I was in her closet, looking for a leather jacket she wanted to take with her because it had been a gift from her mother, when I heard him say, 'Going somewhere, Henrietta?' I froze." She squeezed her eyes shut, wishing she could bleach her mind of the rest.

"Did he know you were there? He had to have seen your car."

"No. Their mansion had a separate five-car garage behind the house. The entrance to it is separate from the front drive. Robert had a driver, and he always used the back road."

Dallas wrapped his hand around hers. "What did you do?"

"I hid like a coward."

"No, you did the smart thing."

"It doesn't feel like it. Anyway, they got in a terrible fight about the things he was involved in, and she told him she was leaving. Then…then she yelled, 'Rachel, he's got a gun.' So much for hiding, huh?" She tried to laugh but sounded a bit hysterical instead. "Seconds after she said that, a gun fired, and I heard Henri make a grunting sound." She shuddered again. "Not a sound I ever want to hear again."

The tears were now flowing down her cheeks. "Hiding wasn't an option anymore, so I grabbed a pair of Henri's stilettos, the closest things I could find for a weapon. I knew if I had any chance of getting away, I had to surprise him. He would be expecting me to walk out of the closet, fearful and begging for my life. So I did the opposite. I ran out, threw one shoe, got lucky that it hit him in the face, and then threw the other one straight at his junk."

Dallas smiled. "Good for you."

"Yeah, but it didn't do the damage I hoped for. He laughed. Said he was going to enjoy having some fun with me before he sent me straight to hell to join Henri." Strangely, Dallas's growl warmed her. "I looked at my friend, there on the floor, and knew she was dead. I've never felt such rage in my life, and that's what saved me…that rage. It made me a little crazy and fearless. I went at him like—"

"A wildcat?"

She smiled for the first time since starting her story. "Yeah, I guess so. Because I have to do fight scenes sometimes, I take kickboxing lessons, and that helped. Honestly, though, I don't even remember what all I did to him, but I managed to get one finger in his eye, then I tore open his cheek with my fingernails. I also did some damage to his junk with my knee. It was weird, but I forgot he had a gun until it fell to the floor. I kicked it under the bed."

"How'd you get away?"

"That's where being a stuntwoman came in handy. He started yelling for his men, and if I tried to escape down the stairs and out the door, they'd catch me. I only had one option, and that was their bedroom balcony. I jumped."

"You're just full of surprises. Did you hurt yourself?"

"I'm trained how to fall, but usually there's an air mattress to land on. I got lucky, just had a sore ankle for a day. I drove straight to the police station and reported a murder. The police went to the mansion, but no one was there. Based on my statement, they were able to get a search warrant. Henri's body was gone, and Robert had disappeared."

"They believe you, right?"

"Yeah. They used one of those ultraviolet lights where I told them Henri's body was, and it showed blood."

"Maybe Robert left the country."

Wouldn't that be wonderful? "I don't think so. Before I ditched my phone, he called me. I didn't recognize the number, and I wouldn't have answered if I'd known it was him. He said there was nowhere I could hide from him. Then I came home the next day after a meeting for my next movie. There was a black SUV in my condo's parking lot with two men inside, one I recognized as a man I'd seen with Robert. I kept going and went to a motel. The next morning, I went to my bank, cashed in a pretty big check, went shopping for both regular and decoy clothes and a burner phone." She shrugged. "You know the rest."

"What I know is that Rachel Denning is one badass woman."

He was pretty badass, too. She traced his scar again, her heart melting a little when his eyes slid closed at her touch. "I think maybe you have a story to tell me when you're ready."

"It's not a story you want to hear. I could kiss you instead."

She laughed and wasn't that something after dredging up her story again? "In your dreams." She'd never ever tell him, but that smirk of his was growing on her.

"I need to borrow a gun."

Jack stopped in his tracks. "For?"

"Thought I'd do a little target practice." Dallas had expected that question, and target practice seemed the most believable and least suspicious answer. It was breakfast time for the dogs, and he waited outside the kennel as Jack went in to fill one of the dogs' food bowl.

"We can go to the range. I could use some practice," Jack said as he exited the kennel and moved to the next one.

He'd also planned for that response. "Sure. But I'm up with the sun, before the sun actually, and it will give me something to do in the mornings instead of sitting on the porch and…" An involuntary shudder traveled through him.

"Remembering?" Jack softly said.

"Yeah. I found a clearing behind the cabin where I can set up a target." It didn't sit well to lie to his friend, so he was going to make it a truth and actually do some target shooting. And it was true that he was up before the sun since he basically didn't sleep.

"I'll give you a gun when you come over tonight."

"Thanks, brother." A SEAL didn't loan out his guns, and Dallas understood the trust Jack was giving him. He also appreciated that Jack's first thought wasn't that Dallas might turn that gun on himself. He might have nightmares, but he'd never take his own life and put his family through that kind of heartbreak.

"Noah and Peyton are coming to dinner, too, so you'll get to meet her."

"Great. It'll be interesting to see the woman who managed to catch Double D."

Jack grinned. "You'll like her. She's got Noah wrapped around her little finger."

"Like Nichole has you?"

"Exactly like that." Jack's goofy grin was a clear testament to how besotted he was with his wife. "Why don't I have Nichole invite one of her friends over?"

"Thanks, but not this time around." Not only was he not ready for any kind of relationship, even a casual one, it felt wrong to spend time with another woman when Rachel was at the cabin alone. He'd told her he would be having dinner with Jack tonight, had tried to talk her into revealing her presence, but she'd adamantly refused.

Somehow, he was going to have to get her to let him bring Jack in on this operation. Dallas could protect her by himself, and he would, but if Hargrove was as deadly as she claimed, he would feel a lot better knowing Jack had their six. And since Noah lived here now, Dallas would take his help, too. It would be almost half of their team back together, and anything Robert Hargrove could think to throw at them, he wouldn't be a match against the three of them.

"What's my agenda for the day?" He wasn't under any orders to spend his time at Operation K-9 Brothers like Noah had been, but he'd come to Asheville to spend time with both Jack and Noah, so here he was. He'd briefly considered staying at the cabin with Rachel, making sure she stayed safe, but that would make Jack suspicious.

"Why don't you spend some time with Bella. Also, you might enjoy watching some of the training we have going on."

"Sounds like a plan."

"Noah's over at our future site, but he'll show up in a while. He said he could use your input while you're here if you're up for it."

"I don't know how much help I can be, but sure." He appreciated that they were trying to make him feel useful. Maybe it would keep his mind off worrying about his future. He was on medical leave, but he couldn't see himself returning. A medical discharge had appeal, but he didn't know what to do with his life.

"We're thinking about including an equine center, but neither one of us knows a thing about horses. Noah wants to pick your brain on that."

"Equine therapy?"

Jack nodded. "I'm liking what I'm hearing about it."

"There's a ranch in our area that does that for children. Annie, the owner, is a good friend of my sister. Any questions you have, I can give her a call."

"Great. Let Noah know that. I've got a meeting at the bank this morning, so I'll catch up with you around lunchtime."

Dallas headed for the kennels. Curled into a ball, Bella didn't look like she'd moved an inch since he'd left her the day before. He went inside and sat a little closer this time, near enough where he could touch her.

"Hello, Bella." She trembled as she buried her face deeper into her fur. "I don't know what was done to you, but I'm sorry that some poor excuse for a human hurt you." He kept his voice soft, but her body violently shook. "I promise that I'll never hurt you, pretty girl."

Because her reaction to him was so strong, he suspected that a male had abused her. He had never dealt with a mistreated dog, but his family had taken in several abused horses over the years. Dallas had worked with his brother Phoenix in gaining the trust of those horses. Out of all the Manning kids, the two of them had a way with the horses. Phoenix even more than Dallas, which was why Phoenix headed up their equine operation.

The Manning ranch was one of the biggest in Montana. Oldest brother Austin was the chief operating officer of the entire spread, Denver was in charge of their cattle enterprise, and Cheyenne and her husband had the dude ranch. That left him and his sister Shiloh, the two youngest, with only the option of working under one of their siblings, which neither one was agreeable to. He'd joined the Navy and Shiloh was a search and rescue Coast Guard helicopter pilot, which was way cool.

He thought back to the times he'd spent with Phoenix, a true horse whisperer, and what he'd learned from his brother. Calmness, patience, no threatening moves or raised voices, and a gentle touch were all things Phoenix had stressed. "Don't look them in the eye, as that's an aggressive act, and talk to them in a soft voice. Talk to them a lot," Phoenix often said.

Okay, so talk it was. "How about I tell you a wildcat story? Would you like that? She's something else, that wildcat. Actually tried to bash my head in." He chuckled. "Yeah, she tried to brain me senseless. Crazy, huh? She's a stunt double. What do you think of that? I watched two of her movies last night, and let me tell you, she's pretty awesome."

It seemed that she was listening, so he continued on, keeping his voice soft. "I have a real dilemma though, and maybe you can give me your opinion. She's a friend of Jack and Nichole's, but she's refusing to let me tell them she's here because there's a bad guy out to hurt her and she doesn't want Jack involved."

She still had her face hidden, but she wasn't trembling anymore, and he counted that as a win. "So, Bella, what do I do? Keep her trust or tell Jack that a friend of his needs our help?"

"A friend needs our help and you're not telling me?" Jack said.

Well, hell. There was going to be one pissed-off wildcat when she found out he'd outed her, even if accidently. He glanced up. "Thought you were gone." When Bella whimpered, Dallas pushed up. "We're upsetting the dog. Let's take this outside."

"Weren't you headed to the bank?" he said when they were away from Bella.

"My meeting got delayed for an hour. Who's at the cabin and what's going on?"

"Your friend Rachel. She—"

"And you weren't going to tell me?"

Yeah, Jack was angry, but Dallas didn't blame him. He wouldn't be so happy either. "I wanted to, but she begged me not to. I would have eventually if I couldn't talk her into telling you herself, which I've been trying to get her to do. She doesn't want you involved because she's trying to protect you."

"You need to start at the beginning."

Dallas leaned back against the building. "Well, the beginning would be when she tried to crack my head open with a tree branch." He related everything Rachel had told him. "If this Robert Hargrove has the resources she says he does, he'll eventually find her, but she covered her tracks pretty impressively, so there wasn't the urgency to tell you immediately. I wanted telling you to be her decision if I could get her to accept that she needed to. If not, I planned to."

"And this is why you want a gun?"

"Yep. Sorry for the lie."

"Well, now I know. Bring her to dinner tonight."

"Not sure that's a good idea. She's not going to be happy with either one of us. She doesn't even want me at the cabin with her because she's afraid I'll get hurt, but I told her I wasn't going anywhere. Besides, I think you, me, and Noah need to put our heads together, come up with a plan without her there."

"Yeah, maybe we need to do that before she knows I know she's here. We're going to have to talk about this without Nichole and Peyton hearing. They'll both want to rush right over to the cabin."

"Copy that. I still want a gun."

"I'll give you one tonight. Why don't you head back

to the cabin and keep an eye on her? I'm not real comfortable with her being alone."

"Yeah, I'm not either. That's another reason I wanted her to tell you, so the three of us could have eyes on her, making sure she stays safe."

Jack glanced at his watch. "I need to head to the bank. Come over around five. We'll eat early, talk about how we're going to handle this, and then you can get back to the cabin before it gets too late."

"That works." Jack left, and Dallas went back to spend a few more minutes with Bella before returning to the cabin. He sat even closer this time, and it seemed to him that the dog wasn't shaking quite as much.

"So, Bella, how angry with me do you think our wildcat's gonna be?"

Chapter Six

Rachel was bored. She'd gone for a run, cleaned the cabin even though it didn't really need it, and had finished reading the book she'd started last night when she couldn't sleep. The restless night, she blamed on a cowboy.

She really needed the distraction of him gone, but the blasted man had dug in the heels of his boots, refusing to leave. A few years ago, she'd stunt doubled for an actress in a western, and at the time, she'd thought casting had picked the perfect male lead for the cowboy role.

Ha! She was reevaluating her opinion on that. Dallas…what was his last name, anyway? Dallas whoever was the personification of a real cowboy.

Duh, Rach, that's because he is a real cowboy.

She was scouring the contents of the freezer for something to make him for dinner since he'd cooked last night when she remembered he was having dinner with Jack and Nichole.

What she wouldn't give to see her best friend, but if she told Nichole she was in Asheville, Nichole would tell Jack, and Jack would go all into hero mode, putting his life on the line to protect her. She refused to let him do that. If Robert hurt Jack, or God forbid, worse, and Nichole lost her husband, Rachel wouldn't be able to live with herself. So no, no matter how much Dallas pushed her to tell Jack she was here and why, she'd stand strong.

She hadn't heard from Detective Diaz since she'd arrived, so she called him, got his voice mail, and left a message. Now what? She was too restless to start another book, and the cabin was spotless, so… She could go for another run. It was important that she stay in shape, but the thought of running up the mountain again had her groaning.

While she was trying to decide what to do, her phone buzzed, Detective Diaz's number showing on the screen. "Thanks for calling me back, Detective."

"I wish I had good news for you, but so far, we haven't been able to find Robert Hargrove."

That wasn't what she wanted to hear, but she wasn't surprised. "So what happens now?"

"We keep looking. Also, because his wife told you he was dealing in illegal arms, we've passed everything we know about him on to the FBI, so they're involved now."

"That's a good thing, right?"

"Definitely. They want to talk to you, but I told them I needed to let you know before I gave them your number. I was going to call you today, in fact, to update you."

"I'll talk to them, but I'd rather be the one to make the call." Could the FBI trace a burner phone? She wasn't sure she wanted the FBI to know her location.

"Fair enough. You have a pen handy?"

"Yeah, hold on a sec." She grabbed her purse and fished out a pen and her notepad. "Okay, go."

"Where are you, Rachel?" he said after giving her the information.

"Someplace safe." At least for now.

"You don't trust me?"

"No offense, but I don't trust anyone right now. Henrietta told me Robert had the police…and I'm not accusing you, but that he had some police on the payroll. That was one reason she wouldn't go to the police herself."

"I promise you I'm not on his payroll. I want to see the man behind bars if he really did kill his wife."

"You doubt me?"

"No, I believe you, but lack of a body makes it just your word."

Lack of a body. That sounded so cold. "The body has a name," she snapped. Tears burned as the loss of her sweet friend hit her again. "I'm sorry. I know you're doing the best you can."

"And we won't stop until we find him, Rachel. Call the FBI. They're waiting to hear from you and having them involved will only help."

"I'll call them today." After she figured out the best way to contact them. Dallas would probably know if a burner phone could be traced. He was a SEAL, and SEALs knew all kinds of secret stuff, right?

Dallas had put his number in her phone, and she thought about calling him to ask about tracing burner phones but decided against it. If Dallas was with Jack, it wasn't a conversation she wanted Jack to overhear, so she'd wait until Dallas got back to the cabin.

After another run, she showered, ate a late lunch, and then made a cup of tea to take out to the porch. This business with Robert needed to be over so she could get her life back. Her next movie started filming in three weeks, and surely the police or FBI would have found him by then. Actually, she needed to be back in LA by the end of next week as the stunt doubles had a meeting with their stunt coordinator to learn what stunts would be required. It was a meeting she couldn't miss.

The movie was about a female FBI profiler targeted by a serial killer, and two of the biggest names in Hollywood were starring in it. She was doubling for the female lead, and there was already talk that the movie would be a blockbuster.

She'd just finished her tea when the Jeep came down the drive. Dallas was returning sooner than she'd expected, and when he parked and got out, her heart gave a little twitch of excitement at seeing him. That wasn't good.

He came up the steps, stopping in front of her. "Soaking up some sun? That's a very catlike thing to do."

"Ha-ha. More like thinking."

He settled in the rocker next to her. "About?"

"My life and how it pretty much sucks right now. I talked to the detective in charge of the case today. No trace of Robert so far, but Detective Diaz has brought in the FBI and I'm supposed to call them."

"That's good, right?"

"I hope so, but I'm nervous about them tracing the call. According to Henri, Robert has some police on the payroll. I'm not saying the detective or FBI are included in that, but I really don't want them to know where I am." She glanced over at him. "I'm not feeling very trusting these days. Can the FBI trace a burner phone?"

"Yes." He stretched out his legs. "I'd say you could trust the FBI, but if you're uncomfortable with them knowing where you are, let's think of a way for you to make the call without them being able to locate you."

"How?" Even if she used someone else's phone, they'd still know she was in the Asheville area. "Who are you calling?" she said when he took out his phone.

"A friend."

"I don't want—"

"You can trust him." He scrolled through his contacts, then put his finger on one. "I'll put it on speaker so you can listen."

"Well, if it ain't a ghost calling me. Hell must've frozen over," a male voice said.

Dallas rolled his eyes. "Boo!"

The man on the other end laughed.

"Listen, I've got someone here, and she needs some help that I think you can give her. I've got you on speaker. Rachel, this is Carter."

"Hi."

"Hello, Rachel. What can I do for you?"

"Um…" How much was she supposed to tell him?

"She needs to call the FBI, but she doesn't want them to trace her phone," Dallas said.

Okay, he didn't need the whole story. That was good. "I have a burner phone, but Dallas said they could trace it."

"They certainly can, but you've come to the right place. I can route you through so many countries they'll never be able to track the call back to you."

"Oh." Who was this guy? "Okay, that's good. I talked to a police detective this morning. Do you think they might have traced that call?" She hadn't even thought about that when she'd talked to Detective Diaz.

"How long ago was that?"

She checked the time on her watch. "About three hours. The detective's in LA, and I'm in…" She hesitated, but Dallas said she could trust this guy. "North Carolina." He didn't need to know exactly where.

Carter chuckled. "Sweetheart, you're in Asheville. I've already traced your location."

Her heart lurched, and panicking, she grabbed for Dallas's phone to disconnect. He held it away from her.

"You scared her, TG."

"Sorry about that, Rachel. I just wanted to show you that I'm good at what I do. As for the police tracing your call, they probably didn't, or you'd have an Asheville officer on your doorstep by now. Which brings up the question, do you trust the detective?"

"I think so, but I can't swear to that." But no more direct calls to Detective Diaz.

"If it's okay with you, I'll dig into him a little."

"That's definitely okay, and thanks."

"Not a problem. You need to make this call now?" Carter asked.

She glanced at Dallas, and he shrugged, telling her that it was her decision. She'd never been so unsure of what to do in her life. Damn Robert to hell for doing this to her.

"Yeah, I might as well get it over with." She pulled the notepaper out of her pocket and read off the FBI agent's name and number.

"Just so you know, I'll be listening in," Carter said. "If anything feels off, I'll disconnect."

"Who are you?" She hadn't meant to say that out loud, but really, without even seeing the man, he was scary.

"Just an ordinary man who can help you."

Dallas snorted. There was nothing ordinary about his friend. Carter Jeffers, now the owner of Titan Group, had been a brilliant and deadly Delta Force operator. Those men were even more secretive than the SEALs. Dallas, along with Jack and Noah, could physically protect Rachel, but Carter could make her invisible to anyone trying to find her.

If he was willing, and Dallas hoped Carter found the situation with Rachel intriguing enough to catch his interest, he could help track down Robert Hargrove. For one thing, he didn't have to follow the rules the FBI did, and he wasn't shy about crossing a line in his investigations if it was for the greater good. He also had resources and the kind of technology the FBI only dreamed of.

"One last thing before you talk to them, Rachel. The number of the phone you're talking on isn't going to show up when we call them, and that's going to tell them you've figured out how to hide it, which is going to up their curiosity. If they ask how you did that, don't answer. If they ask for your number, give them this one… you have a pen?"

"I'll remember it," Dallas said, handing her his phone.

After Carter rattled off the number, and while he was doing his magic to hide her location and connecting her with the FBI, Dallas went inside. He found a pen and wrote down the number. Returning to the porch, he settled down to listen to the conversation.

"Special agent Jim Rhodes speaking."

"Mr. Rhodes, this is Rachel Denning. Detective Diaz said you wanted to talk to me."

"Yes, and thank you for calling, Ms. Denning. We'd like to sit down with you and discuss the situation you've found yourself in with Robert Hargrove. Special agent Laura Macklin and I can come to your home if you'd be more comfortable talking to us there. Or you can come to our office. Your choice."

"That's not possible. I'm not in LA at the moment."

"Where are you? We can have agents from a local field office meet with you."

"Someplace safe. You'll have to ask your questions over the phone."

"Rachel...may I call you Rachel?"

"Sure."

"Thank you. Rachel, we can't protect you if we don't know where you are, and if Robert Hargrove is as dangerous as we believe, you want us at your side. Are you within driving distance to LA?"

Dallas could envision Carter rolling his eyes at their attempt to find out where she was.

"If I am, I'm still not meeting you in person. If you want to talk to me, you'll have to do it by my rules."

He grinned. She wasn't giving the agent any clue as to where she was. His wildcat was no one's fool. He'd bet his favorite horse that they already knew she wasn't at home.

The agent sighed. "I understand you're afraid, and for now, we'll do it your way. But at some point, we need to meet with you."

"We'll see. What do you want to know?"

"Everything. Start from the beginning. We will be recording what you tell us."

As Dallas again listened to her tell the story of her friend's murder, he wanted to personally hunt down Hargrove and teach him a lesson. There were a few seconds of silence when she finished, as if the agent and whoever else was listening were digesting everything she'd told them.

"Finding Robert Hargrove is a priority," the agent said. "We can put you in a safe house until then, and I urge you to consider letting us protect you."

"Thanks, but I'm in a safe place."

"One other thing before you go. I'm going to be real honest with you. The number you're calling from is blocked and we haven't been able to trace your call. Unless you know how to do that, you have someone helping you. If you'd tell us who, we can work with them on protecting you."

Dallas shook his head.

"I'm sorry, but I'm not giving you any names," she said.

Another sigh sounded. "You're not making this easy, Rachel. I wish you'd trust us. We are going to insist that you give us a number to contact you if we have more questions or need to update you on our progress."

Dallas handed her the paper with the number Carter had given them, and she read it off to the agent. When she finished, Dallas took his phone. He didn't say anything until Carter came on the line.

"I've severed the connection, so we can freely talk now. Sounds like you've stepped in some bad shit, Rachel."

"Ya think?"

"You mind if I do a little snooping, darlin'?"

That was exactly what Dallas had been hoping for. "By all means," Dallas answered for her. "We'd appreciate anything you can learn."

"Good. Take me off speaker, Dallas."

He did, then put the phone to his ear. "You're off."

"Text me Rachel's burner number so I can route any

calls to it through me, and put my number in her phone so she can reach me if she needs to. Call me back when you can talk without Rachel listening. We need to make a plan for keeping your girl safe."

"Will do." He'd make that call tonight when he was with Jack and Noah.

"It's good talking to you, brother. You need to unload any of that shit I know you got going on in your head, I'm here for you."

"I'm good."

"No you're not. No one's good after what you went through. The biggest mistake you can make, Ghost, is keeping it all bottled up. Hooah."

After giving the army's battle cry, Carter disconnected before Dallas could respond with the Navy's. Asshole. "Hooyah," he said anyway.

"Hooyah? What does that mean?"

Dallas set his phone on the table between them. "Hooyah is the Navy's battle cry."

"You're going to battle with Carter?"

She was cute when she scrunched up her eyebrows like that.

"Nope." He didn't know how to explain the military brotherhood and their quirky sense of humor, so he didn't try. "You feel better after talking to the FBI?"

"I honestly don't know. I guess it's good they're involved, but I think Robert's like a snake. Hard to catch and dangerous. Why did Carter say a ghost was calling?"

"Ghost is my call sign. He was trying to be funny."

"Like Jack's was Whiskey?"

"Yeah, and Noah was Double D."

"So, Carter's is TG? What does that stand for?"

"Tech Geek." He needed to tell her that Jack knew she was here, even if it made her angry that he'd let it slip. "I have to head over to Jack's shortly. Why don't you come with me?" The plan was for him, Jack, and Noah to talk about how to keep her safe, but it was her life, and he wasn't comfortable making decisions for her without including her. He sure wouldn't appreciate being excluded from discussions that concerned him.

"No. I've already told you I don't want him get involved."

"Sorry, but he already is."

Chapter Seven

"You told him?" Rachel was furious. He'd promised he wouldn't. Had he actually promised, though, or had he just let her think he had? She couldn't remember his exact words, but he knew how she felt about Jack and Nichole knowing she was here.

"Not on purpose."

"What does that mean? The words just came out of your mouth on their own?"

"No, I was telling Bella about you, and—"

"You talked about me to another woman? What the hell, Dallas?" And who was Bella? She thought he was spending the day with Jack. The streak of jealousy just added to her anger. She went inside, slamming the door behind her. He followed her in.

"Bella's a dog."

Oh. Now she felt stupid, but she was still not happy with him. She faced him and crossed her arms over her chest. "You said you wouldn't tell Jack."

"And I didn't. Jack wasn't supposed to be there. Bella's an abused dog, afraid of everything. I was sitting in her kennel, talking to her, trying to get her used to me." He shrugged. "I just started telling her how you tried to brain me with a tree branch, and I didn't know Jack had walked up behind me."

Well, drat. How was she supposed to stay mad at him? "Is he angry I didn't tell him I'm here?"

"He's angry with me for not telling him, but he's worried about you. There's no way you can keep him out of this now that he knows. Noah and Peyton will be there tonight, and the conversation will be how to keep you safe. You can stay here and let us plan your life until Hargrove's caught, or you can come and be a part of our discussion."

"Well, when you put it that way." She wanted to stomp her feet and throw a tantrum, but it wouldn't change anything. "I'll go get dressed."

As soon as Rachel stepped inside Jack and Nichole's house, she was attacked.

"I'm so mad at you!" Nichole shrieked as she tackled Rachel. "How could you be in Asheville and not tell me?"

"I didn't want—"

"No, no excuses." She stepped back. "When Dallas called and said he was bringing you with him, I said to Jack, 'What's he talking about? Rachel isn't here.' If you were, I'd know about it." She put her hands on her hips. "But wrooong! Did I tell you I'm mad at you?"

Rachel glanced at Dallas, and he raised his brows as if saying, "I told you so." She was tempted to stick out her tongue at him.

"You have a lot of explaining to do." Nichole grabbed her hand. "This calls for booze."

She was dragged straight out to the back deck where a bucket of beer on ice was on the table, along with a pitcher of margaritas, and a bottle of wine. She went straight for a margarita, in an already salt-rimmed glass.

Nichole poured herself a glass of wine, then plopped down in a chair. "Start talking. Tell me why you thought it was okay to sneak into town and not tell me."

"How much do you know?" Rachel scooted onto a chair across from her best friend.

"Nothing! I know nothing. Dallas called, said he was on the way, said you were with him, and I thought he was delusional. He didn't know you. How could you be with him?"

"About that." Before she could explain, Dallas and Jack walked out. Jack went straight to the empty chair next to Nichole, and Dallas slid onto the one next to her. She wished he was on the opposite side of the deck so his scent wasn't all up in her nose. Swear to God, he smelled better than any billion-dollar-earning actor she'd ever been around. He smelled like a man she would never get tired of sniffing.

It had to be a cowboy thing, that scent that made her think of wide-open plains and the men who wore spurs on their boots as they raced their horses across fields while doing…well, whatever real cowboys did.

In reality, those men probably didn't smell so good, but she spent most of her life in pretend worlds, and she was fully capable of ignoring reality when she wanted.

Nichole nudged Jack. "Tell her there's nothing she can say that makes it all right for her to sneak into town without telling us."

"She's right, you know," he said.

Noah and Peyton came around the corner of the house, saving her from having to respond. They were holding hands—which was really cute, and she was expecting to see a wedding announcement soon—and they took the seats on the other side of Nichole.

"I didn't know you were in town," Peyton said.

"It's kind of an unplanned trip. It's good seeing you again." They'd become friends during the week she'd been here for Nichole's wedding, had bonded over her maid of honor duties and Peyton's bridesmaid tasks.

"Well, whatever the reason, it's a nice surprise. The three of us girls need to have a play day."

"No," Dallas said.

Peyton's eyes widened. "Who are you?"

"That's Dallas Manning, a teammate of mine and Jack's," Noah said. "He's usually better behaved."

"Really? I've not seen that side of him." Rachel glanced at Dallas. "So you can play nice when you want?" She laughed when he only grunted.

"Well, since no one seems inclined to introduce me, I'm Peyton Sutton, Noah's fiancée. Nice to meet you, Dallas, even if you don't play well with others." She grinned to let him know she was teasing. "Why can't Rachel have a play day with Nichole and me?"

"We'll talk about that after dinner," Jack said. "For now, let's just kick back and enjoy some good brew with friends." He pulled a beer from the ice bucket and handed it over to Dallas. "Peyton's a master beer brewer. This is one of hers."

Dallas eyed the label. "Not My Grannie's Tea. Interesting name." He twisted off the cap and took a swallow. "Damn good."

"Thanks. There are some other flavors in the bucket you might want to try," Peyton said.

As Dallas held the bottle, Rachel noticed that two of his fingers were misshaped, as if they'd been broken and not set right. Was that from when he'd been held captive? While the others talked, she subtly studied him. Jack and Noah had on short-sleeve T-shirts, but Dallas wore a long-sleeve Henley. She'd never seen him in anything but long sleeves. Again, she wondered about his time in captivity.

She probably wouldn't have thought much about it if not for a stuntman she'd worked with whose arms had been burned in a stunt gone wrong. After that, he always wore long-sleeve shirts, even on the hottest days. Was Dallas hiding scars?

Her gaze was caught by the way his throat flexed as he swallowed, by the long fingers wrapped around the beer bottle, by his mouth when it pressed the bottle to those full lips, and… *Stop it! Just stop drooling over his body parts.* But they were such mouthwatering parts.

"You keep staring at me with those soft eyes, and we're going to leave this party and go get down and dirty."

"Asshole," she hissed. The others were talking and not paying attention to them, and he'd kept his voice low to not be overheard. That was good, but she'd go after him with her tree branch again to keep him from discovering how down and dirty she'd like to get. With him.

The dratted man laughed.

Jack swung his gaze to Dallas. "Good to hear you laughing, brother. Want to share?"

She narrowed her eyes at Dallas in the deadliest glare she could manage. If he gave one hint as to why he was laughing, she would sneak into his room later tonight and smother him in his sleep.

"Nothing to share," he said, staring back at her as hard as she was staring at him. He could melt icecaps with the fire he was directing at her. Rachel vaguely wondered if Jack and Nichole had a fire extinguisher handy.

There had never been this much chemistry and heat between her and any other man in all of her twenty-nine years. Why—seriously why—couldn't the cowboy have stampeded into her life when she wasn't afraid of Robert killing her and anyone associated with her?

She tore her gaze away. No good could come of anything happening with the sexy as all get-out man sending her heated looks. Would it seem odd to the others if she moved her chair to the other side of the table? Yeah, that would look weird.

"Time to get down to business," Jack said when everyone had finished their dinner. His gaze settled on Rachel. "I'm not real happy with you, girl."

Nichole glanced between the two of them. "What's going on?"

"Your best friend is running from someone who wants to hurt her, and she wasn't going to tell us that she's hiding out at the cabin."

"What?" Nichole reached across Dallas and grabbed her hand. "Is that true?"

"Yes."

"But why wouldn't you tell us?"

Dallas pushed his plate away. "She didn't want to bring trouble to your door." He looked at her. "Admirable but misguided."

"I'm still not happy that you let the cat out of the bag," she said, shooting him a glare.

He shrugged. "Too bad, wildcat. You don't have to

like it, but you have three men sitting at this table who can and will protect you."

"Wildcat?" Jack said. "She's who you were referring to when you asked about wildcats around the cabin?"

"Told you I thought there was one nosing around." He grinned at her. "This one tried to brain me with a tree branch."

She punched his arm. "Will you give it up with that already!"

"Nope. It's a story we'll tell our children and grandchildren." Silence followed his statement, and he glanced around the table to see everyone looking at him with varying degrees of interest, or in Jack's case, a frown. "Inside joke." Marrying her was just something he'd gotten used to teasing her about, and he'd forgotten they had an audience.

"Wait. Back up." Nichole waved a hand toward them. "I need to hear that story."

He told them about coming into the cabin, not knowing she was there and how he'd ended up with an arm full of wildcat.

Peyton clapped her hands. "That's hilarious." She grimaced. "I mean it is and it's not. You had to be so scared when you heard him come in, Rachel."

"Yeah. I thought it was Robert or one of his men, that they'd found me."

"Who's Robert?" Noah said.

Rachel sighed. "Can't you guys just leave this alone?"

"Not a chance." Dallas sat back. "Start from the beginning and tell them everything."

Her gaze dropped to the table, and he understood that she was worried about putting her friends in danger, but that concern was misguided. She really didn't have a clue how highly trained and deadly the three of them were. Add TG to the mix, and she couldn't have a better team on her side. She lifted her gaze, her eyes flashing that fire that made him want to see just how hot she could burn.

He still wasn't sure what to do about that. The smart thing would be to shut down his growing desire for this woman, but he was finding he didn't particularly want to be smart where Rachel Denning was concerned.

Another sigh, longer than the last one, then she shook her head in defeat. As she told the story he'd heard twice before now, his rage at Robert Hargrove again went from simmering to boiling over. If she hadn't gotten away that day, she would be dead. When they found him—and they would—the man was going to be one sorry bastard.

"My God," Nichole said when Rachel finished. "How could you even think you shouldn't tell us this right away? You need to come here and stay with me and Jack."

Dallas shook his head. "Not a good idea. It's common knowledge that she was here not long ago for your wedding. This is one of the first places Hargrove will look when he realizes she's not still in LA. In fact, you need to be hyperaware of your surroundings and be very cautious, especially when you're alone."

Jack scowled. "She's not going to be alone until we see Hargrove behind bars."

"I'm so sorry," Rachel said, her voice trembling. "I've put all of you in danger. I never should have come here."

Dallas put his hand over hers. "This is the best place you could have come."

"Why don't you both come stay with us until this is over?" Noah slid his gaze from Rachel to Nichole. "Hargrove doesn't know who we are or where we live."

"I'd love that," Peyton said. "We can have girlfriend time. Eat popcorn and make Noah watch a bunch of sappy movies."

"Rachel stays with me." Dallas realized that sounded possessive, but he didn't care.

Nichole shook her head. "I need to be home. I have orders I'm committed to fill, and my studio is here."

"We'll figure something out." Jack put his arm around the back of his wife's chair. "But bottom line, your life is more important than any plate or cup."

Nichole was a successful potter, and Dallas could appreciate that she wanted to honor her commitments, but Jack was absolutely right. "The question is, how long will it take Hargrove to come nosing around here? We can't take any chances." He squeezed Rachel's hand. "No more leaving the cabin unless you're in one of your disguises and one of us is with you."

"I hate this so much," she said.

"Let's continue this discussion tomorrow." Jack stood and picked up his and Nichole's dishes.

"We'll be in my studio," Nichole said. "I want to show Rachel and Peyton the Victorian-era teacups I'm doing for one of the gift shops at the Biltmore Estate."

Dallas carried his plate and Rachel's to the kitchen. He suspected the girls wanted time alone to talk about what Rachel had told them. He'd met Nichole previously and really liked her. She was perfect for Jack. And Peyton was hilarious, especially when she got on a roll. It was obvious that Noah was besotted with the woman. He was glad to see his brothers happy.

Could he find what they had someday? He'd always wanted a family eventually. Unlike many of his team-mates, he hadn't planned to stay in the Navy until they kicked his tired bones out. Three more years was what he'd given himself before he was captured, then the plan was to figure out what to do with the rest of his life and find a woman to fall in love with. They would have babies and live happily ever after.

Overnight, those plans had changed. Now he was on medical leave and had no intention of returning to active duty. He was rudderless, and not in a good place to bring a woman into his life. He wasn't sure he ever would be.

Yet Rachel made him feel alive again. Damn if he understood why. It was a puzzle he wanted to solve. Being around her...well, she gave him hope that his mind could heal. He'd always have the scars on his body, and he could live with that, didn't have a choice.

So what was he going to do about his wildcat? He didn't have an answer, not yet anyway.

Four dogs trotted into the kitchen, including Dakota and Lucky. Dakota had been the team's dog, Jack her handler. An IED had exploded, wounding them both, ending their military careers. "Who are your friends, Dakota?"

"These other two are Rambo and Maggie May." Jack set the dishes on the counter and swept his hand downward. All four dogs sat. "It's really good to have you here."

"Better than I thought it would be." He leaned against the counter as Jack loaded the dishwasher.

"If it's helping, then I hope you stick around for a while." Jack started to say something else, then stopped.

"You got something on your mind?"

"Just that I see the way you look at Rachel. She's a good friend, Nichole's best friend. You're not in a good place for a relationship, and Rachel's not a woman you just have a fling with. I love you, brother, but I won't stand by and watch you hurt her."

"Think much of me, do you?" Dallas pushed down the anger bubbling up before he said something he couldn't take back.

"I think the world of you. Hell, you know that. That's not what this is about. I don't want to see either of you get hurt. You've been through more recently than any person should have, and Rachel will soak that up. She'll feel your pain and be drawn to you. She'll want to heal you."

"What do you mean, soak that up?"

Jack closed the door to the dishwasher, then leaned back against the opposite counter. "She hasn't told you?"

"I have no idea what you're talking about."

"Rachel's an empath. She feels your emotions, your pain."

He didn't want anyone, especially her, feeling his pain. Why hadn't she told him?

"I know that sounds farfetched," Jack said. "But there is such a thing. I've seen it happen with her."

"My sister Cheyenne's mother-in-law is Crow, and she has that ability. I guess I just thought it was a First Nations thing and the way the Indigenous people are in tune with the earth in a way we've forgotten." He'd always thought it was a cool thing that Chenoa could do, but he didn't so much like Rachel *feeling* him. What he'd lived through was for him alone to deal with.

"We talking about what we're gonna do?" Noah said, coming in with his own stack of dishes.

"I was about to tell Jack that I'm supposed to call TG later tonight," Dallas said, cutting off anything Jack might say about warning him off Rachel. He needed to do some thinking about her, what she was, and what he planned to do—if anything—without more input from his well-meaning brothers.

Noah made a funny face. "That man scares me."

"He's definitely spooky," Jack said. "Rachel only said that he'd made the call to the FBI so her phone couldn't be traced. He have anything else to say?"

"Not really. He's going to do some digging, see what he can find on Hargrove."

"Okay, that's another member of the team and a good one to have." Jack glanced at Noah. "You free first thing tomorrow?"

"Yeah. The concrete truck will be at the site in the afternoon to pour some foundations for the cabins, but I'm free until then."

"Good." He turned to Dallas. "Let's meet for breakfast and make some plans. Then you can hang with Noah after that. I'd like you to see what we're doing." He glanced at Noah. "Show him where we're thinking about an equine center and get his input on what we need."

Dallas was curious about Jack's plans for his new center, but having a meeting that involved Rachel behind her back? That was a no-go. "If we're going to meet to make plans on how to protect Rachel, then she needs to be there."

"Why did I know you were going to say that?" Jack narrowed his eyes. "I'm telling you right now, brother, she's off-limits."

Noah laughed as he slapped Dallas on the back.

"Papa tried to warn me off Peyton, yet she's wearing my engagement ring. If you ask me, if Rachel's the one, go for it."

At any other time in his life, she could be the one, but not now. There was also her empath thing. For the first time, he was uncomfortable around her.

Chapter Eight

"Tell me how this empath thing works."

Halfway to her room, Rachel froze. Who had told him her secret? Returning to the cabin from Jack and Nichole's, Dallas had been strangely quiet. She'd been thankful for that after the exhausting time she'd spent telling her friends why Robert wanted to kill her. She prayed it was the last time she had to relive Henri's murder.

Even though she was grateful Dallas had left her to her thoughts, his silence had unnerved her. Stupid that. He was nothing to her other than a ridiculously sexy man she was accidently sharing a cabin with until they both returned to their own worlds.

She faced him. "Who told you?" Lord, he was something to look at, standing there with his long legs braced apart, and those troubled hazel eyes focused on her.

"Jack. I would have rather heard it from you."

"Why? It has nothing to do with you, so I don't understand why you think I owed you an explanation."

"You don't think I should know that you can…what, read me?"

He was bothered by the idea of that. Why? "It's not that I can read people. I don't know what they're thinking, what's in their heads. I just feel their emotions."

"Well, don't feel mine."

She laughed. "You think it's something I can just turn on or off? But don't worry. For some reason, I don't feel your emotions. It's like you don't have any, but I know you do. I see it in your eyes when they get that haunted look in them. But I don't—" she made air quotes "—feel you. That's interesting, don't you think?"

Why did he seem so relieved by that?

They stared at each other, and as they did, his eyes turned stormy. What he didn't know about her was that she was drawn to storms. To their exhilarating furiousness, to the roaring of the wind through the trees, to the sound of the rain beating against windowpanes, to the jagged white bolts of lightning that lit up the sky, and the rolling thunder booming across the earth that shook the land under one's feet.

The man standing in front of her was a storm in a human body, and was she drawn to him? Yes. Yes, she was.

"Rachel," he rumbled, just like the thunder did.

She didn't register her feet moving, not until she was close enough to reach out and touch him. She glanced down at her feet, wondering how they'd done that without her command.

"Rachel," he said again, his voice raw and a bit wild, like a storm. "Look at me."

Unable to defy him, she lifted her gaze to his. The tropical storm that had been swirling in his eyes only minutes ago was now a raging hurricane. And like a storm, the oxygen was sucked out of the air, or out of her lungs anyway. Her breath caught, and he knew.

"Breathe." He grazed his thumb over her bottom lip.

She sucked air back into her lungs. What kind of witchery was he using on her?

"When I kissed you before, I promised myself I wouldn't do it again. I think I lied." His thumb was still sweeping over her mouth, and that simple gesture sent shivers through her body, all the way down to her toes. "Can I kiss you again?"

Incapable of speaking, she nodded. He chuckled, and she thought he was pleased that her brain and mouth had ceased to work, that he'd done that to her. His lips brushed over hers. *Feathers.* If she closed her eyes, she would think he was teasing her lips with feathers. It was strangely erotic. Erotic because those gentle brushes against her mouth were not only sending shivers through her, but they heated her down to her core. She clenched her legs together, fighting the building heat.

She wouldn't have expected a SEAL cowboy to know how to be so gentle. The man was full of surprises, and she wanted to discover them all. She'd never been kissed like this, like her mouth was the most precious thing in the world, a thing to be cherished. And she did feel cherished. That in itself scared her. She could fall for this man so easily. That would be a mistake, and she was tired of making mistakes. She didn't want regrets because of Dallas. She didn't want to go home and wish she'd never met him because she couldn't forget him.

Just as she thought to run for her life, or at least for her sanity, he deepened the kiss. His tongue traced the seam of her mouth, and in the way her feet had grown a mind of their own, so did her mouth. She opened, inviting him in, and he swooped in and wiped her memory clean of any other man who'd kissed her.

He hummed deep in his throat as their tongues tangled, and the sound of that low hum, the need for her she heard in it, silenced the warning bells ringing in the back of her head. She wrapped her hands around his neck, and he slid his down to her hips and pulled her against him. Kissing him felt right, like they fit perfectly, and this was where she belonged.

That thought alone had the warning bells clanging again. She couldn't fall for this man, and that was the direction she was headed. She had a life in LA. He was a Montana cowboy when he wasn't being a SEAL in some foreign country. Their lives didn't mesh. The last thing she needed was a broken heart.

"Stop," she whispered. He immediately let go of her and stepped back. She curled her fingers into her palms to keep from pulling him to her again. "I'm sorry."

His face blanked. "No, I am. It won't happen again." He turned and walked out the door.

She stared at the empty space where he'd stood only seconds before. It shouldn't feel like he'd taken a part of her out that door with him. She shouldn't feel like she'd just lost something she hadn't known she'd needed. There shouldn't be unshed tears burning her eyes. When she heard the Jeep's engine come to life, she walked to the window and watched it drive away.

Damn you, Robert. This is your fault. If not for him, she wouldn't be in Asheville, wouldn't have met a SEAL cowboy who was able to kiss her senseless. She wouldn't know what she was missing when this was over and she returned home. She wouldn't wonder what he was doing, who else he might be kissing.

Resisting the urge to go find Dallas, she went to her room and called Nichole. "You need to get him someplace else to stay."

"By him, you mean your hot roommate?"

"You have no business thinking anyone other than Jack is hot."

Nichole laughed. "I didn't lose my eyes when I married Jack. What's crawled up your butt?"

"He kissed me."

"And that's a bad thing?"

"Yes, very bad." It so was, because every kiss from a man after him would be judged against his and come up lacking. She slid a finger over her lips, still warm from his kiss.

"You don't like him?"

"I like him too much."

"Then what's the problem?"

Everything. "You know I don't do hookups. I have to like a guy before I'll sleep with him."

"You just said you did like him."

Drat. She hadn't meant to admit that. "It's not just that. I'm only here until the police find Robert, then I'll go back to LA. Dallas lives in Montana. There's no future there." She didn't want to return home with a broken heart. "Plus, with this mess I'm in, I don't need the distraction."

"Maybe that's exactly what you need."

"I can't feel him."

"Really? Has that ever happened before?"

"Never. It's weird, but truthfully, I like that I can't." Especially since she was positive he had horrible memories bottled up inside from his time as a prisoner. You didn't get tortured and walk away unscathed.

"Maybe it's a sign."

Rachel laughed, knowing exactly where Nichole was going with that. "You read too many romance books."

"Impossible. Just think about it, okay? Let yourself have some cowboy fun."

It was tempting, *he* was tempting. Long after hanging up with Nichole, she was still thinking about cowboy fun. Should she? Shouldn't she? She'd never had a fling, and for the first time in her life, she found the idea of it appealing.

Could she have a fling and walk away with her heart intact? Since she'd never had sex just for the fun of it, she didn't know if that was possible for her. She needed to care for the man, needed to know that he cared for her, before she could be intimate with him.

Maybe she could step out of her comfort zone with Dallas. There was no denying that she was attracted to him, and if his kiss was any indication, the feeling was mutual. If she walked away from this thing between them, would she regret it?

If she went for it, would she regret it?

She needed a crystal ball that showed the future. Where was the man, anyway? She glanced at her watch. What if he'd gone to a bar or someplace to find a hookup because she'd put the brakes on? Would he do that?

No, not Dallas, not after kissing her. It helped that she knew that about him. *Are you sure?* "Gah!" She wasn't sure of anything. The bathroom attached to his bedroom had a tub. Soaking in a nice warm bath always helped her think, and since Dallas had taken off on her, she'd just help herself to it.

"Ghost," Carter said on answering. "Is this a private conversation?"

"Yeah. But I won't keep secrets from Rachel on things that involve her." Dallas leaned back against the

Jeep's hood. After fleeing the cabin and Rachel, he'd ended up at Operation K-9 Brothers. He'd almost gone to Jack's, but then there would be questions he didn't want to answer. Hell, he didn't know the answers.

"Whatever you tell her is your call. While she was on the phone with the FBI this morning, I did a search for unidentified bodies found in the past week. There's one that could possibly fit her friend. A female's body was burned beyond recognition and left in the desert a hundred miles from LA. Henrietta's fingerprints aren't in the system since she's never been arrested, and there's nothing identifying the woman as Henrietta, but my spidey senses are tingling."

If TG's spidey senses were activated, there was a strong possibility the body was Henrietta's. "Damn. I don't want to keep things from her, but I think I'll hold off on this one until the body is identified." It would break Rachel's heart to know what was done to her friend, even after death, and he didn't want to put her through that unnecessarily.

"That's why I didn't say anything this morning. I agree that it's best to hold off telling her until we're sure. I sent an anonymous message to the local sheriff to check the woman's dental records against those of Henrietta Hargrove."

"How long will that take?"

"Typically six to eight weeks, but I can help it along."

"How?"

TG laughed.

What was he thinking? This was TG. "Never mind. You won't tell me your secrets, and I don't want to know them."

"It would be a good idea to get her a new burner

phone since she talked to the police on the one she has. They're probably not tracing it, but better to be safe. Send me the one she has now, and I'll have that number travel around the country."

"You're really scary, TG."

"Nah, I'm harmless. By the way, Rachel's detective appears to be clean."

"That's good. Call me if you learn anything else."

"Will do."

After disconnecting, Dallas headed to the kennels to check on Bella. She was curled up, nose tucked under her tail, in her usual corner. "Hey, Bella girl." She lifted her face, and when she didn't hide again, he considered that a major accomplishment.

He called Jack. "Hey, brother. I'm at the kennels. Still okay if I take Bella to the cabin with me?"

"She's your dog to work with while you're here, so your decision."

"Great. Didn't want you to come in tomorrow and wonder where she was."

"Rachel with you?"

"No." Because he was apparently a kiss and run kind of man. "Talked to TG a few minutes ago," he said to divert Jack's attention from asking about Rachel. He told Jack what TG had said, and Jack agreed with not telling Rachel until they knew for sure if it was Henrietta.

"TG also thinks we should give Rachel a new burner since she called the police with the one she has and they'll have that number. He said to send the one she has to him."

"Good idea. I'll pick one up in the morning."

"Okay, see you then." Finished with the conversation, he went inside the kennel, and took a seat close to Bella.

"Well, look at you, poking your face out." Dallas slowly moved his hand to Bella's nose. It was the first time she'd let him see her face, and he smiled, feeling like he'd won the lottery. She sniffed his fingers. "That's it, Bella girl, get the smell of me."

Keeping his voice gentle, he talked to her as he eased his fingers under her chin. Her eyes closed when he scratched her. "You like that, huh?" For a few minutes, he hummed while he roamed his hand over her fur, surprised that she was letting him.

"So, Bella, I have a confession to make. I kissed a girl, then I told her I was sorry. That was a lie. I wasn't at all sorry. I told her it wouldn't happen again. That might be another lie."

That damn kiss. He'd never tasted anything sweeter, and now he was left with a craving he wasn't sure he'd ever satisfy if he kept his word to her. He'd had to leave to keep from kissing her again.

"What would you do, Bella?" She flicked her tail once. He slid closer to her, and his heart melted for this abused dog when she put her chin on his knee. "Starting to trust me, hmm?" Another halfhearted tail wag. "I wonder what you'd think of Rachel. She's an empath. That means she feels people's emotions, but she can't feel me."

He was relieved that Rachel couldn't. He agreed with her that it was interesting she couldn't, but he didn't want anyone to *feel* his pain and despair, especially her.

"The funny thing, if she hadn't tried to bash my brain in with a tree branch, I don't think I would have paid much attention to her. I was… I am in a bad place, and I would have barely tolerated having her as a roommate. There's just something about a pretty woman who tries to brain you that catches your attention." The sight of her in those purple panties might have had something to do with it, too. He needed to get off this floor.

"My ass is growing numb sitting on this concrete, Bella girl. How would you feel about breaking out of this joint?"

Dallas pulled to a stop in front of the cabin. It had taken a lot of coaxing and patience to get Bella in the Jeep. She'd curled into a tight ball in the passenger seat, and her too thin body had shook when he'd started the engine. He'd discovered that as long as he kept his hand on her, she'd calm down. If he removed it, she would start shaking again, so he'd driven home with one hand on the steering wheel and one on her.

"What the hell did that bastard do to you, Bella girl?" He hoped that by getting her out of the kennel and bringing her to the cabin, that she'd be happier, but maybe he was pushing her too soon. If she was still this stressed out tomorrow, he'd take her back.

She whined when he removed his hand, but her face stayed hidden under her tail. "It's okay. We just have to get out of the Jeep. There's someone I want you to meet. I think you'll like her." He hoped so. Maybe he should have asked Rachel if she was okay with him bringing a dog to the cabin, but too late now. He went around to the passenger side and opened the door.

"Come on. You can't stay in here all night. I promise the wildcat won't eat you." The leash was still attached to her collar, and he picked it up, then slid his other hand under her belly. Before he could haul her out, she jumped to the ground. "See, that wasn't so hard, was it?"

She pressed the side of her body against his leg as she looked around. She was shaking but not as violently as the first time he'd sat in the kennel with her. Maybe she really was starting to trust him. He sure would like to get his hands on the man who'd turned her into a dog afraid of humans.

Rachel was walking down the hallway when they entered the cabin, and he stumbled, almost falling on his face. "Uh…" Rachel wrapped in a white towel, water droplets dripping down her chest from her wet hair was not a sight he was expecting. It was definitely one he liked.

She stilled. "Oh, I didn't know you were back." She gripped the towel tighter, and he resisted telling her he wouldn't mind if it slipped off, not at all. "Um, I took a bath."

Obviously.

"In your bathroom." She waved a hand toward his room as if he didn't know where that was. "I hope you don't mind, but…well, I needed to think, and a bath helps me get my head straight."

"Think about what?"

"Oh, ah, stuff."

He sure would like to know what that stuff was because he had a suspicion that he might be a part of that stuff.

"I'll just go get dressed."

That wasn't necessary on his account, but he figured she wouldn't appreciate him telling her that.

She took a step, then stopped when Bella whined. "What is that?"

He glanced behind him. He'd forgotten about Bella when confronted by a wet wildcat. "This is Bella." She was trying to melt into the back of his legs. "She's a bit of a scaredy cat."

"Aren't you a pretty thing?" Rachel kneeled, the towel parted, giving him a glimpse of the insides of her thighs, and he swallowed hard.

"You might want to get dressed before I introduce you to her." Before he decided the floor was the perfect place to become better acquainted with his roommate.

"Oh, crap." She pushed up and dashed to her room.

"She sure is cute when she blushes," he told Bella. "How about you wait here a minute while I get your food and bed out of the Jeep." When he headed for the door, she went right with him, an attachment to his leg. "Bella, stay." He wasn't expecting her to stop, had only thought it was worth a try. Surprisingly, she stilled. "Good girl."

A few minutes later, he was back with her things. She hadn't moved, and if he wasn't mistaken, that was relief in her eyes at seeing him return. "Did you think I wasn't coming back?" She attached herself to his leg again. He set her bed next to the sofa, then took the food to the kitchen. After filling one of the bowls with water, he set it on the floor. She lapped some up while he stood there, but as soon as he moved, she became a part of his leg again.

"You're kind of like having a stalker." They moved as one to the living room, and when he sat on the sofa, she tried to climb on his lap. "No, silly girl, you can't spend the rest of your life attached to me." She looked at him with the saddest eyes he'd ever seen, and he almost relented, but ground rules needed to be set.

She rested her chin on his leg, her sad eyes fixed on him. He put his hand on her head. "Here's the deal. No one will ever hurt you again, so you don't need to have that worry in your head anymore. I think Jack has a future in mind for you as a service dog. That's a good job to have, but it's going to mean you have to get used to being around people, strangers you don't know. I know that's going to be hard, but I have faith you can do it."

He sensed Rachel before he saw her, and he glanced over as she came into the room. "Bella and I were just having a little motivational talk."

Rachel took a seat on the end of the sofa. "She's shaking like a leaf."

"She's afraid you're going to hurt her. Animal Control took her away from her previous owner because he abused her."

"That's so sad."

"Yeah, it is, but Jack has her now, and she'll never be hurt again." Tears shimmered in Rachel's eyes, and it made him wonder. "Can you feel animal's emotions, too?"

"Sometimes. Not as strongly as I do people. Can I touch her?"

"That's up to her. Just hold your hand out, let her smell your fingers." She did, and Bella pushed her face between Dallas's legs. "She just needs to get used to you, to find out you're not going to hurt her."

"How'd you get her used to you?"

"Sat in her kennel and talked to her in a gentle voice. Moved myself closer to her each time until she let me touch her."

"Let me give it a try." She inched closer. "Hey, Bella Boo Baby. I'm sorry you've been hurt. Some people just aren't meant to live. I promise I'll never hurt you.

I sure would love to run my fingers through your pretty black fur."

Dallas sure would love to have her fingers on him.

"Don't you want to smell me, Bella Boo?"

Oh, he could smell her all right. She smelled good enough to lick. He didn't know what she used in her bath, but it had to be something with apple and vanilla scents in it. Warm apple pie had always been his favorite dessert.

Bella sniffed her fingers before hiding her face between his legs again.

"She'll come around. She just needs a little time to get used to you." His gaze dropped to Rachel's lips. Had she been thinking about letting him kiss her again? "What was the stuff you needed to think about?"

Chapter Nine

"Stuff?" The way he was looking at her mouth—raw hunger in his eyes—made it hard to think. He'd kissed her, then had said it wouldn't happen again. It shouldn't, but man oh man, did she ever want him to kiss her again. And then some more.

Having a fling wasn't her…or it hadn't been her before a SEAL cowboy invaded her hideaway. Now it was all she could think about. She'd weighed the pros and cons while taking a bath, and although there were definite cons, the pros won. She was going for the fun.

Yeehaw!

"Rachel?"

"Hmm?" If he could eat up her mouth with his eyes, she could do the same to him, and oh boy, those lips of his were made for kissing. "Are you really a cowboy?"

"That's the stuff you've been thinking about?"

Well, no, but having cowboy fun would require a cowboy. "In a roundabout way."

"When I'm home, I work on the ranch alongside my family, so I guess you can call me a cowboy if you want, but we refer to ourselves as ranchers. Where are you going with this?"

"Are you still in the Navy? Still a SEAL?" She was

delaying because she didn't know how to tell him what she'd decided. What if he wasn't interested? Maybe he'd walked out after kissing her because she sucked at it. If she put her offer out there and he turned her down, she'd die of embarrassment. But she hadn't imagined the way he'd looked at her mouth...had she?

"I'm still a SEAL for now. Are these questions leading to something?"

"I want to have some cowboy fun." There, she'd said it.

"Okaaay." His lips twitched. "And this fun would involve what exactly?"

Sheesh, now she was amusing him. Not the reaction she was going for. "Um, you know."

"How about you spell it out so I don't go jumping to conclusions?"

She huffed an exasperated breath. Bella lifted her head and looked at her as if to say, "Just spit it out." Why was this so hard? It was a modern world, and women had every right to express their desires. The problem was, it wasn't her.

She loved June to death, but her grandmother was brazen and had no filter, especially when it came to men. Although she applauded June's ability to be herself, Rachel had sometimes been embarrassed by her grandmother's antics around men. The result was that she'd decided at a young age she would never throw herself at a man the way June did. She needed to like a man, to take the time to get to know him before she could have sex with him. Until Dallas, anyway. Well, she did like him, so that counted.

"Rachel?"

The way he said her name in that soft, intimate voice

and the way his eyes had softened gave her courage. "I want to…" She waved her hand between them. "Um, sleep with you."

"Do you now?"

She was out of words, so she nodded. Goodness, he had a lethal smile. If she was a block of ice, she'd melt right at his feet. While she waited for his answer, her heart was pounding so hard she could hear it thump in her ears.

When he didn't say anything, only looked at her like he was trying to think of how to refuse without hurting her feelings, heat burned its way up her neck and into her cheeks. She was so stupid to think she could be someone she wasn't.

"Forget it. It was a dumb idea." She stood, wanting the refuge of her room. "Just so you know, I don't go around propositioning men."

"Never thought you did." He rose and stepped around Bella. "See this?" He took her hand and flattened her palm against his cheek, over the scar, keeping his pressed over hers. "I can't stand to be touched anymore, not even by my mom, the person I love most in the world." With his free hand, he tugged on the tip of his hair. "I need a haircut, but the thought of someone's hands on me makes my stomach turn over."

What? He'd never given any sign that he didn't want her touching him. She tried to jerk her hand away, but he tightened his grip.

"Funny thing, though. I like you touching me." His eyebrows furrowed, puzzlement on his face. "Why is that?"

"I don't know," she whispered. His admission was a weight she wasn't sure she wanted. She didn't even want to think of the implications of that if her touch was the only one he could tolerate for the rest of his life. She almost laughed at the importance she'd just assigned herself. His avoidance of touch was only a temporary result of what he'd endured. It would pass, and the day would come when she would be a distant memory.

"I don't either," he said, his fingers still wrapped around her hand.

She wanted to wrap her arms around this man and hold him until he believed he was safe from ever being hurt again. She couldn't feel him the way she could other people, but she felt his pain the way a normal person would. "What are you saying?" Did he like that he could tolerate her touch? Not like it?

His gaze captured hers. "I want you, Rachel."

"But?" She had definitely heard a *but* in there.

He let go of her hand, then traced her bottom lip with his finger. "But…" He glanced away for a few seconds before his eyes found hers again. "I don't know if I can handle that much closeness."

Red tinged his cheeks, and she realized that admission had been hard for him. Her embarrassment at being so forward vanished. "I understand." She lifted onto her toes and brushed her lips over his. "I'm going to bed." She stepped back, gave him a smile, then turned to leave.

"Rachel."

She paused and glanced over her shoulder. "Yeah?" She liked when he called her wildcat, but when he said her name in that soft way, her insides went all marsh-mallowy.

"Maybe we could work up to something happening. Test my boundaries."

"Right now?" Lord help her, there was that lethal smile.

He didn't answer as he strode up to her. "Only this." He lowered his mouth to hers. He didn't touch her anywhere else, didn't put his hands on her. Yet, when he teased his tongue along the seam of her lips and she opened for him, when nothing but their mouths were pressed together and their tongues tangled, it was one of the most sensual things she'd ever experienced with a man.

Too soon, he pulled away. "Good night, wildcat."

"Good night, cowboy." Her feet didn't want to move, didn't want to leave him, but she forced them to walk away.

"I almost forgot," he said when she reached the door to her room. "We have a meeting in the morning with Jack and Noah."

"Okay. What time?"

"Plan to leave here at nine."

"See you in the morning." Bella was pressed against his leg. "Good night, Bella Boo." She smiled, then went in her room, and after closing the door, she leaned back against it.

A part of her wanted to wrap her arms around him and promise no one would ever hurt him again. The other part, her smarter side, thought she should run as far from him as possible. He was dangerous to her heart.

"How many are in your camp?" the interpreter said, translating the question.

"My name is Dallas Manning. My rank is—"

The interrogator, the biggest and meanest of his captors, hit him so hard that he heard the crunch of bone in his nose. Dallas squeezed his eyes shut and pressed his lips together to keep from giving them the satisfaction of hearing him scream. White stars exploded behind his eyelids, and he swallowed hard to keep from losing the meager bite of food he'd consumed before they dragged him out of his cell.

"Where is your camp located?"

"My name is Dallas Manning." Since he still had his eyes closed, he didn't see the knife coming at his face. It was only because of the slight change in the air that he jerked his face to the side. That move had saved his eye, but the pain of his cheek being sliced open was impossible to silently bear and he screamed.

Dallas shot straight up in bed and gulped air into his lungs. He shoved the covers aside, dropped to the floor, and did pushups, emptying his mind of anything but counting.

Three hundred, three hundred one, two, three, four... What was that noise?

He paused with his face halfway to the floor, listening. The dog's crying almost sounded like a baby. "Bella?" She whined again. He rolled over and reached for the bedside lamp, turning it on. The dog was curled up in the corner of the room, shaking as hard as she had the first time he'd seen her. Shit, he'd scared her.

"It's okay, girl," he softly said as he eased over to her. "No one's going to hurt you. I just had a bad dream." He leaned back against the wall and put his hand on top of her head. "You're okay." She crawled onto his lap. "We're two messed-up creatures, huh?"

"Two beautiful creatures."

Dallas lifted his gaze to the woman sitting in his doorway with her legs crossed and her hands clasped together. How long had she been there? He was losing his skills if she could sneak up on him like that.

"I woke you. I'm sorry." He'd never wanted her to see his body. He should have shut his door, but he'd left it open so he could hear if anyone tried to break into the cabin.

"You didn't. I was reading a boring book, hoping it would put me to sleep. I heard you, and I just couldn't pretend I didn't." Her gaze traveled over his scarred chest and arms. Since he was only wearing boxer briefs, he was glad Bella's body was hiding his messed-up legs. The expression in her eyes went from appreciation to pity.

"Don't," he said, almost cringing at the snarl in his voice, but he couldn't take anyone's pity, one reason he'd fled from his family. He especially couldn't take hers.

"What? Don't what, Dallas? Hate that someone hurt you? That your body is marked by their cruelty but still beautiful? Sorry, but I get to own my feelings about you." She tilted her head as she stared back at him. "Do you think you can handle me touching you right now?"

There was nothing he wanted more, but he was still too raw after his nightmare. "I don't think I can."

The ride to K-9 for their meeting with Jack and Noah was the quietest time he'd had with Rachel in the few days he'd known her. He hated that he was to blame for the distance between them, but it was for the best.

As he turned onto the gravel road that led to K-9, he glanced at her. She was wearing one of her disguises, probably the one she wore on the plane, that of a college student.

If the college girl with long blond hair, black skinny

jeans riding low on her hips, and the pale blue off-the-shoulder blouse had been in one of his classes, he would have begged her to go out with him. The man he was now wanted to see the real Rachel sitting next to him, not this pretty sorority girl who was ignoring his existence.

He couldn't stand her silence. "Hey, I'm sorry."

"For what?" She finally looked at him.

"For last night." He parked the car, then shifted to face her. "I'm giving you mixed signals, and that's wrong of me."

"What you're giving me is whiplash, but apology accepted." She put her hand on the door handle. "No more kissing, okay?"

His first impulse was a resounding no, he didn't agree, not after knowing how sweet she tasted, how soft and warm her lips were. And even more than those reasons, was this one…she was the only person since his rescue that he could tolerate touching him. How was he supposed to turn his back on that?

"Fine, no more kissing." Because he couldn't resist messing with her a little, he said, "Until we get married. Then all bets are off." She laughed, and he felt a hundred feet tall for putting that light in her eyes.

"Someday I'm going to accept your proposal just to see you panic."

He wasn't sure he would, but that was his secret. He already knew he'd pursue a relationship with her if he'd met her before his time in Hotel Hell, but now he was a mess. And it wasn't just that holding him back.

Dallas loved working with the horses, and he was good at it. He could work for Phoenix, who'd taken what had been a minor segment of the family business and built it into a substantial training and breeding operation, but Dallas wanted something of his own. If he could just figure out what that was.

As much as he tried not to, he envied his siblings. They had found their places in life. Money wasn't an issue. Each sibling had a trust fund and owned shares in the ranch, even he and Shiloh, and they were all wealthy. But he wanted a purpose, and he wanted to love whatever that might be. Until he figured out his future, it wasn't fair to involve someone else in his life, not when he didn't even know where he'd end up living.

"Whoa, who are you and what have you done with Rachel?" Noah said when Rachel walked into K-9's conference room with Dallas.

Dallas grinned. "Meet college girl, Rachel's alter ego."

Jack walked in and came to an abrupt halt at seeing Rachel. "Incredible. If I passed you on the street, I'd walk right by never realizing it was you."

"That's the intention of doing this," Rachel said. "Hopefully, Robert won't realize it's me if I show up on any security cameras he manages to see."

Jack pulled out a chair at the table. "There's always the chance he can find out you flew into Asheville, and that concerns me."

"Nope, I flew to Atlanta, then paid cash for a junk car and drove it here disguised as an old lady."

Noah whistled. "You're one clever woman, Rachel Denning."

She really was, and Dallas loved the big smile that blossomed on her face at the praise. He put his hand on her back and guided her to the chair next to Jack, then took the seat next to her, across from Noah.

"You have that phone with you that you used to call the police?" Jack asked Rachel.

She nodded. "Why? Do you think the police are tracing it?"

"No way to know, but we're not going to risk it," Dallas said as Jack slid a new phone across the table. "Give Jack the one you have. From now on, any calls you make will go through TG. That includes calls to any of us."

Jack tapped the screen on the new phone. "TG's number is already programed in the new one."

"What about my grandmother?" She handed Jack the old phone. "I need to be able to talk to her."

"You can talk to anyone you want to as long as the calls go through TG. He'll make sure they're all untraceable," Jack said. "I put TG's number in the notes section. Give it to your grandmother or anyone else who might call you."

She rubbed a hand over her face. "I hate this. Why can't the police find Robert?" She glanced at Dallas, tears in her eyes. "If only I'd gotten Henri out of there faster."

"Hey." He put his hand over hers. "You can't think like that. None of this is on you." Out of the corner of his eye, he noted that Jack and Noah were both looking at the hand he had over hers. The difference was that Noah was grinning and Jack was frowning. Jack was right to be concerned, and he almost snatched his hand away but stopped himself. She was hurting and it didn't mean anything that he wanted to comfort her.

Well, he wanted to scoop her up in his arms and carry her away to somewhere safe where men weren't trying to kill her. He supposed it did mean something, that he wanted to wipe those tears from her eyes and find a way to make her smile.

Her old phone chimed, and Jack eyed the screen. "Detective Diaz." He glanced at Rachel. "Call him back on your new phone."

"Using the number for Carter?" she asked. Dallas nodded, but before she could call TG, her new phone buzzed, TG's name showing up on the screen. She jumped, then stared at the phone as if it was a possessed thing.

"Go ahead and answer," he said. "Put it on speaker."

"Um, hi, Carter. It's like you have ESP or something. I was about to call you."

"Hi, darlin'. Who all's with you?"

"Dallas, Jack, and Noah."

Was it his imagination or had she said his name softer than Jack's and Noah's? His gaze slid to her, and she smiled. Eff him. He would move mountains for this woman to keep that smile on her face.

"Double D! Dude, where you been hiding?" TG said.

Dallas was curious to hear Noah's answer. Noah had been through hell but had managed to climb his way out. Dallas wanted to know how he'd done it.

Noah rolled his eyes. "Like you didn't know exactly where I am."

That was true, and Dallas chuckled. TG could likely tell you where every single operator he'd come in contact with was and what they were doing.

"Can't deny it," TG said. "So, Rachel, darlin', your detective is calling to give you what he considers bad news, but I find there's a bright side to everything."

Chapter Ten

Rachel flattened her hands on the table to keep from putting them over her ears. The last thing she wanted was more bad news. Dallas slipped his hand under the table, put it on her knee, and squeezed. His touch reminded her that she wasn't alone. She glanced around the table at the three men who'd put themselves in the middle of her troubles without her asking for their help.

Then there was the one on the phone who seemed to be some kind of all-knowing oracle. Carter Jeffers really was spooky, and from what little the guys had said about him, she'd never want to get on his bad side. She straightened her spine, taking courage from these men who had skills she could only guess at.

"Okay, spooky man, lay it on me. What's the bad news?"

"Your apartment was broken into last night. Detective Diaz is calling to tell you that."

She couldn't say she was surprised, but it enraged her. That was her home, the place she was supposed to feel safe. "How do you know?"

"I have my ways. Was there anything there that would give any indication as to where you are?"

"Not that I can think of…oh, wait. My laptop has

all my friends' names and addresses in it…my grand-mother's, Jack and Nichole's."

"Does your grandmother live in LA?"

"Yes, but she's hiding out at a dude ranch in Wyoming." She sucked in a breath. "Oh God, I never went back in my apartment when I saw Robert's men. My grandmother emailed me when she arrived, telling me how much she loved the Lazy Horse Ranch. That email is still on my computer. If Robert has it, he can find her." She pushed away from the table. "I have to go get her."

"Take a breath, darlin'. We'll make sure she's safe."

She turned pleading eyes on Dallas. "Please, I have to go to her." Her grandmother was the only family she had left, and if something happened to her, Rachel would never forgive herself.

"Listen to Carter," Dallas said. "We'll keep her safe. Exactly where is she?"

"The ranch is in Jackson Hole." She sat back down. "She can't stay there, not if there's any chance of Robert finding her."

Dallas nodded. "She's right. You got anyone near there, TG?"

"Yeah. I've got a husband and wife team that can be there in two hours. They can take your grandmother to wherever you want."

"The Big Sky Ranch in Butte, my family's spread," Dallas said. "I've got three brothers, one sister, one brother-in-law, parents, and a shitload of ranch hands who all can hold their own in a shooting contest against any SEAL team. I'll call my sister. Cheyenne will have a room ready for…" He glanced at Rachel.

"June. June Denning. She's going to be disappointed

to have to leave her hot cowboys at the Lazy Horse, so tell your team to take her kicking and screaming if they have to."

"Not to worry, darlin'. We got this. As soon as she's safe in Montana, I'll call you so you can stop worrying about her."

Dallas chuckled. "Trust me. There are plenty of cowboys at my family's ranch for your grandmother to drool over. She'll just be trading one dude ranch for a better one."

"Thank you, all of you." She glanced around the table, wishing there were better words than just *thank you* to express her gratitude. Not one of these men had to be here for her.

"You're one of us." Dallas squeezed her hand. "We protect our own."

"The bright side of this is that my team in LA has been watching your apartment, meaning they're now tailing the man who broke in," Carter said. "Eventually he'll lead them to Hargrove. In the meantime, call your grandmother and tell her to expect my team. Their names are Zeke and Stephanie Cress. After that, call Detective Diaz, but don't let on that you already know about the break-in."

It occurred to her that Carter's services wouldn't be free. "Okay, but you have so many people working on this. I…ah, can you give me an estimate on how much all this is going to cost?" She had money saved, and she'd use it all to keep June safe. She just hoped she had enough.

"Darlin', you don't owe me a thing. I live for meting out justice on men like Robert Hargrove. Your boys will tell you that's true."

"It is," Dallas said. "Besides, TG doesn't need any more money. He has more than God."

Carter chuckled. "Well, that's not quite true, but I'm running a close second. You make those phone calls, and I'll call you when I have more news."

"Well, *thank you* doesn't seem adequate, but thank you so much." Carter had already disconnected, and she realized she was thanking a dial tone. "Wow," she whispered. "I'm glad he's on our side." She slid her gaze over each of the three men at the table. "That goes for you guys, too. Thank you. I still worry about what will happen if Robert finds out you're helping me."

"I ain't afraid of stinkin' Robert," Noah said.

"Hooyah!" Dallas and Jack said in unison, with Noah echoing them.

Dallas gave her a smile full of confidence. "The man has no clue what he's up against. Call your grandmother so she knows what's going on, then you need to call the detective back. Remember to use TG's number to make your call."

"Got it." While she talked to her grandmother, the guys moved to the other side of the room. What were they talking about? She tried to eavesdrop, but their voices were too low, and along with her grandmother talking, she couldn't catch their words.

While half listening to June express her excitement over getting to meet a whole new host of hot cowboys, Rachel allowed her gaze to roam over Dallas. Talk about hot cowboys…the man stole her breath. After seeing his body last night, she understood why he always wore long-sleeve shirts.

To her, his body was beautiful, a work of art. The scars were forever a part of him, which made them beautiful too, a testament to his courage and bravery. After returning to her room, she'd let the tears fall for the man who'd been tortured so brutally and now couldn't stand to be touched.

He caught her staring at him and winked. A hundred butterflies fluttered in her stomach. Why had she said no more kissing?

Dallas didn't have to look over at Rachel to know her eyes were on him. He felt her gaze roaming over him, and unable to resist catching her in the act, he glanced at her and winked. Her cheeks pinked, and he expected her to divert her eyes, but she didn't. She winked back at him, and he laughed. Man, he liked this girl. He liked kissing her even more. He was trained to follow the rules, but no more kissing might be one worth breaking.

"Stop flirting with Nichole's best friend, and pay attention," Jack snapped.

Noah snorted. "He is paying attention, just not to you."

True that. "That's all I have until TG finds out if the body is Henrietta. We also need to know if Rachel's laptop is missing. If it is, we'll need to put protection on Nichole."

Jack's eyes turned steely. "He touches my wife, and he'll die slowly and painfully."

"Her parents live in Florida, right?" Noah said, getting a nod from Jack. "Maybe she should pay them a visit until Hargrove's behind bars."

"That's a good idea," Dallas said.

Jack sighed. "She's not going to like being sent off with Rachel here, but she can be mad at me all she wants if it means she's safe. Maybe we should send Rachel with her."

"No." Panic surged at the thought of being separated from her. "He's only after Rachel. If we send her, too, we'll all have to go to guard them. Plus, you'd be putting Nichole's parents in danger."

"Yeah, bad idea," Jack said. "Let's finish up here so I can go break the news to Nichole."

"Give me a few minutes to call my sister." He clicked on Cheyenne's number as he left the room.

"You're an ass, baby brother" was Cheyenne's greeting.

He winced. Yeah, he pretty much had been, considering he'd fled without telling everyone except for his father that he was leaving. He'd been drowning, and his father understood. As a boy, Laramie Manning had been tortured by his stepfather until his biological father had learned of his treatment and had rescued him.

When he'd said he had to leave, his father had nodded as if he'd been expecting it. "Son, if that's what you need, I'll take you to the airport. When your mother kicks me out of our bedroom for sending you off without telling her, you're going to owe me a new horse. I've got my eye on one and he's not cheap."

Damn, but he loved his father. His mother, too, but he didn't know how to tell her he couldn't handle all the hugs she kept giving him, that even her touch was unbearable.

"Yeah, I guess I am, but I had to get away for a while, Cheyenne. Dad understood."

"If that's what you needed to do, I'll accept you had to leave, but you're still an ass for sneaking away."

"If I promise to never do it again, will you forgive me?"

"Maybe. Probably. Hell, I never could say no to you. That doesn't make me happy, Dallas."

He smiled. He loved and respected his three brothers, but his two sisters had him wrapped around their fingers. Cheyenne was the second oldest, a mini-mommy. They'd never been as close as he and Shiloh because of the age difference, but she was a mama bear, always protecting those she loved.

"I have a story to tell you." He told her how he'd found a wildcat in the cabin when he'd arrived in Asheville, and why Rachel was hiding out.

"She really tried to bash your brains in?"

"There's entirely too much delight in your voice about that, sis."

She laughed…for much longer than he thought necessary. "So, moving along. Her grandmother is the only family she has left. Her name is June Denning, and I'm sending her to you. It will break Rachel's heart if any harm comes to her grandmother, so tell the family her life is important to me. You all keep her safe, Cheyenne."

"Of course, we will. But I have to say, you fall in love way too easily, baby brother. You always have."

He pulled the phone away from his ear and scowled at the screen. What. The. Hell? "Cheyenne, I'm not asking for your opinion. I've only been in love once, or thought I was at the time, and you know it. Just keep Rachel's grandmother safe. She'll be there sometime tonight. Have a room ready." He gave her the names of the couple bringing June, then disconnected before she could answer.

Her observation might have been true before he'd joined the Navy. He'd never been *in love*, but he'd loved all his girlfriends. Nothing wrong with that. After enlisting, he'd realized that long deployments weren't conducive to relationships. Even when he was home, the team was always training, so there was little time for dating. Like many of his SEAL brothers, he'd kept his hookups to women who weren't looking to get his ring on their finger.

He returned to the conference room and slid back into the seat next to her. "Your grandmother okay with moving?"

She made air quotes. "New hot cowboys, new meat."

He snorted a laugh along with Jack and Noah. "She actually said that?"

"Yep. June dances to her own bongo drums."

Noah sang "Save a Horse (Ride a Cowboy)," making her laugh. She'd been around Noah enough to know that his parlor trick was singing a song that fit the moment. It was always funny, not to mention that he had a fantastic voice, so she loved listening to him.

"My grandmother's theme song." She glanced at Dallas. "You might want to warn the boys on the ranch that she's headed their way."

"No, I think it will be more fun to let them be surprised." The love she had for her grandmother was there in her voice. He put his hand over hers. "I promise my family will keep her safe."

"I believe you. Knowing that means more than I can say, so thank you."

"No thanks necessary. Go ahead and call the detective. Put him on speaker."

"Rachel, thanks for calling back," Detective Diaz said. "I'm afraid I have some bad news."

"Well, that wasn't what I wanted to hear. I was hoping you were calling to tell me that you'd caught Robert."

"Not yet, but we will find him. Your apartment was broken into."

"No way! When did that happen? Did they take anything? Do you think it was Robert or one of his men? Were there fingerprints?"

Her shock sounded real, and Dallas gave her a thumbs-up.

"It happened last night, and we need you to come tell us if anything is missing."

"Sorry, but I can't do that right now. Did they trash my apartment?"

"Yes, it's a mess. Rachel, we need you to come here, and I'm not asking. I'm telling you what you have to do."

Dallas shook his head. Unless they had a warrant for her arrest, she was under no obligation to do anything they asked.

"I can't, not right now. I need to know if my laptop is missing. I left it on my coffee table."

"I don't remember seeing it, but I wasn't specifically looking for it. If you'll come to the station, I'll take you to your apartment. At the moment, it's a crime scene and you can't enter by yourself."

She squeezed her eyes shut at hearing her laptop was probably gone, and Dallas couldn't help it. He had to touch her. He put his hand on her knee, hoping his touch reminded her that she was safe. He'd make sure of it.

She opened her eyes and gave him a grateful smile. "You're not hearing me, Detective. I can't come there. It's important for me to know about my laptop. Could you or maybe an officer go see if it's there?"

"Where are you? You can trust me, if that's what you're worried about."

"Someplace safe. I told you why I'm not trusting

the police so much right now. I don't believe you're on Robert's payroll, but if you know where I am, others who don't have my best interest could find out. Can you please find out about my computer?"

"Why is that so important?"

"Because it has my family and friends' names and addresses in it. Robert will use them to get to me."

"Okay, I'll go myself. You're calling on a different phone. Why is that?"

"Just trying to stay safe."

"Good answer," Dallas mouthed, getting another smile.

"Rachel, I'm going to be real honest with you here. We've been trying to trace this call, and we're being blocked. You either have some interesting talents, or you have help."

She chuckled. "Funny, the FBI said the same thing. Let's just say…" She glanced at him.

Dallas muted the phone. "Tell him you have friends in high places." That would put the detective on notice that she was being protected. Let him wonder just who those friends were that could keep the police and FBI from tracing her phone. He glanced at Jack. "That okay?"

Jack shrugged. "I don't see why not."

He unmuted the phone.

"Well, Detective, let's just say I have friends in high places." She grinned, giving him the impression that she liked saying that.

He sure liked seeing a smile on her face. If they were alone, he'd kiss her, his agreement not to be damned.

Chapter Eleven

For a moment, Rachel thought Dallas was going to kiss
her, right there in front of Jack and Noah. She would
have let him. Oh, yeah, she would've. *What happened
to no more kissing, Rach?* Why had she even thrown
that rule out there? She must have had a reason, but she
sure couldn't remember it, not when he looked at her
like he wanted to devour her.

Someone cleared their throat, breaking the eye connection she and Dallas had going. Jack was scowling
and Noah was grinning. The grinning she got. He had a
front row seat to an *almost* scene right out of a movie…
boy kisses girl, girl goes all dreamy, forgetting they
have an audience.

Jack's scowl, though? She didn't get it. What was his
problem? She'd caught him several times giving Dallas
a stink eye. Men, they were strange creatures. They—
okay, him, the SEAL cowboy one—confused her. Jack
did, too, but she wasn't concerned about him and what
he was thinking. Not when all she could think about
was kissing the man next to her.

"I'm off to tell Nichole to pack a bag." Jack tapped
on the table in front of Dallas. "When you go out to

the site with Noah, think about where and how on the property you'd set up an equine center."

"Copy that."

She noticed how Dallas's eyes brightened at the mention of horses but wait. What? "Where's Nichole going?"

"To her parents' until this is over," Jack said.

"Because of me. I'm sorry." She hated being the reason Nichole had to be sent away so Jack could be sure she stayed safe.

"I shouldn't have come here."

Jack shook his head. "You're exactly where you need to be. Both Nichole and I would be upset if you hadn't come to us when your life is in danger."

"I'm still sorry."

"Don't be. I'll catch up with y'all later."

After Jack left, Dallas said, "He's right, you know. You're where you need to be. Why don't we grab some lunch and you come with me and Noah to the site?"

She stuck a finger under the wig and scratched. The stupid thing was getting itchy, and she was more than ready to get it off. "I think I'd rather go back to the cabin. Besides, we left Bella alone, and she's probably scared."

"You sure? I'm not crazy about you being alone."

"I don't see how Robert could have tracked me this soon. The cabin's address isn't in my contact list. I'll be okay." Besides, she needed some time alone to think. Did she want to kiss Dallas again? Well, duh. Silly question. The better question was, should she?

"Since you're taking Rachel back to the cabin, I think I'll go have lunch with Peyton," Noah said to Dallas. "Meet back here in two hours?"

"That works. I'll grab a bite at the cabin."

As they walked out, Dallas put his hand on her lower back. She liked that, probably too much. She'd never dated a man who was as protective as Dallas, as attentive. Not that they were dating, but at any other time, she would sure love to have a man like him interested in her.

After this was over, they'd go their separate ways, and if her heart gave a sad ping at that, it was what it was. While they were here, though, she wanted to have a little fun with the hottest man she'd ever met. If she let this opportunity pass by, she'd go home regretting it.

"A penny."

"Huh?" So deep in her head, she hadn't even registered that they were in the Jeep, heading to the cabin.

"You were a thousand miles away. A penny for your thoughts."

"Oh, ah…" *Say it, Rach.* Okay, going for it…well, kind of. "I was thinking of you, but I'm freaking out a little because those thoughts are a little…" X-rated, but she couldn't bring herself to say that. She was such a chicken.

"A little?"

"Nothing." She glanced out the window to keep him from seeing the truth in her eyes, the lust that she was sure was in them, shining as bright as the North Star. She'd had crushes on guys before, but she'd never been in lust like this and wasn't sure she liked it. A change of subject was in order. "How long do you think it will take Carter's people to get my grandmother to your ranch?"

"Not sure, but probably sometime this afternoon." He parked in front of the cabin, and after turning off the ignition, he turned to her. "This conversation you started but can't seem to finish for some reason isn't over. You're going to tell me about those thoughts you're having." He tapped her nose, then exited the Jeep.

She blew out a breath while admiring the back of him as he jogged up the steps. Okay, she was mostly admiring his butt because it was mighty fine. At the door, he glanced back at her, giving her a sly smile. She'd never had such sexy thoughts about a man before, and embarrassed heat burned her cheeks that he seemed to know exactly where her mind was.

Why had she said anything, opened a door he apparently wasn't going to let her close? She'd never had sex just because she wanted to jump a sexy hot guy's bones and wanting to was out of her comfort zone. But boy, did she ever want to now. They'd flirted around the idea of it, and she had gone back and forth, one minute kissing him and the next telling him no more kisses. Was she brave enough to ask for what she wanted?

After he disappeared inside, she got out and followed him in. Her plan was to dash to her room and stay there until he left.

"Water, soda, or beer with your sandwich?" Dallas said.

She stumbled to a stop. "Oh, um, nothing, thanks."

He pointed a butter knife coated with mustard at her. "So you'd rather hide in your room than have lunch with me?"

Was it possible for an ability to jump from one person to another? Had her talent for reading people deserted her for him? Because he was reading her like an open book, had been from the start. She searched her brain for a snarky retort, but before she could come up with one, her phone buzzed.

"It's Detective Diaz," she said after checking the screen. "I can answer it, right?"

Dallas nodded. "Yeah. TG's made sure that number's safe." From her side of the conversation, he gathered that her laptop was missing. How long would it take Hargrove or his men to show up in Asheville? Because he was sure they would now that the man had her laptop. Bella crept into the kitchen, and he kneeled in front of her. "There you are. You sleep away the morning while we were gone?" She put her chin on his knee and peered up at him with her soulful brown eyes. "You missed me, huh?"

"Why can't you find him?"

Bella whined at Rachel's raised voice. "It's all right, girl. She's not mad at you." Rachel was losing her patience with the detective, and he didn't blame her. Was Hargrove really that elusive, or were the police not trying very hard to find him?

"I feel sick," she said after disconnecting. "He has my laptop with all my contacts in it. I'm bringing Robert straight to Jack and Nichole. It was a mistake to come here."

She turned away, but not before he saw the tears filling her eyes. "Hey, none of this is your fault." He dropped the knife on the counter and caught up with her halfway down the hall. "Listen to me. With Hargrove having your laptop, the chance he would come here looking for answers is high, whether you were here or not. Jack wouldn't have known to keep Nichole safe, and we wouldn't have known to be on guard, so you actually did everyone a favor. No one blames you, and there's no safer place to be than here. Is there anything in your laptop about this cabin?" She leaned her head on his chest, and he wrapped his arms around her.

"No, nothing."

"Okay, that's good. Since there's no way for him to know about it, you're safe here."

"I'm more worried about everyone else. My grandmother, Nichole, you, Jack, Noah, even Peyton. I'll never forgive myself if something happens to any of you."

"Nothing's going to happen to us. Nichole will be safe at her parents', your grandmother's in good hands at my family's ranch, and as for me, Jack, and Noah, we've been in situations considerably more dangerous than anything Hargrove can bring our way."

She felt good in his arms, like this was where she belonged. It wasn't real, though. Here at the cabin, it was as if they were in their own little world, and that had to be why he wasn't climbing the walls the way he had been at home. Also, he had a mission to concentrate on. Keeping Rachel safe.

"Nichole has to leave Jack because of me. She probably hates me."

"She would never hate you. Why don't you call her, then come eat some lunch?" He reluctantly dropped his arms and stepped back.

"Okay." She smiled. "Thank you. You have a way of making me feel better."

He tapped her nose. "I'm a man of many talents." A few of which he'd like to show her.

Her gaze traveled over him, then she lifted her eyes back to his, and she rolled her eyes. "I just bet."

The tears that had been in her eyes were gone, and she was smiling as she went to her room. He almost stumbled over Bella when he turned to head back to the kitchen. "You're more attached to me than my shadow, Bella girl."

Apparently, he had two girls who needed some TLC. Bella padded along beside him. Since she'd been cooped up all morning, he grabbed her leash and took her outside. His phone buzzed, his mother's name appearing on the screen. It was a miracle that she'd waited two days to call him.

"Mama mine," he said.

"Well, you sound better than when you left."

That was true. "You got that from two words?" He made a quick bet with himself that she was calling about Rachel's grandmother.

"You're my son. I know all your voice emotions. Why am I hearing from Cheyenne instead of from you that we have a special guest arriving?"

Ding. Ding. Ding. "I was going to call you tonight. It all happened pretty fast."

"Cheyenne said she's coming here so we can protect her. What's going on, Dallas? I thought you were going there to spend some relaxing time with your friend."

"You know me. I get bored easily, so I'm just keeping myself entertained."

"Dallas Manning, you don't need to be courting trouble after your ordeal."

"It's nothing to worry about, Mom." She referred to his imprisonment as his ordeal—as if his time in hell hadn't been much more than an inconvenience—and he would go to his grave before he'd tell her the things that had been done to him. And he sure wasn't going to tell her how serious the situation with Rachel was or she'd have the whole family on a plane to Asheville to make sure her baby boy was safe.

"Just who is this woman coming here, and what kind of danger is she bringing with her? How do you know her? What have you gotten yourself involved in? What—"

"Give the boy a chance to answer, Bonnie," he heard his dad say in the background. "Put it on speaker."

Oh, man. Now he'd have two of them interrogating him. "Hi, Dad. You find Old Arnie?" The old bull was more pet than anything and had a habit of wandering off.

"The stupid fool went down in the ravine again and couldn't get out," his father said with fondness in his voice.

"Probably looking for you." Old Arnie followed his dad around like a devoted dog.

"Enough about Old Arnie," his mother snapped. "You need to come home, Dallas. You should be with your family, not out looking for trouble. Tell him to come home, Laramie."

No, that was not what he needed. Without hurting their feelings, especially his mother's, how could he tell them he had to leave because they were smothering him?

"I know you're worried about him, honey, but our son is a kickass SEAL. I think he's capable of taking care of himself."

"I don't care how kickass *our son* is, he needs to be with his family after his ordeal so we can take care of him."

"He'll come home when he's ready. What's for dinner?"

"Broiled chicken and a salad. It's a new recipe I found on Google."

Dallas grinned. His mother loved Google. Ever since she'd discovered the search engine, she spent hours looking up things.

His dad groaned. "Come on, Bonnie. Enough of this broiled chicken shit. We're cattle ranchers. We eat beef, big fat juicy steaks."

And there they went. Dallas chuckled because this was often how a three-way conversation went with his mom and dad, whether they had him on the phone or one of his siblings. At least the attention was off him. He'd give them a minute or two, then he'd say a quick goodbye and quickly disconnect before they remembered he hadn't answered any of their questions.

"Dallas? Oh, there you are."

He put a finger to his lips to hush Rachel, but it was too late.

"Who's that?" his mother—who could hear better than a bat when you least wanted her to—said.

"Just a friend. Gotta go."

"Dallas Manning, don't you hang up."

He hung up. "That was my parents. My mother seems to think I'm still her little boy, needing her to take care of me."

She looked him over from his head on down, pausing on the zipper of his jeans, then lower, and then back up. "There is nothing *little boy* about you."

"Glad you noticed." He gave up on his resolve to not touch her, stepped in front of her, and wrapped a lock of her hair around his fingers. "How locked down are you on us never kissing again?"

"I was going to talk to you about that tonight."

"Yeah? And what—" His phone rang again, and he rolled his eyes at seeing his mother's name on the screen. He hadn't answered any of her questions, and now there was a mystery woman to investigate. She wasn't one to easily give up.

"Do you need to answer that?"

"Nope." Cheyenne had all the information and had already told their mother all she needed to know. "My mama's worse than an old hound with a bone. Now, back to kissing." And whatever that might lead to.

Before coming here, the last thing he had on his mind or wanted was to find himself interested in a woman. For one thing, his body was a roadmap of his torture, not a thing any woman would want to see. But there hadn't been any disgust in Rachel's eyes when she'd come into his room and found him close to naked. Unless he was completely off base, and he didn't think he was, he'd seen desire in those golden-brown eyes when her gaze had roamed over him.

"You're supposed to meet Noah soon." She put her hand on his waist. "We'll talk about kissing tonight." She frowned. "What's this?" She lifted his shirt. "A gun?"

"Yes, that would be a gun." He pulled his shirt back over the holster.

"Is that really necessary?"

"Yes. Let's have some lunch."

Chapter Twelve

"Guess it's just you and me, Bella Boo," Rachel said after Dallas left to meet up with Noah. He'd wanted her to go with him, but she needed some time by herself. Bella walked to the front door and stared at it.

"You miss him, huh?" As much as Rachel wanted some alone time, she missed him, too. "He'll be back in a little while. What should we do?" He'd made her promise that she'd stay inside with the door locked, so she couldn't go for a run. Bummer that. She did some of her best thinking when she ran.

That Dallas had a gun on him really bothered her. She'd tried to hide how much, but it had hit home how dangerous her situation was. It wasn't the gun itself that bothered her as much as the reminder that she'd brought danger to her friends.

Maybe she should let the police or even better, the FBI, hide her away somewhere. Bella sighed, then padded to the sofa and peered at her with her sad brown eyes. Rachel patted the cushion. "Why don't you come up here and snuggle with me."

Bella gave another doggy sigh, sounding as if Rachel was a poor substitute for her favorite man, then jumped onto the sofa. Rachel combed her fingers through the dog's soft fur. "Hey, pretty girl. What do you want to talk about? Dallas, huh?"

She pulled Bella's legs over her lap. "There. That's better. So, if we're going to talk about your best guy, I have a question. Should I stick to the no-kissing rule or not?" Bella didn't seem to have an opinion.

If she dropped the rule, they wouldn't stop at just kissing. Not that she would want to stop. It was that having an affair wasn't her. But how many times in her life would she get a chance to meet someone like Dallas?

She wasn't worried about risking her heart. They both had lives they'd return to in different parts of the country. She'd go home with some great memories with an honest-to-God SEAL cowboy in the starring role.

Carpe diem, right?

Now, if only Dallas was here so she could jump his bones before she talked herself out of it. Since he wasn't, and she was bored, she turned on the TV, flipped through the channels, and stopped at seeing the movie *Arsenic and Old Lace.*

"This movie's hilarious," she told Bella. "Let's watch it." Never mind she'd seen it a dozen times, at least it would be something to do.

"Now what, Bella?" she said when the movie was over. What she really needed was a run and she couldn't even do that. The dog had fallen asleep during the movie, and she opened her eyes, yawned, then closed them again. "Humph. You're a lousy conversationalist." Maybe she should find something to make for dinner.

When she was halfway to the kitchen, her phone rang, and her heart skipped a beat before she considered that Carter wouldn't put through a call from Robert. Returning to the living room, she picked it up from the coffee table, breathing a sigh of relief at seeing Carter's name on the screen.

"It makes me nervous when this phone rings," she said.

"Just me, darlin'. Your grandmother's a hoot."

"I could have told you that, but you talked to her? She's safe?"

"She's in Montana and on the phone waiting to talk to you. She thinks I have a sexy voice and wanted me to send her a selfie without my shirt on."

"Okay, that's embarrassing."

"Nah, she's funny."

She heard the amusement in his voice. "Just how long did you talk to my grandmother?"

"Oh, we're besties now. I'm putting her through."

"Rachel? Are you there?"

"I am. You're in Montana now, right?" It was so good to hear her grandmother's voice.

"Yes. It was so exciting, like being in a spy movie. That nice couple sneaked me out of the ranch in Wyoming in the back of a utility truck. Then when we were miles away, we switched cars to a black SUV, and would you believe we changed that car for a bread company van to sneak me into the dude ranch. This place is amazing, even better than the last ranch. And my goodness, the cowboys here are right off the cover of a romance book. Except they have their shirts on. Do you think they might take them off when—"

"Please don't ask them to take their shirts off. I mean it, June."

"Aw, you're no fun. I was thinking you should come here so I don't have to worry about you. We could find you a smoking hot cowboy."

She had one of those, thank you very much. "I'm fine. I've got a team of highly skilled men watching over me. Just promise to stay on the ranch until this is over, okay?"

"I promise. The lady who owns this dude ranch is beautiful, so I'm glad she's married, or she'd be competition. Did you know she and her husband are on the cover of a romance novel?"

"No, I didn't know that." She smiled as June gushed about Cheyenne and her husband, how awesome the dude ranch was, and how beautiful Montana was. When June finally took a breath, Rachel said, "Listen, I need to go. You have fun, and I'll talk to you in a few days."

"Okay. I love you, honey pie."

"Love you, too."

She chuckled after disconnecting. Maybe she should tell Dallas to warn the men on his ranch to keep an eye on their shirts. She wouldn't put it past June to steal them.

"What you and Jack have planned here is pretty impressive," Dallas said after Noah had taken him on a tour of the site. The location was in a valley surrounded by the Blue Ridge Mountains. A forest of trees, each a different shade of green—reminding him of a patchwork quilt—rose up behind the one cabin already built, and where others were planned. A river snaked its way through the land, and on the other side, a mama deer and her fawn were grazing. It was an idyllic spot, peaceful and perfect for a retreat.

Noah nodded. "The kennels will be finished next week. Jack will move the dogs over then so he can be onsite. We're aiming for the lodge and cabins to be done before winter sets in. We're pretty much on top of everything except for the equestrian center. We know jack shit about horses."

"I might be slow, brother, but I do eventually catch on." He narrowed his eyes at Noah. "The equestrian center is why I'm here."

"No, you're here because when Jack talked to you, he picked up on the fact you needed some downtime with people who'd understand what you're dealing with even if you don't want to talk about it. However, since you're here, might as well make yourself useful."

"Jack's a sneaky bastard. This how he got you to work for him? Had you roped in before you knew what he was up to?"

Noah laughed. "More or less. Pretty sure he had a plan for me from day one." He stared at the mountains for a moment, then turned his gaze to Dallas. "I thought I'd be a SEAL until they ran me off when I couldn't pass the physical, but after what happened, I just couldn't go back. What if I messed up again and…" He shook his head. "I try not to go there."

"Yeah, same here," Dallas quietly said. Noah was thinking of the mistake he'd made. No one on the team blamed him, but Dallas understood why Noah did. Truthfully, although he'd been brutally tortured, he wouldn't trade places because he'd feel the same guilt as Noah did.

"I was drowning my guilt in the bottom of a bottle, no idea how to climb out, and facing a bleak future. Jack saved me." He swung an arm out, taking in their surroundings. "To be involved in something that will help people like us is more satisfying than I can explain." His voice cracked, and he cleared his throat.

Then he grinned. "And because Jack brought me here, I met Peyton, and that, brother, is the best thing that's ever happened to me."

"How the mighty have fallen."

"'Cause I'm a man in love," Noah sang.

Dallas rolled his eyes. "You're ridiculous, is what you are." And amusing. Noah had kept them entertained on deployments with his ability to come up with a song that fit any situation.

The man actually had an amazing voice and could play a guitar as well as any rock star, could have been a rock star himself, he had that much talent. Dallas had asked him once why he hadn't pursued a career in music. Noah claimed he had no desire to be famous and have to deal with all that came with that.

"Credit for that one goes to Eric Clapton, if you're wondering."

He wasn't. He did, however, envy the peace and happiness both Jack and Noah had managed to find. Maybe there was hope for him. A girl with whiskey brown eyes popped into his mind. He pushed the image away. He had to figure out his future before he brought a woman into his life. "So, where are you thinking of putting the equestrian center?"

"Haven't a clue. That's what we're hoping you can help us with. Like, how many horses do we need, what kind of staff, what kind of building, and any other questions we don't know to ask."

Dallas surveyed the site again. "I'd suggest starting with a dozen or so horses but build a barn with at least two dozen stalls so you'll have room to grow if need be. You want horses that are mature, steady, and calm. You'll want some paddocks so a horse can't run away if it spooks. Map out two or three riding trails for those more experienced. The barn and paddocks need to be on flat land. As for staffing—"

"Whoa, I've already forgotten half of what you just said."

"Bullshit." He tapped Noah's head. "Your mind is a steel trap, but I see what you're doing here. So, how about, to quote you, I make myself useful while I'm here and work up a business plan for an equestrian center?"

"Jack said you'd come around." Noah slapped him on the back. "Welcome to Operation Warriors Center."

"All I'm doing is creating a working plan for the equestrian part, so don't go getting any ideas."

"I said close to the same thing and look at me now." Noah's laugh sounded a bit like *you don't stand a chance against Jack.*

"Yeah, well, I'm a Montana boy, so I won't be sticking around."

Noah's only answer was a sly smile, which Dallas ignored.

"You got anything planned for that level spot off to the right?" Dallas pointed to an area in the distance.

"Nope. That look like a good place for your barn and paddocks?"

"Not my barn. Not my paddocks, but yeah, it does."

"Then that's where we'll put it. Let's take a ride over there."

"Yeah, I'd like to walk the area." They got in Noah's four-wheel-drive truck and were halfway to the spot when his phone rang, TG's name coming up.

"You got some news for me?" Dallas said.

"Good and bad news. Rachel's grandmother arrived at your ranch and is settling in. The bad news, the body has been identified as Henrietta's. I imagine the police will be calling Rachel soon to tell her."

"She's not going to take that well." It would hurt her to know how her friend's body was disposed of.

"It would be a good idea for her to hear it from you. Still no sign of Hargrove. His men, the two my people are following, haven't made contact with him yet. By contact, I mean they haven't led us to him. I'm sure they've been talking to him. The car they're driving is registered to Hargrove's company, so we don't have an ID on the two so I can't tap into their phones. It's only a matter of time, though, before we figure out who they are."

"Hopefully that will happen soon. Thanks for the heads-up on Rachel's friend. I'm going to head to the cabin now. It'll take me about fifteen minutes to get there. If her detective calls before that, don't put him through."

"Copy that."

Noah started singing "Secret Agent Man."

"Is that Alba sounding like a cat in heat?"

Dallas laughed as he put his phone on speaker. "How'd you guess?" TG and his team had worked one of the most dangerous operations Dallas had ever been on with his SEAL team two years ago. He glanced at Noah. "Dude's dissing your singing."

"Hey, asshole," Noah said. "Correct me if I'm wrong, but weren't you the one who told that bartender in South America that if he could get me to sing, he'd go home with pockets full of pesos?"

"Don't know what you're talking about, Double D."

As was typical of the man, he disconnected without

another word. Dallas glanced at Noah. "I need to get back to the cabin."

"I figured." Noah turned his truck around. "What's going on?"

"The police have identified Henrietta's body and will probably be calling Rachel soon to tell her. She needs to hear about that from me first."

"She definitely does."

"You still carry those dice?" he asked as Noah drove him back to the Jeep. The team called him Double D because of the pair of dice he always had in his pocket.

"Nope. Don't need them anymore."

"You ever going to tell me why you were always fondling them?"

Noah stopped his truck next to the Jeep. "I might tell you and Jack together if the two of you get me drunk enough."

"That bad, huh?"

"The worst. Go take care of your girl."

"She's not my girl."

"Uh-huh."

Dallas parked in his usual spot, and before he went inside, he walked around the cabin, checking for footprints and anything suspicious. When he reached the main bedroom window, he stopped and studied it. If Hargrove or his men found the cabin, they'd cover the front and back doors, intending to trap Rachel inside. He returned to the Jeep and parked it next to the bedroom window instead. If they had to escape, they could go right out the window and jump in the Jeep.

"Honey, I'm home," he called out when he entered the cabin.

Chapter Thirteen

From her corner in the kitchen, Bella scrambled to get her feet under her, then took off for the door. "I see where I rate," Rachel muttered. She ignored the way her heart fluttered at hearing Dallas's voice. Well, she tried to, anyway.

Dallas walked into the kitchen with Bella at his side, stopped mid-stride, and said as his gaze roamed over her body, "You're killing me, sugar."

She hadn't been expecting him back this early and had planned to change before he returned. The denim shorts barely covered her butt cheeks, and the midriff top was a little snug, not to mention she wasn't wearing a bra under it, so no surprise his eyeballs were about to pop out of their sockets. Although she hadn't intended him to see her dressed like this, she liked the appreciation in his eyes. A lot.

He rubbed a hand over his face and muttered something that sounded a lot like, "My new fantasy." Then he gave his head a shake, lifted his nose in the air, and sniffed. "Something smells good in here. Did the little woman spend the day sweating over a hot stove?"

She wanted to laugh at his silliness, but she leaned back against the counter and glared. "The little woman is going to bop you over the head with a frying pan if you keep calling her the little woman."

"You really have a thing for wanting to bash my brains out." He grinned. "Should I be worried?"

"Yeah, you might want to sleep with one eye open."

"Duly noted." He opened the oven door and peered inside. "Pot roast?"

"Get your nose out of our dinner." She didn't cook much, but a pot roast was easy. Just pour some red wine and beef broth over the meat, add some potatoes, carrots, and onions, and then cook it forever.

"Yes, ma'am." He closed the oven door. His eyes slid over her again. "When I was fifteen, I saw a rerun of *The Dukes of Hazzard.* I had erotic dreams about Daisy for months after that. You—" he pointed at her "—are the new Daisy Duke in my dreams."

Okay then. "I don't even know what to say to that." Other than she liked the idea of being in his dreams.

A smile curved his lips as he inched close enough to touch her. He trailed the tip of his finger over the top of her shorts, his fingernail lightly scraping against her skin, leaving goose bumps in its wake. "Wear this outfit when we get married, and I promise you we'll burn up the sheets on our wedding night."

She sputtered a laugh. "You're ridiculous." Before she decided they should get an early start on their wedding night, she stepped away. "You're back early. How'd your day go?"

"Great." He dropped his hand down to Bella's head, and the dog sighed. Rachel knew the feeling. "I'm impressed with what Jack and Noah are creating for our brothers and sisters who are having problems now that they're back in civilization. You should come with me tomorrow. Check it out."

"I'd like that." It beat spending another boring day hanging around the cabin.

"Good. To why I'm back early, there's something I need to talk to you about. Why don't we grab a beer and sit on the porch?"

"Okay." She took two bottles from the refrigerator and handed them to him, then opened a drawer to get a bottle opener. Before she could find it, he'd twisted off the caps with his hand.

She followed him and Bella to the porch, and when he settled in a rocker, Bella attached herself to his leg. The dog was head over heels in love with him, and Rachel wondered what would happen to Bella when Dallas returned home.

"I think you're a dog whisperer."

He smiled down at Bella. "No, just the first person who was nice to her. We'll bring her with us tomorrow. Jack wants to start working with me and her."

"I'd love to watch that." The way Jack had with dogs had always fascinated her. She glanced at the yard, then frowned. "Where's the Jeep?"

"Parked on the side, next to the bedroom window." He absently scratched Bella's head. "Keeping it there will make it easier to get away if it comes to that. If the worst happens, and Hargrove and his men have the front and back doors covered, we can go out the bedroom window, jump in the Jeep, and beat feet."

"Beat feet?"

"Haul ass in military lingo."

"Oh. Okay, that sounds smart. I just hope it doesn't come to that."

"Me, too, sugar. Me, too."

"So, what did you want to talk about?"

He combed his fingers through his hair. "I really need a haircut."

"Then get one." She was sure that wasn't what he wanted to talk about. What was so bad that he was delaying telling her?

"I… I can't."

Oh, Dallas. You're breaking my heart. Because he'd said he could bear her touch, she put her hand on his arm. "I can cut your hair."

He stared at her hand, then lifted his gaze to hers and grinned. "Like what, you'll just put a bowl on my head and cut around it?"

There went her heart, hurting for the man who was using humor to try to hide his vulnerability, to downplay the result of what his being tortured did to him. She purposely rolled her eyes. "Yeah, and you'll be so sexy with a bowl cut. You'll have to fight the girls off."

Those pretty eyes of his heated as he looked at her. "Are you going to be one of those girls?"

"Mmm." She was pretty sure she was, but that was all she'd give him until they had that talk about kissing. Speaking of talking… "So, you had something you wanted to tell me?"

"Yeah."

Concern replaced the heat in his eyes, and suddenly she didn't want to hear whatever he had to say because whatever it was, it wasn't going to be good news.

"You're probably going to get a call from your detective soon, and I wanted you to hear it from me, from a friend. There's no easy way to say this. They found Henrietta's body."

She knew they would eventually, but even so, tears burned her eyes. "Where?"

"In the desert."

"He just dumped her out there, thrown out like the trash?" Dear God.

"Yeah, and it's even worse than that. She was burned beyond recognition. I'm sure Hargrove was hoping she wouldn't be identified."

She'd cried for Henri after she was murdered, but her tears turned to sobs as she cried for her friend again. She deserved so much better.

"I'm so sorry." He stood, scooped her up, and sat in her rocker with her on his lap.

She didn't know how long she cried with her face buried against his chest while he held her, but finally, the tears slowed. "Sorry, I got your shirt wet." When she tried to push away, he put his hands on her hips and held her in place. She didn't fight him. She was right where she wanted to be.

He'd held her, comforted her, and let her soak his shirt. Her male friends were all either actors or stuntmen, and she couldn't name one who would have held her and made her feel safe the way Dallas did. They would have been too busy with their own lives to involve themselves in hers.

With that thought, it hit like a zap of lightning that except for Nichole, all her friendships were superficial. Her friends in LA weren't ones she could count on, not someone who would be there for her no matter what. If Nichole had known she was in trouble, she would have dropped everything to be at Rachel's side, no questions asked.

For a while now, she'd been pushing away her discontent, ignoring that little voice in her head asking if she was really happy. Because her hours on the sets were often long and exhausting, she hadn't had a relationship in a long time. Her last somewhat serious one had been two years ago, and that had ended because he grew tired of waiting around for her to find time to be with him. She was lonely, something else she'd been trying to ignore. Unless she changed occupations, she didn't see that changing.

Coming back home this time made her miss Asheville more than ever. She was born and raised here, and always knew she'd come back someday. Maybe she was ready sooner than she'd thought she'd be. It would sure make June happy to come home. Her grandmother had followed her to LA, for moral support she'd said. Rachel was of the opinion that June had wanted a closer look at her favorite hot actors.

It always both thrilled and amused Rachel to be able to take June to Hollywood events where her grandmother got to flirt with the pretty boys. It didn't surprise her that June was a favorite of Rachel's acquaintances. Lately, though, June had mentioned a few times that she was thinking of moving back home. Maybe they were both ready, or close to it.

"Some deep thoughts going on there," Dallas said.

"Hmm?" She lifted her gaze to his, got caught in those hazel eyes staring back at her, watched them darken. He wanted her. She could see it in the heat swirling in his pupils. She wanted him, too. Why not let this thing simmering between them happen?

She could stop being lonely for the short time they were both here, and for him, he could handle being touched by her when he couldn't tolerate it from any other woman. Win-win. They could both have something they wanted. Maybe the memories she made with him would keep her from being so lonely when she returned home.

He tapped her forehead. "What's going on in there?"

Go for it, Rach. For once in your life take what you want. "Just this."

The last thing Dallas was expecting was Rachel's mouth on his. Not after she'd cried her heart out. He would give anything to know what thoughts had been churning in her mind the last few minutes, because something was going on in that brain of hers. But she was kissing him, and whatever had brought her to put her mouth on his, he could only cheer her on.

When she wrapped her arms around his neck and pressed her breasts against his chest, he was afraid he was going to embarrass himself. Because of his deployment, then his capture, his time in the hospital, and his coming home a damaged man, he hadn't been with a woman in almost a year.

Just her tongue seeking his had him teetering on the edge. Damn if the first time they were bare skin to bare skin it would be in a rocking chair. And the biggest damn, he was going to make sure this was what she really wanted. That she was thinking straight and not reacting to hearing how her friend's body had been, in her words, "thrown out like the trash."

The last girl he'd been serious with had been during his senior year of high school. He would have married her. It would have meant working for one of his brothers, but he would have done it for her.

Turned out Cindy had other plans, though. Ones she hadn't shared with him until the night of their graduation when he'd taken her to the fanciest restaurant in Butte, planning to propose. He'd even taken from his pocket the ring Cheyenne had helped him pick out and was holding it on his lap. Before he could say the words, she told him she had some awesome news to share. An unexpected modeling opportunity had come her way, and she would be moving to New York. He'd slipped the ring back into his pocket.

She grinned at him as if he should be in on why there was more excitement in her eyes than he'd ever put in them. He'd had a choice then. Tell her he thought it was the most unawesome thing he could imagine or be happy for her. He had his pride after all, so he said, "Wow, Cindy, that's awesome." She had obviously been meant for bigger things since he occasionally saw her picture on a magazine cover. It took a while, but he'd reached a point where he couldn't imagine himself being married to her.

Now, here was this girl who was…well, he didn't know what she was doing to him, but for the first time since Cindy, he wanted more than a simple hookup. After years of avoiding relationships, he wasn't sure how to process that.

He let the kiss go on for another minute, then forced himself to pull away. Her eyes were dilated and dreamy, and he almost dove back in. "Hey." He smiled as he trailed his thumb over her bottom lip, damp from his kiss.

"Hey," she whispered back.

"Before we take this any further, we should talk."

"Talk about kissing and other stuff?"

He laughed. "Yeah, that."

"Well, I thought about it all day, and I want the kisses and maybe the other stuff."

"Maybe, huh?"

She trailed her finger down the front of his shirt. "If you're lucky."

"So you know, I intend to get real lucky."

"Pretty sure of yourself there."

"No, just hopeful. You good, or do we need to talk some more about kisses and stuff?" He ached for this girl, and that in itself was a miracle. After his rescue, he hadn't been interested in anything, and he'd worried that would be a permanent condition. Yet, from the moment he'd had his arms wrapped around a belligerent wildcat, life had gotten interesting again.

"I'm good."

She sure was. Bella tried to climb on his lap and join them, and Rachel laughed. "What's the matter, Bella Boo? You feeling left out?"

He held out his hand, palm up, and Bella laid her chin on it and stared at him with her soulful eyes. "How much longer does your pot roast need to cook?"

"Another hour."

"We need to get started on your workout regimen." He grinned when she turned up her nose. "Get up, lazy bones. We'll take Bella for a run up the mountain." Maybe the exercise would settle down his urge to carry her to the bed for some of that *stuff* she said might happen.

He stood, bringing her up with him, and she wrapped her legs around his waist. "Hmm, I like you there."

"In that case, I'll just hang on to you while you run up the mountain." She squeezed the muscles in his upper arms. "You being a manly SEAL cowboy and all, it would be a piece of cake for you."

He snorted. "Nice try." He carried her inside and dropped her legs, letting her slide down his body. Pure torture. "Go put on your running shoes." He watched her walk down the hallway, chuckling when she exaggerated the sway of her hips. "Killing me, sugar."

She glanced over her shoulder and gave him a sultry smile. Yep, killing him. After exchanging his Henley for a long-sleeve T-shirt and his jeans for lightweight sweats, he returned to the living room to find Rachel waiting. She'd changed into running shorts that clung to her skin and a sports bra, no T-shirt over it. He swallowed hard.

"Ready?"

"Beat you up the mountain." She took off, letting the door slam behind her.

He grabbed Bella's leash and clipped it to her collar. "Silly girl thinks she can beat us."

When he caught up with her, he raced past her, then turned and ran backward. He ran that way for five minutes or so, amused when she tried to pass him. He just moved faster. She was getting annoyed, which was his objective.

He'd learned in BUD/S that the way to get through the exercises was to get mad. Anger gave you energy, one reason the instructors yelled things at you that would piss you off. Getting pissed off also made you stubborn—at least, it had him.

When his back leg muscles began to protest, he turned but stayed ahead of her. He glanced over his shoulder. "Need a break yet?" He laughed when she glared at him.

She really was in good shape for a civilian. Most people, men and women, would have legs like rubber by now and would be begging to stop. Not only was she in good shape, but she was stubborn, and he liked that. He liked a lot of things about her.

They ran for another fifteen or so minutes, and he could see that she was tiring. He slowed to a fast walk to let her cool down.

"I hate you." She sucked in air. "You're not even breathing hard."

"Training. Lots and lots of it." Although he wasn't back to his best. Two weeks of being starved and tortured tended to take a toll on one's body, but it was good getting back to physical activity. He slowed to match her pace.

"That dog is head over heels for you," she said. "She's going to be crushed when you leave."

He glanced down at Bella. Unlike most dogs that strained at the end of their leash when out for a walk, she stayed right next to him. "Jack will find her a good home with someone who needs a dog like her." He was trying hard not to get attached to her, but that wasn't working so well.

"You could take her home with you. She'd probably love living on a ranch."

If he went home. And where had that thought come from? Of course he was going home. To do what, he had no idea. He supposed he'd end up working for Phoenix, although that didn't thrill him.

His brother's hired hands kept the stalls clean and the horses groomed and fed. Phoenix did not allow anyone else to work with his horses. Not even Dallas. No matter that Dallas was pretty damn good with horses himself.

"Deep in thought over there."

"Just thinking about some stuff." He pushed the uncertainty about his future aside. He'd deal with that when he got home. While he had a sexy wildcat in his life, he'd enjoy the time he had with her.

"What kind of stuff?"

"About our wedding night." He waggled his eyebrows, cartoon style. "And you wearing those hot little shorts."

She punched his arm. "You're ridiculous."

"So you keep saying." Bella's ears perked up, and for the first time since starting on their run, she left his side. Curious about what she was up to, he followed her to the edge of the trail. Bella went down a small path that obviously wasn't used much. She stared ahead, her ears still standing at attention, then she looked back at him and whined.

"She wants us to follow her," Rachel said, coming to stand next to him.

"Looks like." He wasn't sure what the dog was leading them to, and he was glad he had the gun Jack had lent him strapped on under his shirt. "Stay close to me."

"You don't think she hears a bear or mountain lion, do you? Do they have mountain lions in North Carolina?" she whispered.

"Good question," he whispered back.

Chapter Fourteen

The path was too small to walk next to Dallas, so Rachel stayed right behind him. She didn't think Bella would lead them into danger, but they didn't really know the dog all that well and what she might do.

She put her hand on his waist, hoping to feel that gun strapped there that she hadn't been so happy about and let out a sigh of relief that he was wearing it. He chuckled, and she knew he remembered when she'd asked if having a gun on him was necessary. She pinched him, and he glanced back at her with way too much amusement in his eyes.

Because of her job, she'd met every kind of man out there, and not a one of them had anything on Dallas. Not in her eyes, anyway. It hit her then, and she groaned. *I'm in so much trouble with this man.*

"What?" he said, making her wonder if she'd said that aloud.

"Nothing. Nothing at all." They were still whispering, afraid the bear or mountain lion might hear them… if a killer animal was what Bella was leading them to. The trees were growing thicker, cutting out the sunlight, and it was getting spookier with each step forward.

She was reminded of a horror movie she'd stunt doubled in, where a bunch of teenagers decided to play a game in the woods where an evil ghost supposedly lived. The only problem, in the movie, the ghost turned out to be real.

"Evil ghosts aren't real," she muttered. She was pretty sure that was true.

"You say something?"

"Nope." She hooked her fingers into the back of his sweats. Now that she was thinking about evil spirits, she was nervous, which was pretty stupid. There was no such thing as ghosts. Still, she wasn't chancing getting separated from him. "Maybe we should go back to the trail."

"We will in a minute. I'm curious what has Bella's attention."

She leaned around him to look at the dog. Bella was at the end of the leash, pulling Dallas along. Her ears were still up, and now she was making a whining noise. That made Rachel feel a little better. If there was danger, she'd be growling, right?

They came to a downed tree, and Bella jumped over it, then disappeared around a boulder that seemed to suddenly appear. Dallas stepped over the tree, and Rachel followed, hearing a mewling sound.

"What was that?" she asked.

"Don't know." He walked around the boulder, then stopped. "What have you found, Bella?"

Rachel moved next to him. Bella was flat on her stomach at the entrance to a small cave, and her whine grew louder. She was also wagging her tail, which eased Rachel's mind. She wouldn't be wagging her tail at danger.

Dallas squatted and peered into the cave. "Too dark

to see." He pulled his phone out of his sweats pocket, clicked on the flashlight, and shined it into the cave. Bella belly crawled forward, disappearing until only her wagging tail was visible.

"Well, well, well," Dallas murmured.

She tried to see what was in there, but Dallas's body was blocking her view. "What is it?"

He leaned his upper body inside, then came back out, and in his hand was a tiny gray-and-white kitten. Bella hopped around him, her gaze glued on the little thing.

"How in the world did that get in there?" she said. "Where's the mother?"

"Don't think there is one. Look how skinny it is."

Poor thing. It really was skinny. "Do you think the mother brought it here, then something happened to her?" She glanced around. "Like a bear or mountain lion?" She made a mental note to google bears and mountain lions in North Carolina.

"Haven't a clue."

"Well, we can't leave it here." She almost laughed. She'd come here to hide out, and so far, she'd collected a starving kitten, a traumatized dog, and a hot SEAL cowboy.

Bella jumped up and put her paws on Dallas's waist, then tried to take the kitten from him.

He chuckled. "I don't think Bella would let us leave it behind even if we tried."

The kitten found one of his fingers and tried to suckle.

"Aww, it's hungry. What is it, a girl or boy?"

He turned it over so they could see the kitten's belly. "Looks like we have a little boy."

She tried not to feel all fuzzy warm inside at the *we* but failed. Bella, still with her paws on Dallas's waist, licked the little guy. The kitten wiggled his tiny body until it was upright again, then stuck his nose against the dog's. Bella gently took the kitten in her mouth, lowered her paws to the ground, and then headed back the way they'd come.

"Shouldn't you get the kitten back before Bella hurts him?"

"Nah. She won't hurt him. Kittens and puppies are used to their mamas carrying them around like that. It probably makes the little guy feel safe."

They followed Bella and her newly adopted baby back to the main path. When they reached the trail, Dallas scanned the area around them. "We should come back tomorrow to check and make sure there's not a mom or other kittens around."

"What if we can't find the cave?"

He walked to a good-size rock that she wouldn't be able to lift, picked it up, and set it at the beginning of the path. "We'll look for this."

Just watching him do that while barely flexing a muscle did something to her girly parts. Was she that shallow that brawn made her want to jump his bones? Well, she'd be lying to herself if she tried to pretend she hadn't wanted to explore whatever this was between them since he'd kissed her—since before that, really.

"My grandmother called this afternoon," she said, scrambling for something to talk about other than how much she couldn't stop thinking about Dallas and sex.

"She okay being at the ranch?"

"Ha! She's in heaven. She said your cowboys are hotter than the ones at the other ranch." If they all looked like him, June would definitely be in heaven.

She grinned. "Maybe you should warn them to lock their doors at night."

"And spoil all her fun?"

She laughed. "I'm just kidding. She won't sneak into their rooms at night… I don't think."

"Your grandmother actually sounds like a fun woman."

"Most of the time." There were times she was over the top, but June had reached an age where she could get away with her antics. "Apparently she and Carter have a flirtation going. She asked him to send her a picture of himself without his shirt on. He sent her a picture of Dwayne Johnson."

"That's funny because TG is a dead ringer for The Rock, except he has twice as many tattoos."

"That is funny. I can see her now, showing that picture to her friends and telling them that's her new boyfriend."

"I think I would like your grandmother." He watched Bella for a moment, pulling at the end of her leash as if she needed to be back in the cabin like right now. "You never talk about your parents. Are they in the picture?" She talked about her grandmother a lot, and the love between them was obvious. Not once had she mentioned her mother or father.

"Nope. My mother died giving birth to me, and the sperm donor skipped town as soon as he found out she was pregnant."

Dallas wished he could take back the question when her face blanked. He heard the sadness in her voice and couldn't imagine not having a large family, or to think of the man who sired him as only a sperm donor.

"You're welcome to some of mine," he said, wanting to see her smile again. "They're nosy and get all up in your business, but they mean well." She smiled, and it felt like the sun had come out on a rainy day.

"I'll take two of your cowboy brothers."

"The hell you will." He clamped his mouth shut. His outburst surprised him, but his brothers couldn't have her. She shot him an amused grin, and he wondered how much trouble he was in with this girl.

They reached the cabin, and as soon as he unlocked and opened the door, Bella pushed past them. He stood aside to let Rachel enter. They both followed Bella into the kitchen, and he guessed Rachel was as curious as he to see what the dog was going to do with the kitten.

Bella stopped at her food dish and gently set the kitten on the floor, then sat and waited for her adopted baby to eat. When the kitten didn't chow down, Bella looked up at him with worried eyes.

"Don't think he cares for dog food, Bella." Dallas dropped to the floor. "He's probably dehydrated." He stuck his hand in the dog's water bowl, then put a finger to the kitten's mouth. The little thing started sucking on his finger, so he repeated the process a few times.

Rachel dropped down beside him. "How do we feed him? We have some milk."

"That might upset his stomach. We need to take him to the vet tomorrow, get him checked out. I'm guessing he's between five to eight weeks. Hard to tell since he's likely malnourished. He probably hasn't been weaned from his mother, so we'll need to teach him how to eat." He pushed up, went to the pantry, and searched the shelves for something that might work. "Let's try this for tonight." He held up a can of tuna.

"Can he eat that?"

"I'm going to mash it up until it's like paste, then we'll try finger feeding him."

"Blue."

"As in the color, or you're sad?" He mashed up the tuna and some of the juice.

"As in that's his name. Blue for the Blue Ridge Mountains where we found him."

He eyed the kitten, now trying to find a nipple in Bella's stomach while the dog was diligently giving the little guy a bath. "It's a good name for him." He sat on the floor again with the bowl of tuna and picked up the kitten. "Sorry, buddy, no milk for you there."

"I hope he'll eat the tuna."

"Let's find out. Dip your pinky in the tuna, then put it to his mouth." The kitten turned its face away. "Smear a little over his lips."

"Oh," she said, excitement in her voice when the kitten licked his lips, then got an expression on his face as if realizing that was some good stuff.

"Give him some more." He watched her feed the scrawny thing, his eyes on her, not the kitten. In spite of fearing for her life and grieving the loss of her friend, she managed to still laugh and smile. He had no doubt she was at heart a happy person. Maybe her joy of life was bleeding over to him.

The only reason he'd accepted Jack's invitation was to get away from his smothering family. He'd expected to come here, spend as little time with Jack and Noah as he could get away with, and the rest of his stay holed up with his misery.

Then a wildcat tried to bash him in the head, and he forgot to be miserable. His gaze locked on her mouth when she grinned at the kitten. He wanted to kiss her until she couldn't remember her name…until he couldn't remember his.

"Ouch, Blue." She laughed. "His teeth are like little needles."

"He was definitely hungry. We should probably let what he's eaten settle in his stomach. We'll give him more later." He inhaled the aroma of pot roast, and his stomach growled in anticipation. He grinned back at her when she laughed. "Speaking of hungry…"

"Well, then we better feed you." She set Blue on the floor. "Here's your baby back, Bella Boo."

Bella picked Blue up by his neck, then took him to her bed in the corner of the kitchen. Within minutes, the kitten was asleep, nestled in the dog's fur.

"That's just so sweet," she said, a soft smile on her face. "What's going to happen to them when we leave?"

"Pretty sure Jack intends Bella to be a service dog. As for Blue, he'll help us find him a good home."

"I've never had a pet. Maybe I'll take Blue home with me."

"Something to think about. What can I do to help with dinner?"

"You can set the table."

"On it." That only took a few minutes. "Wine, water, or something else?"

"Wine would be nice."

Normally he'd go for a beer, but he decided to pour himself a glass, too.

She had her back to him as she dished up the pot roast and vegetables. Her hair was pulled back in a ponytail, and it had been teasing him on their run. The temptation to wrap it around his fist while he kissed her soft skin had been there all afternoon, and he finally gave in.

He walked up behind her and put his hands on her shoulders. "You can stop me at any time, but I have to do this." He fisted her ponytail, then pressed his lips to the skin below her ear and paused, giving her a chance to stop him. When she bent her head, inviting him to continue, he sighed in relief.

Musk from their run mixed with her apples and vanilla scent, and for some reason, that was hot as hell. Like sex combined with innocence and cookies. He swallowed a chuckle at that thought.

How did this girl turn him on like no other ever had, make him laugh when he'd not expected to ever laugh again? "Rachel," he murmured.

There were things he wanted to say to her, but he wasn't even sure what those things were. He was straddling a fence, not sure which way to go. While he belonged to one of the wealthiest ranching families in Montana, he was lost. Being lost meant he had nothing to offer her. But he could show her how special she was, how much a man could want her. So, as long as she would let him, while they were together, that was what he would do.

He slipped his arms around her, resting his hands on her stomach. He wanted—was dying—to go lower, but she hadn't given him that permission yet. He nipped his teeth across her skin.

"If you want dinner, you have to stop," she said.

"Hmm, a choice of dinner, which smells amazing, or kissing you? You drive a hard bargain." He pressed one last kiss just below her ear. "Let's eat, then get back to kissing. That work for you?"

She leaned her head back on his chest and peered up at him. "Sounds like a very good plan."

"I have my moments." He stepped to the side, picked up both plates, and carried them to the table. He took his first bite of the pot roast, closed his eyes, and sighed. "This is good." It was great to have his appetite back.

"Thanks. I don't cook much, but it's one thing I can cook pretty good. Hard to mess up a pot roast." She took a sip of her wine. "So, tell me about your family. June said the dude ranch was awesome, and that your sister was really nice. Cheyenne, right?" He nodded. "She said Cheyenne and her husband were models for a cowboy romance cover. What book? I need to check it out."

"I'll find it after dinner. The author is a friend of Cheyenne's and talked them into modeling for the cover. Cheyenne's husband said never again."

"I've watched photoshoots for movie posters and stuff. It really isn't fun."

"Yeah, he said he'd rather stick his arm up a cow, and believe me, that's saying something." He almost laughed at how wide her eyes grew.

"You have to do that?"

"Sometimes during birth, but that's not good dinner conversation."

"True. What about the rest of your family?"

"Mom's Bonnie, my dad's name is Laramie, then from oldest down, Austin, Denver, Cheyenne, Phoenix, Shiloh, then me." He waited for the question he knew was coming.

"You all are named after places?"

"It's a generations-long Manning family tradition."

"I think it's cool. I love those names. And they all work at the ranch?"

"All but Shiloh and me. She's a Coast Guard rescue helicopter pilot."

"For real? Wow. That's awesome."

"I think so." He told her each of his siblings' roles at the ranch. "My dad stepped back from the day-to-day operation a few years ago, but he still has opinions on how things should run." He chuckled. "His expertise is with the cattle side of the business, so he and Denver lock horns the most."

"Are they all married?"

"Only Cheyenne. Austin came close a few years ago, but when she found out she'd have to sign a prenup, she broke up with him. Obviously, he dodged a bullet with that one. The rule was put in effect by my great-grandfather when one of his daughters got divorced, which was pretty unheard of back then. Her husband tried to claim ownership of the ranch. Any Manning who marries without getting a prenup now loses their inheritance."

"That sounds kind of harsh…losing your inheritance. I can understand the prenup, considering the size of your ranch and all. I checked out the ranch's website when I found out June was going there. Talk about impressive." Pink stained her cheeks. "I wasn't snooping, just wanted to make sure she was going someplace safe."

Pink was pretty on her. He wondered where else on her body she blushed…where he could make her blush. "The website is public, so you weren't snooping. Your grandmother's safe. I promise."

"I believe you. So, what about you? Where do you fit in?"

And that was the million-dollar question, wasn't it?

"I don't know." How'd the conversation get turned to him? He stood. "You cooked. I'll clean. Why don't you take the rest of your wine to the living room and relax? Or have a nice bath."

She put her hand on his wrist. "Dallas. Where do you fit in?"

He dropped back down in the chair. "Nowhere. Shiloh and I are the youngest, and all the jobs were taken by the time we were out of school. That was why I joined the Navy, and she joined the Coast Guard."

"If you could, what job would you choose?"

"The horses, but Phoenix has that covered."

"So you'll stay in the Navy when your leave is up?"

"Not sure." He was sure, and the answer was no, but he couldn't stand seeing the sadness in her eyes that was for him. "Nothing I have to think about today." He stood again, and this time, she didn't stop him. "Go relax."

"Why don't I help?"

"Nope. I got this." Her phone buzzed, and he picked it up from the counter. He glanced at the screen. "It's the detective."

"I guess he's calling to tell me they found Henri's body. I'm not supposed to know that, right?"

"Right." A minute later, his phone buzzed, TG's name on the screen. "Talk to me." He walked out to the porch. TG would know that Rachel was on the phone with the detective, and that meant TG had information he didn't want her to overhear.

"How's Rachel holding up?"

"Pretty good, although she took it hard learning how Henrietta's body was disposed of."

"Not surprising. That was harsh. I'll leave it up to you whether to tell her or not, but a man showed up at the Wyoming ranch looking for her grandmother. He claimed to be her son."

"Does June have a son?" Rachel hadn't mentioned one.

"Negative. Unfortunately, they don't have cameras. I've got a vague description and that he drove a black Escalade, and that's it."

"Shit."

"My sentiments, exactly. But we got Rachel's grandmother out of there before Hargrove's men found her, and that's what counts."

"Thank you for that. I don't think she could get over losing June. What about the FBI? I'm surprised Rachel hasn't heard from them again."

"Their focus at the moment is on diving into Hargrove's involvement in his illegal activities. Most especially, they want to know who he's selling arms to. They've decided that Rachel can't help them with any of that for now, nor can she help them find him, so she's not on their radar. She will be after they find him, and he goes to trial. She'll be their star witness on the murder charge."

"How the hell do you find all this stuff out?" He snorted. "Never mind. It's one of those if you told me, you'd have to kill me things."

"Affirmative, and I really don't fancy taking you out. I know you're being vigilant, but it's time to start being extra cautious."

"Copy that. Speaking of being cautious, I need you to do me a favor. Rachel and I went to a grocery store the first day I was here. Can you hack into their security and erase the footage they have of us?"

"I thought you were going to give me something hard to do. What store?"

He gave TG the store's name and the date they were there. "I'm expecting Hargrove or his men to show up any day now."

"Just keep our girl safe."

As usual in conversations with TG, he disconnected before Dallas could respond. TG was right. It was time to raise the threat level.

Chapter Fifteen

"I think you could use a hug," Dallas said, coming back inside.

Rachel attempted a smile. It hadn't been any easier hearing what Robert had done to Henri the second time around. "Hugs are always welcome." Especially from him.

He wrapped his arms around her and put his hand on the back of her head, pulling her face against his chest. "He'll pay for what he did to your friend. He's got every cop and federal agent on the lookout for him."

She squeezed her eyes shut against the burning tears. Hopefully they'd find him soon. She'd never thought this about anyone, not even someone she didn't like, but she hoped he burned in hell.

"Go take a nice bath." He kissed the top of her head. "I'll get the kitchen cleaned up and take Bella out."

"I can help."

"Nope." He leaned back and looked at her. "By the way, you're sleeping in the big bed with me from now on."

"I am?" She wasn't ready for that yet.

"Yes, ma'am. But all we're doing tonight is sleeping. From now on, when we're at the cabin, I want you close.

Hopefully Hargrove won't find out about this place, but we can't take a chance. If you can't handle being in the same bed with me, I'll sleep on the floor."

"No, I can handle it." No way would she make him sleep on the floor, and he was right. Sleeping in a separate room wasn't safe any longer.

"Good." He stepped away, then patted her butt. "Go take your bath."

She saluted him. "Yes, sir." She stopped in her room. What should she sleep in? Not that she had much of a choice since she'd only bought the necessities when she'd shopped for clothes before leaving LA. Since she hadn't unpacked, she gathered up her Kindle, phone charger, and grabbed her suitcase, taking everything to the bigger room.

After deciding on a T-shirt and her running shorts, she headed for the bathroom, opting for a quick shower instead of a bath. Dallas wasn't in the room when she came out, but he'd moved Bella's bed in, and she was busy giving her baby a bath. Rachel kneeled on the floor. "Aren't you just the best mommy?"

Bella nosed her hand, then returned to caring for her kitten. The dog had come a long way in the short time she'd been with Dallas. He really was great with Bella, and she was sure that carried over to other animals. It was sad that what he'd most like to do on his family's ranch wasn't an option for him.

"Sweet dreams, Bella Boo and Blue." She chuckled. "Sounds like a nursery rhyme. Bella Boo had a kitten named Blue…" She tried to think of words that rhymed with blue.

"…and off they went to the zoo where a cow taught them how to say moo."

Laughing, she glanced over her shoulder. "Now there's a surprise talent I never would have guessed you had."

He was leaning against the doorframe, and he'd obviously showered in the other bathroom since his hair was damp. Even though he was covered from neck to ankles in a light gray long-sleeve T and plaid pajama bottoms, he still took her breath away. "I have all kinds of hidden talents, sugar."

She just bet he did. He sauntered toward her, and her gaze fell on his bare feet. Who knew men's feet could be sexy? She gave Bella one last head scratch, then stood. "So, um…ready for bed?" She'd never gone to bed with a man just to sleep, and she was a little weirded out. It wasn't like they both didn't know that something would happen between them, but she wasn't ready…not tonight.

"Oh, I'm definitely ready for…." He grinned. "Sleeping."

And just like that, he'd un-weirded her. She rolled her eyes, then walked to the bed. "Which side do you sleep on?"

"Doesn't matter. Take your pick."

Since she was standing next to the right side, she'd take that one. When they were both in bed, him facing her, he got a funny look on his face. "What?"

"Just trying to imprint on my brain not to dream about you, thinking I'm making love to you, and try to do it for real."

"You dream about me?"

"Since the night you tried to brain-bash me."

"Oh," she whispered.

"Yeah, not sure why you trying to kill me is such a turn-on."

This man. She could easily fall in love with him if she let herself. She wouldn't, though. There was only heartbreak if she went down that road. "Hot cowboy aside, you're strange, you know that, right?"

A grin stretched across his face. "Damn, girl, you're funny. I really like you." He brushed away the lock of hair that had fallen over his forehead.

She grabbed his hand and traced her finger over his two bent ones. "Did this happen when you were a prisoner?"

"Yeah." He curled his hand around hers. "So, tell me about a day in the life of Rachel Denning."

He didn't want to talk about that time. Had he talked to anyone about it? His family. Jack or Noah? A therapist? She wasn't an expert on what he'd gone through, but it seemed to her that it wasn't something he should hold inside.

"A day in the life of Rachel Denning is pretty boring. Making movies involves a lot of sitting around in makeup and costume waiting to be called on the set when it's time to film a stunt. I read a lot."

"I guess you don't have lines to learn?"

"Nope. They can make me look like the actress I'm stunting for, but they can't change my voice." She really did lead a boring life, but she wanted to know more about his. "How old were you when you had your first kiss?"

"Seven."

"For real?"

"Uh-huh. Leah Ann Sorenson. She dared me to kiss her." He shrugged. "What was a boy to do but follow through when challenged? So, I kissed her, and she slapped me." He grinned. "That was before I was an enlightened male."

She laughed. "Doesn't seem fair that she dared you to do it and then slapped you. Okay, what about your first real kiss? How old?"

"Thirteen. Leah Ann Sorenson. At least that time I didn't get slapped."

"That's hilarious."

"What about you? Who and how old?"

"Fifteen. Steve Cochran. I had the biggest crush on him, then he kissed me, and it was yucky. It was a very slobbery kiss."

"Gross. Okay, who gave you the best kiss you've ever had?"

"You." She wasn't sure she should have admitted that, but it was the truth. And oh, his smile made her glad she did.

"Yeah?"

"Mmm-hmm. But I haven't kissed a lot of guys, so check back with me in a year or two."

"Hell no. I'm always going to be your best kisser." He brought her hand up to his lips and pressed his lips to her palm.

No man had ever kissed her palm, had ever made her feel so special. They talked late into the night, telling each other their favorite colors, favorite foods, and sharing stories from their childhood.

When she yawned, he said, "Turn around and scoot back, sleepyhead."

She fell asleep with him spooned around her, and her last thought was how much she was going to miss him when she returned home.

* * *

Rachel hadn't known what to expect Operation K-9 Brothers to be like. Maybe some cages with dogs in them, but it was nothing of the sort. The dogs were housed in large kennels with plenty of room to move around. All the dogs looked happy and healthy. Her favorite part was the building housing the puppies. She'd played with them for a while, then had come outside to watch Jack work with Dallas and Bella.

"Someone trained her very well," Jack said as he stood in front of Dallas and Bella. "I'm having trouble believing that same person was the one who abused her."

Rachel had come to the same conclusion. How could someone take so much care in a dog's training only to hurt the dog? "Maybe someone stole her from her owner?" She sat in a lawn chair Jack had set out for her while he worked with Dallas and Bella. They hadn't found a command that Bella didn't know.

Jack nodded. "Possibly. We had her checked for a chip, but she doesn't have one. Surprising for a pure-bred." He studied Bella for a moment. "She's scared to death. I think before we work with her anymore, she needs more time to start believing we're not going to hurt her."

Although she performed on command, she kept her still too skinny body pressed against Dallas's leg whenever possible. Rachel had the impression that as long as Bella was touching him, she felt safe. Rachel knew the feeling.

They'd found a vet near the cabin and had dropped Blue off on the way over. Bella hadn't liked the kitten taken from her and had refused to leave the vet's office. Dallas had had to pick her up and carry her out to the Jeep.

"Let's walk her over to the kennels for a minute," Jack said.

When they were out of earshot, they stopped and seemed to be having a serious conversation. Rachel wished she could hear what they were talking about. Dallas glanced at her and winked. Silly how those winks of his sent warmth streaming through her, made her heart skip a beat, and put a goofy smile on her face.

Dallas noticed Rachel watching them, and by the frown on her face, he was sure she thought they were talking about her, which they were. He winked, and her frown morphed into a smile. He liked making her smile.

"She's doing okay," Dallas said in answer to Jack's question. "Better than most people would be if someone was out to kill them."

"I'm not liking the way you look at her. You're not messing around with her, are you?"

"Say one more word, brother, and I'll put you on your ass." Whatever happened between Rachel and him was their business.

"You can try." He sighed. "Look, I wouldn't blame you if you were interested in her. She's pretty and smart, but you're not in a good place for a relationship. You'll end up hurting her, then I'll have to hurt you."

Dallas threw Jack's words back at him. "You can try." He wouldn't know how to explain the peace he felt in his mind when he was with her, that she spoke to his heart. The touching thing didn't make sense either, and he didn't even try to explain that. For one thing, he hadn't told Jack that he had a problem with touching.

"I just don't want to see either one of you get hurt."

"We're just friends, okay?" And they were. He hoped that when all this was over and she returned home, they could stay in touch. He didn't like the thought of not having her in his life somehow.

"Yeah, okay." Jack pulled a small package out of his pocket. "Here's your paracord."

"Thanks." Dallas slipped it into his pocket.

"You're not going to put it on?"

"Nope." He lifted his sleeve. "I have one. You should get yourself one. Never know when it will come in handy." He saw the question in Jack's eyes. "It's for Rachel. She saw mine and said she wanted one."

Before Jack could comment on that, he decided to divert the conversation to a different subject. "I talked to TG yesterday. Someone showed up at the Wyoming ranch, looking for Rachel's grandmother."

"I'm not liking that. Does Rachel know?"

"No, and there's no reason to tell her. It will only worry her, and her grandmother's safe. There's nothing to lead anyone to my family's ranch."

"I'm thinking it's time to step up our vigilance. If someone showed up in Wyoming, that means Hargrove got into her computer. He'll have her contacts."

"Agree, and TG said the same thing. Rachel decided that she'll stay in her college girl disguise whenever we leave the cabin. College girl has been seen with me. For all appearances, we're boyfriend and girlfriend, and to change her disguise would be suspicious." Although, the first time they'd gone out, she'd been a flashy, big-chested girl, but TG was going to take care of that.

Jack glanced at her. "She does look like a college girl. If I didn't know it was her, I really wouldn't recognize her."

"Same. I don't think she should be left alone at the cabin anymore."

"There's something I want you to do for me, and she can go with you. Let's walk back over there."

The whole time they'd been talking, Bella had glued herself to his leg. Dallas reached down and scratched her head. "Let's go see your second favorite person in the world."

"You guys been talking about me?" Rachel said when they stopped in front of her.

"Yep." Dallas grinned when she wrinkled her nose. "Jack has a job for us." Hopefully it was something he was willing to do.

Jack told her his plans for Operation Warriors Center, listing the activities he wanted to offer their visitors.

"Wow, that sounds really ambitious and pretty awesome," she said. "I love the idea of a rock-climbing wall. That's one of my favorite downtime things to do." She grinned. "Not to brag, but I'm considered an expert at it. What grade wall are you planning? I'm thinking maybe an average wall, something around a five point eight or so?"

Jack gave her a look she couldn't interpret. "Maybe you can consult with us when we plan the wall. You like hiking?"

"Love hiking." She looked around. "You have some great trails in the area. I'd map out some easy ones, some intermediate ones, and a few difficult ones. Some of those should have waterfalls included. People love seeing those."

"Hmm."

What was that hmm for? What he was planning really was awesome, and she couldn't imagine how satisfying it would be to be involved in something like Operation Warriors Center.

"Dallas already knows this, but I want to also include equine therapy in what we're offering. I've been hearing good things about it. Problem is, I need the right horses for something like that, and all I know about horses is that you can ride them." Jack eyed Dallas. "You know horses, and I want you to find me some that will suit our needs. I have a couple of places in the area you two can check out."

"Oh, I'd like that," Rachel said.

"You ever ride?" Dallas would enjoy an afternoon of riding with her.

She nodded. "I had to fall off once for a stunt. In order to fall off, I had to learn how to ride a galloping horse. It was fun."

Of course she'd think that was fun. "We'll go tomorrow."

Noah showed up with Lucky trotting along beside him. "Dudes and dudette, what's happening?"

"I'm sending Dallas and Rachel out horse hunting," Jack said. "We get the okay to start construction on the lodge?"

"Affirmative. The contractor will have his men here on Monday to start." He bumped Dallas's shoulder. "Sure am glad you're here to do that. I was afraid it was going to be my job, and I don't know a horse from a donkey."

"Oh, hell, he's going to sing," Dallas said, seeing that mischievous gleam that always appeared in Noah's eyes when he was about to come up with a song for the occasion. And sure enough, he sang a song about riding a donkey to the honky tonky.

"He's weird," Dallas told Rachel when Noah finished the song. "Never bet against him that he can't come up with a song that fits whatever you're talking about."

She laughed. "That's a great talent to have. I actually know that one. It's 'Donkey' by Jerrod Niemann."

"Give the lady a prize." Noah glanced at Lucky, who had his front legs flat on the ground and butt in the air, tail wagging, trying to get Bella's attention. Bella had her face buried against Dallas's leg. "I know she's pretty, buddy, but she obviously has no interest in you." He snapped his fingers. "Leave her alone."

Rachel had to smile at the disappointed expression on Lucky's face as he came to Noah's side. "Aww, it sucks to be rejected, doesn't it, Lucky?" At hearing his name, his ears perked up, and he trotted over to her. "I think Bella's just playing hard to get," she stage-whispered to him. "She's also very shy, so don't give up."

"You tell them about Saturday morning pancakes?" Noah asked Jack.

"Not yet."

"We get together on Saturday mornings for pancakes," Noah said. "Jack's grandmother and Dirty Mary join us, and—"

"Dirty Mary?" That sounded to her like a rude thing to call someone.

Jack rolled his eyes. "My grandmother's friend, and her pals at assisted living nicknamed her that. You'll see why Saturday."

"And she's okay with that?"

He nodded. "Actually, she loves the name and does her best to live up to it."

"She's a hoot," Noah looked at Dallas and grinned. "She's in her eighties and harmless…mostly. Just keep your ass away from her grabby hands, and you'll be fine."

Rachel decided she couldn't wait to meet Dirty Mary with the grabby hands. She'd miss seeing her friend, though. "Nichole make it to Florida okay?"

"No, she did not," Jack said. "Stubborn woman refused to go. We did come to a compromise. She's staying at her brother's house until Hargrove isn't a threat." He frowned. "Mark's name and address isn't in your contacts, is it?"

"No."

"Okay, good."

The only names from here in her contacts were Jack and Nichole's. She'd never forgive herself if something happened to any one of them. "I… I need to go."

Chapter Sixteen

Dallas leaned against the bedroom doorframe as Rachel threw things in her suitcase. "What are you doing?" She'd been fine back at Operation K-9 Brothers one minute, and in the next, all the color had drained from her face.

On the ride to the vet to pick up Blue, then on to the cabin, she'd closed up tighter than a clam. Even Bella's excitement at having her kitten back hadn't put a smile on her face.

"Rachel." He strode into the room. "What's going on?" She was packing; he could see that. What he didn't understand was why. What had set her off?

"What does it look like? I'm leaving."

"The hell you are." He stepped behind her, wrapped his arms around her, and pulled her away from the suitcase she'd put on the bed. "Talk to me, Rachel."

She deflated in his arms like a balloon losing air. "I'm going to get people killed. I… I can't live with that."

"What people?"

"You're seriously asking me that?" She twisted away from him and poked him in the chest. "You. Jack and

Nichole. Noah, maybe even Peyton. That's what people." She slapped her hands over her face.

He wrapped his fingers around her wrists and pulled her hands away from her face. "Listen to me. You're not going to get anyone killed. You have some of the best-trained and deadliest men in the world protecting you. Me, Jack, Noah, TG, and God knows who all he has poking their noses into this. Not a single one of us is going to walk away and leave you to fight this on your own. If you run, I will come after you." He put his fingers under her chin, lifting her face, forcing her to look at him. "You hearing me?"

"I can't live with seeing one of you hurt or worse." She squeezed her eyes shut. "Especially you."

She was killing him. "So you think taking off will keep us safe? Maybe, but probably not. And how do you think your leaving will make us feel, not knowing if you're safe or not?"

"I'll disappear somewhere. Change my name and appearance."

"And be all alone? Do you know why horses are herd animals?"

She shook her head.

"Because there's safety in a herd. A horse alone is prey. Herding makes them smart. Tell me a horse isn't smarter than you."

She didn't answer, so he grabbed his duffel bag and tossed it on the bed next to her suitcase.

"What are you doing?" she yelled.

He paused with a pair of socks in his hand. "Packing. I'd think that was obvious."

"You're going home?"

He tossed the socks into his duffel. "I'm going with you."

"Dallas." She sat on the bed. "Please let me disappear. I'll find someplace that Robert will never think to look for me."

"Sure, we can do that." He wadded up a shirt and stuffed it in the duffel. Normally, he would neatly fold his clothes, but he was mad. She didn't trust them to not only keep her safe, but themselves as well. If she thought any one of them would stand by and let her take off by herself without protection, she had no clue how tenacious a SEAL could be.

Not that he expected her to understand how extensively trained he, Jack, and Noah were, how specialized their skills were. No, what bugged the hell out of him was that she didn't trust him to stay out of harm's way. She was willing to sacrifice herself for him, and that wasn't acceptable.

He glanced at her, and ah, hell, tears were swimming in her eyes. He dropped to his knees in front of her and took her hands in his. "Listen. I can't let you take off by yourself. I don't have it in me to do that. We can go, find a place to hide, you and me. Hargrove would probably never find us, but there's no guarantee on that, so we'll always be looking over our shoulder. Or we can stay here where we have Jack and Noah watching our six. Those are your two choices."

"You promise you won't let him hurt you?"

He wanted to promise her anything she asked for, but he wouldn't lie to her. "You know I can't promise that, just like I can't promise a piece of space junk won't fall on my head tomorrow." There was a hint of a smile. "What I can promise is that I'm very good at what I do, as are Jack and Noah. We have no intention of letting Hargrove hurt us. So, what will it be? Are we staying or going?"

"I guess we're staying."

"That's my girl." He squeezed her hands, then stood. "Oh, almost forgot. Got you something." He pulled the package out of his pocket and handed it to her.

"What is it?" She held the small envelope up, then shook it.

"Open it and see."

She tore the end off, peeked inside, and then lifted wide eyes to him. "You got me a paracord bracelet?"

"It's a good one, the same as mine."

"Thank you. Thank you so much!" She launched herself at him. "This is awesome."

"Well, hello there." He wrapped his arms around her. How many women would get this excited about such a simple and inexpensive gift? She was something else, something special.

She leaned her head back and grinned up at him. "For a paracord, I might even let you kiss me."

"Yeah?" His gaze fell to her mouth. "Like right now?"

"If you want."

"Oh, I want."

She tossed the paracord on the dresser. "You can show me all the things this does later, after we lock lips."

He chuckled. "Lock lips, huh?" He lowered his mouth to hers, and as he kissed her, he had the crazy thought that she was the only woman he wanted to kiss for the rest of his life.

She had her hair in a ponytail again, and he wrapped

it around his fist the way he'd wanted to do every time that ponytail bounced along her back during their runs up the mountain. She softly moaned, telling him she liked that. He lowered his other hand to her hip, pulling her against him, letting her feel how much he wanted her.

"Please," she whispered into his mouth.

"Yes," he whispered back. He'd never wanted a girl the way he wanted Rachel, and that scared him a little. There wasn't a future for them, but he was beginning to think that he wanted more than a fling. Their lives were in two different parts of the country, though, the distance too great to even see each other on the weekends.

There was no way he'd move to LA. That place would suffocate him, and he'd never ask her to give up her career and move to Montana. She was a city girl with an awesome career, and she'd be bored out of her mind living on a ranch.

She tugged on the hem of his shirt. "Take it off."

"No."

"Yes."

"The shirt stays on." When she frowned, he said, "You don't want to see the mess of my body while I'm making love to you." Because that was what he was going to do…make love to her all night long. His scars were hard for him to look at, and he wouldn't make her, not while they were loving on each other. It was bad enough that he'd have to take his jeans off.

She leaned away, put her hands on his cheeks, and stared into his eyes. "You think I'll be turned off at seeing your body?"

He nodded. "I can barely stand to look at myself in a mirror, so I can't imagine—"

She put her fingers over his lips. "I've already seen you with your shirt off. It hurts my heart what was done to you, but your body is beautiful, your scars a testament to your bravery and courage. Don't feel shame for that."

He had felt shame. Shame at allowing himself to be captured, and his most secret shame? That he'd been close to breaking, and he'd recognized it and knew that if he did, he wouldn't be able to live with himself. Because the things he knew, if those secrets spilled from his lips, he would have put his team—his brothers—in danger. That wasn't acceptable, and he'd made the decision to die. He'd managed to break off a small piece of the wall of his cell, the jagged edge sharp enough to slice open his wrists. All he was waiting for was night, when the guards wouldn't be able to see him in the cell. His team found him that day.

If they'd been one more day in finding him, they would have been bringing his body home, and it shamed him that he'd been weak in mind and body. But maybe he had been a little brave in managing to hold out for two weeks of starvation and torture. Maybe that had taken a bit of courage.

The heaviness he'd carried in his bones, in his soul, were still there, but with her words…for the first time since being rescued, the weight of that burden was lighter. He could breathe easier.

He trailed the back of his hand down her cheek. "Thank you," he whispered, and when she gave him a soft smile, his heart turned over in his chest. She soothed his soul, had from the moment he'd held her in his arms and hadn't wanted to crawl out of his skin. How was he going to give her up when the time came?

She lowered her hands to the hem of his shirt. "Let me see you, Dallas. All of you."

"Okay, but feel free to tell me to put my shirt back on. I won't be insulted." He meant that, but it hit him that after what she'd said, he would be disappointed if she did ask.

"I won't."

He blew out a breath as he pulled his shirt over his head and dropped it to the floor. "Showtime."

"So many," she whispered as her gaze roamed over his scars. She shuddered. "I can't begin to imagine the strength it took to survive what was done to you." She trailed a finger down the worst scar on his chest. "But you're beautiful, Dallas. And I'll add sex on a freaking stick."

He grinned. "I don't think I've ever been called that before."

"Oh, I'm sure you have, just not to your face." She traced the bucking horse on his belt buckle. "I wish I could have seen you ride one of these. I bet you looked hot doing it."

"Come to Montana and I'll ride a bronc for you. You can judge for yourself."

Dallas riding a bucking horse? Oh, yeah. Definitely hot. Rachel bet during his bronc days the cowgirls were lined up, hoping to get noticed by him. She tugged on the belt buckle. "Off."

"Yes, ma'am."

He unbuckled the belt, then unbuttoned his jeans. She lifted her eyes to his to see that his gaze was on her. Mercy, he could melt her on the spot with all that heat in his eyes. When his hand moved to his zipper, he lifted his brows. "Are you sure?"

"Yes." She didn't think she'd been surer of anything in her life, but she liked that he asked. She already knew he was a good man, but he kept proving it each time he did or said something like that. Her gaze followed his fingers as he slowly lowered the zipper, then pushed his jeans over his hips, revealing a pair of dark blue boxer briefs. A thin line of hair dissected his stomach, disappearing below the waistband of his briefs, drawing her gaze downward, to the proof of his arousal. She swallowed hard.

This was really happening.

"Rachel?" He cupped her chin, lifting her face. "You can tell me to stop at any time."

She put her hand on his chest, over his heart, felt it beat hard against her palm. She lifted her eyes to his, saw the raw hunger in them. "Don't stop."

"Thank God." He dropped his hand to the neck of her T-shirt, dipped a finger inside and tugged. "Can I undress you?"

"Yes, please."

"Don't move." He set her suitcase on the floor, then dropped his duffel next to it. "We'll be needing that bed real soon." He picked up his jeans and pulled out his wallet, taking a condom from it. "We'll be needing this, too." He frowned. "I only have one, so we'll need to stop at the store tomorrow."

"Okay."

"You weren't thinking this was going to be a one-time thing, were you?"

Honestly, she didn't have a clue what she expected to happen between them, but... "I was hoping not." Jeez, that smile of his. It could melt a girl's panties right off.

"Me, too." He sat on the edge of the bed and spread his legs. "Come here."

As she stepped toward him, her eyes roamed over him, and she smiled at all the hotness sitting there, waiting for her. When her gaze reached his legs, she gasped. Dear God. His legs were as scarred as his chest and arms, and she tried and failed to will away the tears burning her eyes. He wouldn't want her pity. How had he endured that kind of torture?

"Don't."

His harsh voice was jarring. Did he think she was disgusted by his scars? His eyes, filled with heat and desire a moment ago, were now stormy, turbulence swirling in their hazel depths. "Don't what, Dallas?" She dropped to her knees, put her hand over a scar on his inner thigh, and looked up at him. "Don't hurt for what was done to you? Don't look at the scars scattered over your body and want to do serious damage to the people who did this to you? Don't still look at you and think how beautiful you are, both inside and out? Which of those don't you want me to do?"

"Rachel," he whispered.

She stood and stepped between his knees. Leaning down, she softly pressed her lips to his. A shudder passed through him, and for the first time since she'd met him, she felt his pain. Had he buried what had happened to him so deeply so that he couldn't feel anything? Was that why she hadn't been able to read him? Was he opening up to her now? It was something to think about but later. Right now, she had an almost naked man on the bed, and she needed him as much as he needed her.

"We gonna get it on or what, cowboy?"

He stared at her for a moment, the ghost of a smile appeared, and the storm that had been building in his eyes calmed. "We're gonna get it on." He slipped his hand under her T-shirt and cupped her breast. "There are too many clothes between my skin and yours." He tugged on her bra, then removed his hand and leaned back. "Take your shirt and bra off."

"I thought you were going to undress me."

He braced his hands behind him and stared at her with smoldering eyes. "I changed my mind. I want to watch you get naked for me."

"Do you now?"

He nodded, and she decided to torture him a little. With the speed of a turtle, she lifted her shirt, baring her stomach an inch at a time. When she had it up to the bottom of her bra, she paused, and gave the man who loved to smirk a smirk of her own.

He growled his impatience.

That growly noise coming from deep in his throat did funny things to her, things like made her feel like the room was too hot. "Are you hot?" she said, then wanted to slap a hand over her mouth.

He grinned. "Do you mean that as is it warm in here or am I hot, like are you asking me to rate myself?"

She laughed because by God, he was funny. And based on the amusement in his eyes, he knew it. "We already know you're a hot cowboy."

"Ah. You're feeling all hot and bothered then. Good to know." He trailed a finger down her stomach. "Let me see you, Rachel. All of you," he said, throwing her words back at her.

"I've never done this before."

He stilled. "You're a virgin?"

"No! I meant that I've never stripteased for a man."
She laughed when he let out a relieved breath. "Scared
you, huh?"

"I'd say. Do you want me to take over?"

She shook her head. "No, I want to do this for you."
Even though she was feeling shy about doing it, she really did want to. She pulled her shirt over her head and
tossed it aside. Next came her bra, and she was glad
she'd worn one that clipped in the front. She unhooked
it but held the two sides together.

His gaze was hot and heavy and focused on her
breasts. She loved that she could put that heated look
in his eyes. He fisted his hands in the quilt. Did he do
that to keep from touching her? She thought so—that
she was testing his willpower—and that gave her the
confidence to continue. She slid the straps of her bra
down her arms and dropped it to the floor.

"Beautiful," he murmured. "So beautiful that I have
to have a taste." He leaned forward and swirled his
tongue around a nipple, then lightly nipped it with his
teeth.

"Ohhhh." The sensation was so intense that her
knees threatened to buckle, and she put her hands on
his shoulders to keep from crumbling to the floor in a
quivering mass. She felt his smile against her skin, then
he moved to the other breast.

While his sinful mouth was busy pleasuring her
breasts, he unsnapped her jeans, lowered the zipper,
and pushed them down her legs. She kicked them to the
side. He cupped her sex over her panties, then slowly
toyed with her clit with his thumb.

"Oh, my." She pushed against his hand, needing
more. He chuckled as he increased the pressure while

his fingers stroked her over her panties. "Dallas," she whimpered as something that felt like an electrical charge pulsed through her body. "Please."

"Let it happen, sugar." He flicked a finger over her clit again and again. "I've got you."

Hot waves of pleasure coursed through her, wave after wave after wave. She lost the ability to stand, and as she headed for the floor, he caught her, and settled her on his leg. She buried her face against his neck as she tried to get control of her breathing.

"That was amazing," she said between gulps for air. He'd quite literally ruined her boyfriend criteria. She'd liked sex, but it had always been something she could take or leave. Now though...now Dallas had shown her what was possible, he'd changed the yardstick of what she wanted from a man.

And she hadn't even taken her panties off.

"Want to tell me why you're laughing?" he said.

"Nope." She lifted her head so she could see him and grinned a very happy grin. "But feel free to carry on."

Amusement lit his eyes, then he glanced over at the nightstand. "We only have one condom until we can buy more." His gaze returned to hers...no, his eyes snared hers. That was the only way to describe how he was looking at her. "That means that we're going to have to get creative later, but for now, this very second, I need to be inside you. Are you okay with that?"

She was. She so was. When she realized he was waiting for an answer, she nodded like a deranged bobblehead, getting another chuckle from him. He lifted her to her feet, removed her panties, then took off his boxer briefs. She thought they would stretch out on the bed, but he sat back down.

He patted his leg. "Back on my lap." When she sat on his leg like she'd done earlier, he said, "No, straddle me."

"Well, duh. I guess that would work better." She really liked it when he laughed.

"I'm pretty sure it will." He reached over and grabbed the condom, and when he was covered, she settled on his lap and wrapped her legs around his back.

"I've never done it this way." Come to think of it, her sex life had been pretty vanilla. She was sure Dallas would be able to show her all she was missing.

"No? I'm going to have fun showing you what you've been missing."

"Wow, you just read my mind." She really liked that he was playful and that she felt comfortable admitting her lack of experience.

He put his hands on her hips and lifted her. "Slide down on me."

Chapter Seventeen

Dallas slid his eyes closed as Rachel eased down on him. Not that long ago, he'd curled up in the corner of a cell not much bigger than him and scrolled through a mental list of the things he missed. At the top was food and a pain-free day, but up there with those was the touch of a woman. Of her soft skin, her smell, of the pleasure of wrapping his body around hers and sinking deep inside her.

He'd thought—sitting in that corner, hungry and his wounds throbbing—that more than anything, he wished he could have one more intimate time with a woman before they killed him, or he did the job for them.

After his rescue and his time in the hospital, he'd come home, and hadn't been tempted or interested in fulfilling that wish. How could he when he couldn't stand to be touched? Now here was a woman awakening the desire that he'd feared was gone forever.

He buried his face against her neck, afraid she'd see the grateful tears in his eyes. It scared him how much he needed her, maybe forever. What if she was the only woman whose touch he'd ever be able to tolerate? How was he supposed to walk away?

"Don't be sad," she said.

Before he could think why she said that, she began moving. He wrapped his arms around her, holding her close. He'd thought their first time would be hot and heavy, frantic even. Instead, it was tender and dreamy. He almost felt like he was floating on air. He'd never experienced anything like it, and he never wanted it to end.

But it did. When she clenched her core muscles around him, telling him she was close to the edge, he found her mouth, needing that connection, too. Their tongues tangled, dueled, and explored. Their breaths mingled and he felt like they were breathing for each other. He could feel her heart beating against his chest, and when she moaned into his mouth, and her hands fisted his hair, and her body shuddered, he let go, soaring with her.

"You want me to trim your hair?"

Dallas loaded the last dinner plate in the dishwasher, then stepped behind Rachel and nuzzled her neck. "But then what will you hold on to?" He'd noticed that she liked to curl her fingers around his hair when they kissed.

She peered back at him. "Oh, I think I can find a thing or two."

"Now you have my attention."

"I just bet." She dried her hands on a dishtowel, then turned to face him. "I like your hair the way it is, but you mentioned it was getting too long. Up to you."

"Maybe just trim it up a little?" If he didn't let her cut it, eventually he'd have hair down to his waist. He wondered if she'd have a problem with him showing up once a month for a haircut once this was over and she returned home.

"Sure. I saw scissors somewhere the other day. Go get a towel and your comb while I find them."

"Yes, ma'am."

"Shirt off," she said when he returned.

He grinned. "I like it when you're bossy." If she'd told him to take off his shirt a few days ago, he would have walked out of the room. It was a minor miracle that he didn't hesitate to do as she asked.

Turned out getting a haircut was torture. Every time her breasts brushed across his shoulders or one of his arms, he wanted to pull her onto his lap and make love to her again. To keep from doing just that, he mentally recited the names of all the horses at the ranch.

She stepped in front of him. "You're muttering things."

"No, I'm not." Was he?

"Yes, you are. I clearly heard *Lego*. Is getting a haircut upsetting to you? We don't have to finish."

"No, let's get this done."

"Okay." She moved behind him and combed her fingers through his hair. "So, who or what is Lego?"

Apparently, he had muttered his horse's name out loud, but Lego he could talk about. "My rescue mustang."

"Oh, cool. Why'd you name him that?"

"I didn't, Cheyenne's little girl did. Wasn't what I planned to name him, but I dare you to say no to your four-year-old niece. They cry when they don't get their way."

She leaned around him and smiled. "You're a softie, Dallas Manning."

"Only with little girls who cry."

"Nuh-uh." She pulled the towel from his shoulders and used it to wipe away pieces of hair. "All done. Go look in the mirror and tell me if you'll let me come near you with scissors again."

She followed him to the bathroom, leaning against the doorway as he took a quick look at his reflection. "Well?"

"You can come near me with scissors again." He loved the sweet smile she gave him. Even though his scars didn't seem to bother her, he still wasn't comfortable walking around without a shirt on. He headed for the bedroom to get a shirt.

"Who said you could get on the bed, Bella?" She gave him a quick glance before turning her attention back on the small lump darting around under the covers.

Rachel laughed as she joined Bella on the bed. "What little monster have you got under there, Bella Boo?" She tapped the sheet, and the lump darted for her finger.

Bella looked at Rachel, and Dallas could swear there was a grin on the dog's face. He leaned back against the wall, his gaze going first to Bella, the dog that had been ready to give up on life not so long ago. He'd understood because he'd been there. Now her coat was shiny, she was gaining weight—her ribs hardly showing anymore—and the once dull chocolate eyes were alert and happy.

Rachel was moving her hand over the bedcover for the kitten to chase. His heart took a weird bounce as she played with Blue while carrying on a conversation with Bella. How could he keep them, all three of them?

He couldn't. Well, maybe the kitten, but it would break Bella's heart if he took her baby back to Montana with him. Bella belonged to Jack and would eventually become a service dog for one of their wounded brothers or sisters, so there was no keeping her.

As for Rachel…

There was no way around it. He was going to have to let her go. In the same way he wouldn't be able to survive living in LA, she'd hate living out in the middle of nowhere on a ranch in Montana. If some asshole wasn't out to kill her, he'd leave right now and go home before he fell for her. He was almost there already. Since he couldn't do that, he needed to take a step back. No more falling for a beautiful wildcat.

He was halfway out the door when she said, "Show me what all this paracord bracelet does." He turned toward her but didn't step back into the room. The kitten was out from under the covers and curled up under Bella's chin. Bella was looking at him as if also interested in his answer.

"You can google all the things." He really needed to go somewhere where she wasn't for a while, before he begged her for things she couldn't give him.

"I want you to show me," she said.

Eff him! He couldn't refuse her, even though he totally should. She was going to be the biggest regret in his life. Cursing himself, he stepped back into the bedroom and took the bracelet from her. "Are you familiar with these at all?"

"Well, I know they're made out of parachute cords and can be used for a lot of things." She took it from him and studied it. "I see a compass, a small blade, and what is that?"

"A whistle. If you're lost in the woods, it comes in handy. You can also start a fire, catch fish, and make a

shelter among other things." He showed her how to re-
move the blade. "If you're tied up, you can free yourself
or use it to clean the fish you caught with the paracord."

"This is so cool, the best present I've ever gotten."
She slid the blade back in place.

He laughed. "You're weird."

"Put it on me." She handed it him, then held out her
wrist.

After snapping it on her, he traced a finger over the
bracelet. "You know this means we're engaged now."
Yeah, he was waving a white flag of surrender. There
was no way he could shut her out while he was anywhere near her, so he was giving in. He'd enjoy being
with her until it was time for them to return to their
homes. He'd deal with missing her then, because he
was going to.

"You're ridiculous." She grinned at him, then held
up her bracelet and admired it.

"Is that any way to talk to your fiancé?"

"How about I show you my appreciation?"

"If you insist."

"Oh, I do." She tackled him and spent the next hour
showing him her appreciation.

Someone sounded like they were in agony. Rachel first
thought she was dreaming, but as the voice continued
saying the same thing over and over, an edge of determination mixed in with the pain, she blinked open her
eyes. It took a few seconds to realize Dallas was saying his name, rank, serial number, and birthdate over
and over.

She reached over and turned on the lamp. Bella had
taken to sleeping at their feet with her kitten, but now

she was on her belly next to Dallas, her worried gaze on him. She glanced at Rachel and whined, as if wanting Rachel to do something.

Dallas was curled in a fetal position with his hands over his head, and it didn't take a genius to know that he was having a nightmare of his time as a prisoner. In between his words, he flinched and made a tormented sound deep in his throat, and she sensed that he was determined not to cry out. Because of his scarred body, she knew, without him ever telling her what he'd endured, that his treatment had been brutal.

She hated that he was reliving that time in his sleep. Should she wake him? What if he thought she was one of his tormentors and tried to attack her? He would never forgive himself if he accidently hurt her. But she couldn't bear to let him go on reliving his torture. Even though he was dreaming, the pain was real. She could hear that in his voice.

"Dallas, wake up." She put her hand on his shoulder and shook it. He continued saying his name, rank, serial number, and birthdate. Bella's whines grew louder, and she stood and went back to the foot of the bed.

Rachel wasn't sure what made her do it, but she scooted over and wrapped herself around Dallas's body and held him. It was as if the dam had broken, and she could feel him. The pain pouring from him was almost unbearable, but she didn't let go. If he could endure it, so could she. It hurt, though, so badly. How had he survived weeks of this agony?

She'd never tried to send an emotion back to someone, and didn't know if it was possible, but she had to try. She closed her mind to all but soothing calm and peace, then imagined sending it to him while she quietly talked to him.

"I've got you, cowboy. You're safe with me." As she softly talked to him, he shuddered and grew quiet.

"Are you awake?" she whispered. He answered with a soft sigh, and she realized he was still asleep but no longer dreaming.

Bella returned with Blue in her mouth and dropped the kitten next to Dallas's head.

"You sweet, sweet girl." Rachel was touched and surprised by Bella's gift to Dallas. Blue made Bella happy, so she believed the kitten would make Dallas happy.

The kitten blinked sleepy eyes, yawned, and then curled up where he was and went back to sleep. Seemingly satisfied that all was well now, Bella lowered her body down next to Blue and Dallas.

Rachel couldn't help smiling at the pile of bodies surrounding Dallas, wanting to comfort him while he slept, unaware that he was covered in love. Or maybe he was, even if only subconsciously, as his sleep was peaceful now.

It was no wonder after what he'd lived through that he had shut down to the point that she hadn't been able to feel his emotions. But a person couldn't stay locked down forever before their demons surfaced and demanded attention, no matter how hard a person tried to pretend they were okay.

She was pretty sure that was what was going on with Dallas and why she was starting to sense his emotions now. Should she tell him what she suspected? That he wasn't okay? That he couldn't keep pretending he was hunky-dory when he wasn't? She didn't have answers to those questions, so she'd just hold him, be there for him tonight and the rest of the nights they'd be together.

After that… Well, she didn't know what came after that. But she was pretty sure there would be heartbreak involved. Since she'd never had a broken heart, she wasn't sure how worried she should be. Was it something that could be cured with enough wine and ice cream like in romance novels? Or was it something she'd never get over?

"What makes a good therapy horse?" Rachel asked as she rode along a trail next to Dallas. She filled her lungs with fir-scented air. Even though it was spring, mornings in the mountains were…she first thought chilly, but refreshing was a better word. Purple rhododendrons in full bloom dotted the trail, and she remembered how June loved to take springtime car rides on the Parkway. All of it—the invigorating mountain air, the scent of the trees, and the flowering shrubs—reminded her how much she loved the place she thought of as home.

Dallas had woken her early, telling her they were going to check out some horses that were for sale. Honey, the mare she was riding, and Dallas's gelding, Thunder, seemed pretty docile. She was sure Dallas was used to livelier horses.

"I've been reading up on that, and a good age for one is around eight years or older. Definitely a calm temperament. You want horses that don't tend to spook, although any horse will spook if something scares them. Some breeds are more high-strung than others."

"What are these?"

"Quarter horses, a good breed for therapy horses. They tend to be average in size and have a good tem-

perament. I'm liking these two for Jack's equine therapy program."

"Can we run them?" The trail was wide and flat, and
she was a little bored with just plodding along.

"Yeah, I want to see how they do. Race you to that
dead tree." He winked at her, then kicked his heels into
Thunder's flanks.

"Hey, you didn't say go!"

He laughed, and his laughter was music to her ears.

She spurred Honey. "Come on, Honey. You going to
let him win?" The horse nickered, then took off.

As she raced behind Dallas, she decided she liked
being behind him where she could admire him. He rode
as if he were part of the horse, as if he were born riding
one. They raced until they reached the dead tree, and
he slowed Thunder to a trot. She hated trotting. It was
a bouncy gait, and she could never catch the rhythm
of the horse in a trot, so she looked ridiculous as she
bounced along.

Dallas, on the other hand, was still doing his one-
with-the-horse thing. He halted Thunder and turned
the horse toward her. As he watched her bobble in the
saddle, his lips twitched.

"Are you laughing at me?" she asked as she stopped
Honey in front of him.

"Trying hard not to."

"Okay, Mr. Born in the Saddle, what am I doing
wrong?"

"First, you're squeezing her sides with your legs.
Don't do that."

"I feel like I'm going to fall off if I don't. It's weird,
but I have a good seat on a galloping horse, but let it
trot, and I turn into one of those bobblehead dolls."

"You're trying to stay in the saddle, and that's why you're bouncing around. In a trot, you don't want to do that. Try this. Lift with the horse, but don't sit all the way back down. Imagine that the saddle is too hot to sit on, so you can only touch it as you lower. Like barely touch it. Go ahead and try it."

He trotted Thunder beside her and Honey. "Ouch, that's hot," he said when her entire butt landed on the saddle.

Laughing, she jerked up.

"Stop trying to squeeze her to death with your legs."

That habit was even harder to break, which she didn't understand since she didn't do it in a gallop. It took a few minutes, but she finally caught the rhythm of the horse, and couldn't believe how much easier it was when she didn't try to keep her bottom glued to the saddle and hold on with her legs. When she finally caught on, she was exhilarated.

"Oh, man, that's awesome." She grinned at him. "I had a riding instructor when I was learning, but she was never able to get through to me how to ride a trotting horse. Yet you did in only a few minutes."

"I think I deserve a kiss then." He halted Thunder, and Honey stopped when his horse did.

"Do you now?"

"Yes, ma'am." He edged his horse next to hers, put his hand behind her neck, leaned over, and covered her mouth with his.

"Wow," she said when he pulled away. "Kissing on horseback is sexy."

"Stick with me, sugar, and I'll give you all the sexy times you want."

Yes, please.

* * *

As Dallas rang the doorbell of Noah and Peyton's downtown loft Saturday morning, Rachel wished she could have come as herself and not in her college girl disguise. "It will be okay if I take this wig off while we're inside, right? The thing is itchy."

"And ruin my college girl fantasy?"

She rolled her eyes. "Men!"

He laughed. "Sorry, we can't help ourselves. Give me a kiss before you do away with my college girl."

"Lay one on me, dude." She puckered her lips. He was grinning as he lowered his mouth to hers. He put his hand on the side of her neck, spread his fingers, and caressed her throat with his thumb. The man sure knew how to kiss. Another thing she was going to miss when it was time to go home.

"Should I check back in five minutes to see if you two are done?" Jack stood in the open doorway with a scowl on his face.

Rachel jumped back as heat warmed her neck and cheeks. "Ah, that's okay. We're done."

"Says you." Dallas winked at her, then put his hand on her lower back as they stepped inside.

She should have thought to ask him how she was supposed to act around his friends. Was it a secret that things had changed between them, or did he want them to know that? Since she didn't know, she'd let him take the lead on what he wanted them to know.

"Oh, what have we here?" An elderly woman wearing leopard print leggings, a gauzy black top, and sparkly silver sandals aimed her thin body at Dallas.

Rachel almost laughed when Dallas grunted, then stepped behind her. She guessed that this must be the man-butt-pinching woman Jack and Noah had warned him about. This pancake breakfast was going to be fun.

Jack's grandmother, who Rachel had met at the wedding, stepped in front of the first woman. "You're scaring the poor man, Mary. At least wait until you know his name before you attack him."

"Well, introduce us then," Mary said as she tried to peek around Rachel.

Jack strode over and put his hand on Mary's shoulder. "Mary, this is Rachel Denning, Nichole's best friend." With amusement in his eyes, he looked over her shoulder. "The man hiding behind her is Dallas Manning, one of my former teammates."

"Nice to meet you, Rachel, but step aside and let me check out this handsome man."

Dallas put his hands on her shoulders, keeping her in place, and Rachel was fighting hard to keep her laughter contained. Not that she blamed him for hiding considering that wicked gleam in Mary's eyes.

"My friends call me Dirty Mary." She grinned as if entirely proud of her nickname. "You can call me Dirty Mary, handsome."

Nichole walked into the room with Peyton at her side, and forgetting that she was the barrier between Dallas and Mary, Rachel ran to greet them. She was in the process of hugging them when she remembered she'd abandoned him. She glanced back, and seeing that Mary was squeezing Dallas's upper arm, apparently checking out his muscles, she hurried back to him. He didn't like to be touched, and he was probably about to climb out of his skin.

When she reached his side, ready to do something to divert Mary's attention, she met Dallas's gaze and stilled. There was wonder in his eyes, and she felt astonishment coming from him. Well, how about that? He could bear Mary touching him. She wasn't sure how to feel about that. She kind of liked that she was the only one who could touch him and wasn't sure she wanted to share, even with a little old lady.

Unaware of the miracle taking place, Mary reached behind Dallas and pinched his butt. Rachel expected him to move away from her grabby hands, but he only laughed.

"While your new friend's manhandling you," Jack said, "I'll introduce you to my grandmother. Grammie, this is my good friend, Dallas. Dallas, my grandmother, Lizzy."

"It's always good to meet a friend of Jack's." She leaned toward Dallas. "Do you have a higher rank than he did?"

"Actually, I did, ma'am."

"Good, then I'd like you to order him to get his wife pregnant so I can have a grandbaby before I die."

Chapter Eighteen

"Ah…." Dallas was at a loss for words. He was also trying to process why he wasn't having a problem with the woman getting handsy with his ass. Was he okay with her touching him because she was elderly? To test that theory, he held out his hand to Jack's grandmother.

"It's a pleasure to meet you, Miss Lizzy. I can't tell you how much we enjoyed your care packages to Jack." She put her hand in his, and he immediately wanted to snatch it away. With a smirk at Jack, he added, "When he'd share them. The chocolate chip cookies were our favorites." He let go of her hand, swallowing a sigh of relief.

"I told him he better share with his teammates." She gave him a brilliant smile. "You can return the favor by ordering my grandson to give me a grandbaby, preferably two or three."

Jack sighed. "Grammie, we're working on it."

"Well, obviously not hard enough."

"If she had her way, she'd lock Nichole and me in the bedroom until we showed her an ultrasound proving there's a baby in my wife's belly."

"Now there's an idea," Lizzy said.

Carrying a large bag, Noah walked in at the end of

the conversation. "You should totally do that, Lizzy." He kissed the woman's cheek. "Sorry I wasn't here when you arrived, but I got your favorite breakfast dessert in here." He tapped the bag.

Mary let go of Dallas and cozied up to Noah. "And what did you get for me, McHottie?"

"Snickerdoodle doughnuts for Miss Lizzy and cherry turnovers for my best girl, Dirty Mary."

Dallas stepped back and watched the banter between Noah, Jack, Lizzy, and Mary. The people in this room were fond of each other and were comfortable in their own skins. He got that Jack fit in with his grandmother and her friend, but he was disturbed that he was jealous of Noah for his ease and comfort with these people. As teammates, they had been as close, closer even, than blood brothers, and when stateside, they'd hung out together. But outside of that, they hadn't socialized with each other's families. Looked like things had changed for Jack and Noah.

Rachel moved next to him and he put his arm around her, pulling her against his side. Jack narrowed his eyes at him, and Dallas frowned. He figured he was going to get another talking-to at some point this morning. What was Jack's problem? He was acting like a big brother. Rachel was an adult, fully capable of making her own decisions.

"Mary, let's go help the girls get breakfast ready and give these men a break from you molesting them." Lizzy grabbed Mary's hand and pulled her away.

"You're no fun," Mary grumbled. She glanced over her shoulder and blew them a kiss. "I'll be back, boys."

Dallas laughed. "She's a trip."

"One of a kind," Jack said. "Mostly harmless."

Noah snorted. "I'm not so sure about that."

"I think she's hilarious," Rachel scratched under the wig. "I need to get this thing off for a while. Where's your bathroom?" she asked Noah.

"Down the hall, second door on the left."

After she headed to the bathroom, Dallas raised his brows at Jack's intense stare. "Got something you want to say, brother?" As if he didn't already know.

"What's going on with you and Rachel?"

"Nothing." The lie was bitter on his tongue. Honestly, he really wasn't sure what was going on with them other than they liked each other and were sleeping together. "She's a great girl, and we're friends." That much was true.

"She'll be going home soon, and it better not be in tears."

"Rachel's perfectly capable of taking care of herself." He didn't need this shit from Jack.

"So, did you find us any horses?" Noah said.

Dallas appreciated that Noah was defusing the tension. "Six possible. Four at that place in Asheville, and two over in Weaverville. I'm planning to hit up the other places on the list over the next couple of days. When will you have the barn ready, and the pasture fenced?"

"Now that you've selected where the barn will go, we'll get started on it right away. The fencing will be done this month. If you're sure about the ones you like, see if the owners will board them if we buy them now."

"You have someone lined up to head the equine therapy part?"

Jack and Noah shared a glance, then Jack said, "We'll talk about that later."

The two of them were up to something, and Dallas

hoped they weren't counting on him to stick around. His home was in Montana. Doing what was the big question, but he'd figure it out when he returned to the ranch. Where she won't be, he thought when Rachel walked back in the room without her wig. She smiled at him as she headed for the kitchen to join the other women. That sweet smile was playing havoc with his heart.

He glanced around Noah and Peyton's downtown loft. "Helluva place you got here, Double D."

"Never thought I'd like loft living, but it's great. Got a lot of restaurants and shops right outside the door."

The loft was cool, but there was no way Dallas could live here. He needed wide-open spaces. Laughter came from the kitchen, and he, Jack, and Noah all looked that way.

"Honey, if you ain't hittin' that up, you need to have your head checked," Mary said. "If you don't want him, give him to me. This old broad will show that boy some new tricks."

Rachel met his gaze across the room, and there was pure mischief in her eyes. "Oh, I don't know, let me think about it. But I should probably warn you that he's a grouchy one."

He was not! Not with her anyway.

"Thank God Dirty Mary has new meat in her orbit." Noah rubbed his rear end. "My ass needs a break from pinchy fingers."

"And before that, it was me," Jack said. "Welcome to the Dirty Mary Grabby Hands Club."

Dallas snorted. "Not a club I aspired to." Although it was both weird and interesting that Mary's grabby hands didn't bother him. "She must have been a pistol when she was young."

"Seven husbands," Jack said. "Some she buried, and some she left wanting more…at least, that's how she tells it."

Noah shook his head. "Not sure any one of us would have survived her."

"True story," Jack said.

"You boys get your sexy butts to the table. Breakfast is ready," Mary called.

Dallas wasn't sure how she managed it, but he ended up seated on one side of Mary with Noah on her other. The table was loaded with platters stacked high with pancakes, plates of bacon, bowls of fruit, and assorted syrups, along with pots of coffee and pitchers of mimosas. The various pastries Noah had bought were the centerpiece of the table.

Mary wrapped the fingers of one hand around his biceps and did the same to Noah with her other hand. "Eat up, boys. Gotta keep these muscles strong for the ladies."

He flexed his muscles, getting a giggle from her, and eyed the food. "There's enough here to feed our team several times over."

Noah started singing something about banana pancakes, and Dallas sat back in his chair and stared at his friend. "There's really a song about banana pancakes?"

Peyton laughed. "There really is. Jack Johnson's 'Banana Pancakes.'"

"You really do have a great voice," Rachel said.

Jack shook his finger at her. "Don't encourage him. He'll come up with a song for anything you say."

"You got a song about Dirty Mary rocking a McHottie's world?" Mary asked.

Noah grinned. "I sure do, but I can't sing it in front

of you ladies. You can listen to it on YouTube. The title actually is 'Dirty Mary' by Lady Bouncer. She sings about a horny secretary."

Mary clapped her hands. "I can do horny secretary."

"I just bet you can," Jack muttered.

Rachel sat on the other side of him, and when she laugh-snorted, Dallas glanced at her and smiled. He loved seeing her enjoy herself. She looked at him, and he got caught in those eyes staring back at him. He wanted to grab her hand and drag her back to the cabin with him, back to their cozy little world where he could spend the day making love to her. Instead, he settled for putting his hand on her leg and squeezing.

"How soon can we leave?" she said quietly, letting him know her mind was in the same place as his.

"Real soon," he said, getting one of those smiles that he'd decided was just for him.

"You have a song about a grandson giving his grandmother a grandbaby?" Lizzy said, bringing his attention back to the group.

Jack groaned. "No, he does not, Grammie." He pointed his fork at her plate. "Eat your pancakes."

"The last time I had sex, there was syrup involved," Mary said as she poured syrup over her pancakes. "It was sticky."

Rachel choked on her mimosa. The sound of silverware clanging as the pieces hit the table filled the air, and she glanced around. Everyone except for Lizzy was staring at Mary in stunned silence. Lizzy was happily digging into her pancakes.

"What?" Mary blinked owl eyes at them.

"Kids these days apparently have sensitive ears," Lizzy said, then went back to eating her breakfast.

Jack picked up the fork he'd dropped and studied it as if it held the meaning of life. "Grammie, there are some things *us kids* don't want to hear, and you or Mary having sex is one of them."

"How do you think you got here, Jackie? I had to have sex with your grandfather to have your father, and your parents had sex to have you." She and Mary exchanged eye rolls.

Jack buried his face in his hands, and Rachel didn't think she'd ever been so entertained.

"I was at Woodstock, you know," Mary said. "Somewhere there's a picture of me flashing my titties at the Grateful Dead. Let me tell you, those boys' tongues were hanging out at seeing my awesome boobs."

The silverware they'd all picked up fell to the table again. Beside her, Dallas's shoulders shook, and he had his fist pressed against his mouth. She glanced around the table. Jack still had his hands covering his face, but she could tell that, like Dallas, everyone was trying not to laugh.

There was pure devilment in Noah's eyes. Oh boy, what was up to? When he started singing about ta-tas driving him bonkers, Rachel lost it. The man was ridiculously funny.

Dallas made a strangled sound as he pushed away from the table and disappeared down the hallway. Jack apparently had something important to do in the kitchen, but he sounded like he was choking.

Nichole and Peyton cracked up, and through her laughter, Nichole said, "You made that one up."

Grinning ear to ear, Noah shook his head. "Nope. That one's a Scuzz Twittly song."

Rachel picked up her fork and speared a chunk of

pineapple. "There's really a song about ta-tas? Who knew?"

"Pretty much a song about everything." Noah glanced toward the kitchen. "You gonna be okay, Whiskey?"

"No." Jack walked back to the table. "I'm scarred for life." He leveled a stern look at his grandmother and Mary. "You two try to behave for the rest of our breakfast."

Mary wrinkled her nose. "Where's the fun in that?"

Ignoring her question, he pointed at Noah. "And you, no more songs today."

He had such a severe expression that Rachel would have thought he was mad if she hadn't seen his lips twitch.

Gosh, she was going to miss these people when she had to go home. The one she was going to miss the most returned to the table. "Having fun?"

He leaned his mouth near her ear. "Yep, but I have some other kind of fun in mind."

"You just have ta-tas on the mind now."

"Yours specifically."

Oh, my. That heat in his eyes sent a shiver through her.

Lizzy and Mary settled down, and the rest of the morning was considerably calmer than the first part. After they finished eating, Noah and Jack started picking up plates. "The girls cook, the guys clean," Noah said.

"Sounds fair." Dallas gathered a handful of dishes.

Rachel refilled her mimosa glass, then Peyton's when she nodded. "Some?" she asked Nichole.

"No, thanks."

Rachel narrowed her eyes, studying her friend. She'd been picking up happy vibes from Nichole all morning. Not that Nichole wasn't always happy, but the emotions coming from her today were different.

"Lizzy and I'll help the boys," Mary said.

Peyton laughed. "Of course you will."

Taking her mimosa with her, she followed Nichole to the living room.

"How's Bella doing?" Nichole said after they were seated, she and Nichole on the sofa and Peyton on a chair. "That poor girl was the saddest thing I've ever seen when Jack brought her to the kennels."

"You wouldn't recognize her compared to how she was when Dallas got her. She has a kitten now, and it's the sweetest thing to see."

"The dog has a kitten?" Peyton said.

Rachel told them about Bella finding a kitten in a cave and carrying her home. How Bella wouldn't let Blue out of her sight.

"That's so sweet," Nichole said. She glanced at the kitchen, then leaned forward. "I might be pregnant."

"What?" both Rachel and Peyton exclaimed.

"Shhh. We're not even hinting that I might be to Lizzy. Not until we're sure. We stopped on the way here this morning and bought a pregnancy test."

"Let's go do it now," Peyton said.

"No, I want Jack with me when I do."

"Oh, well, I guess that's only right."

Rachel laughed at how crestfallen Peyton looked. "If you are, Lizzy's going to be over the moon."

"For real." Nichole glanced over at the kitchen again. "She's given us all kinds of potions and crystals that are supposed to enhance the chance of getting pregnant, so she's going to take credit for it happening."

"I'm going to be an honorary auntie," Rachel said. And over two thousand miles away. She'd miss everything. Seeing her best friend's baby smile, take her first steps...all of it.

"Can I be an honorary auntie, too?" Peyton pressed her hands together as if in prayer.

Nichole grinned. "If there is one, the more aunties my baby has the better."

Rachel couldn't be happier for Nichole. She wouldn't say anything to ruin Nichole and Jack's excitement at reading together what the stick said, but she knew Nichole was pregnant. She'd never felt a life growing from a pregnant woman before, but she did from Nichole. A curtain of sadness fell over her. She wouldn't be here for the friend who'd stood by her since third grade.

She downed the rest of her mimosa, then forced a smile she didn't feel. "Call me as soon as you know."

Nichole grabbed her hand. "You know I will."

It was so hard not to tell her that there would be an excited phone call.

Dallas walked into the living room. When he was standing next to her, he put his hand on her shoulder. "You ready to go, wildcat?"

"In a few minutes, cowboy."

"Wildcat and cowboy?" Nichole's gaze darted between them. "Girlfriend, you've been holding out on me."

She had been. Their bond hadn't lessened after Rachel had moved to LA. They talked often and told each other everything, but for the first time whatever it was going on between her and Dallas felt private, even from besties.

"It's just that with hiding from Robert, and now you having to stay with your brother, we haven't had much of a chance to talk." That sounded excusable, right? "You are still staying with Mark?"

"Yeah, and I don't like it. I miss sleeping in the same bed as my guy. When he picked me up this morning to bring me here, I almost jumped his bones, but then we never would have made it to breakfast."

"I'm sorry."

"Stop it, Rach. That man is to blame, not you."

It was impossible not to blame herself, but Nichole wouldn't want to hear it. "I can't wait to find out if I'm going to be an auntie." When she stood, she realized she was a little buzzed from the mimosas.

Nichole wrapped her in a tight hug. "You'll be the first one I'll tell."

After saying goodbyes, she and Dallas left. When they entered the elevator, no one else was in it. As soon as the door closed, Dallas backed her up to the wall.

He pressed his body against hers, curled his fingers around her neck, and stole her mouth.

And God help her, she was falling in love with him.

Chapter Nineteen

Dallas didn't slow his run up the mountain as he answered his phone. When he heard what Noah had to say, he stopped. After he finished the call, he turned to Rachel as she ran in place in front of him.

"That was Noah. He and Peyton have a friend, Joseph, a homeless guy who claims a sidewalk spot near their loft. Noah described us and told Joseph to keep watch. Joseph told Noah there was a man hanging around this morning who seemed unusually interested in the people coming in and out of the building."

"How would he know where they live? Their address isn't in my contacts."

"Just a guess, but he must have followed Jack." He didn't want to tell her the rest, but she needed to know. "Joseph said that when we came out, the man followed us into the garage."

She paled. "Oh my God." She tangled her fingers in her hair. "I forgot to put my wig back on before we left. It's still on the counter in Peyton's bathroom."

And his attention had been on her and not his surroundings. She'd been a little tipsy and more than a bit randy, both with her hands and her words. When they'd arrived at the cabin, they'd barely said hello to Bella and her kitten as they'd raced to the bed. Now they were almost to the top of the mountain, having decided to go for a run before dinner.

"We need to get back to the cabin." He needed to get her locked inside and then do some recon. Make sure there wasn't anyone snooping around the area. Once they got out of town and were on the rural road to the cabin, he would have noticed a car following them if it had been close, so they were probably okay. But *probably* didn't cut it.

Although Bella wasn't happy leaving Blue behind, she was with them. He'd hadn't bothered with a leash, knowing she wouldn't run off. As soon as they started back down the mountain, she raced ahead, eager to get back to her kitten.

Suddenly, she stopped. The dog that had been afraid of her own shadow not that long ago growled as razor sharp fur stood up along her spine. Her ears were up, and her gaze was intent on the woods to their right. "What is it, Bella?" Dallas didn't see any movement among the trees, didn't hear a sound, not even the chirping of birds. That wasn't good. Someone was out there. Bella took off, disappearing into the woods.

He pulled his gun from the holster. As much as he didn't want to chase after Bella with Rachel at his side, he couldn't leave her on the trail, unprotected. He put his hand on her shoulder. "Stay right behind me. If I tell you to run, you haul ass to that cave we found and call the police, then Jack." He'd rather she return to the cabin, but if Robert and his men had found her, the cabin wouldn't be safe.

Gunfire broke the silence, then a man screamed. They ran, following the direction Bella had gone. The man screamed again. A few minutes after entering the woods, Dallas came to an abrupt stop, and Rachel plowed into his back.

"Get it off me!" a man on the ground shouted.

Dallas picked up the gun the man had dropped. Because the bastard had tried to shoot his dog, he let Bella get one more tug on the man's arm before calling her off. "Bella, come." Although her previous owner had abused her, he'd trained her well. She immediately came to his side, but ready to defend her people again if necessary, her attention never left the man.

He reached down and scratched her head. "Good girl."

"That's one of Robert's men," Rachel said, stepping next to him. "He was there the day Robert shot Henri." She pulled her phone out of her sports bra. "I'll call the police."

"No, call Jack." They needed some detectives out here, maybe even SWAT, not a bunch of patrol officers. He glanced around. Were there more men here with this one? Bella's attention was still on this man, not the woods, so he was going to trust that she'd alert him if anyone else tried to sneak up on them.

Dallas pointed his gun at the man. "Who's here with you?"

"Fuck you." The man flipped over and pushed up, causing Bella to growl.

"You try to run, and I'll let the dog have at you." He'd shoot the bastard if he had to, but he was damn tired of shooting people.

"Jack's on the way with Deke, his detective friend." She tucked her phone back in her bra. "Do we stay here and wait for them?"

"No, we need to get back to the cabin." He doubted the man was alone, and he wanted to get her somewhere safe, and here wasn't it. "Walk," he ordered the man.

"He's going to run," Rachel said.

Sure enough, the fool took off. He touched Bella's head. "Go." She shot off like a bullet. It took her less than a minute to catch up with the man, and when she did, she jumped, going for his arm. The man screamed when she sank her teeth into his skin, but he kept running.

As soon as he'd let Bella go after the man, he'd grabbed Rachel's hand, bringing her with him as he chased the Bella and her quarry. No way was he leaving her unprotected. Because of her training and body condition, she kept up with him.

With his free arm, the man swung a fist at Bella's nose, knocking her away. Dallas saw red. The asshole had hurt his dog, and he'd had enough. He pushed Rachel behind him, then aimed his gun and fired.

"Oh my God!" Rachel peeked around him at the man who was again on the ground. "I thought you were going to kill him."

"Just gave him a flesh wound, enough to discourage him from running again." Never mind that this was one man he wouldn't lose sleep over killing, but he'd never shot anyone in the back and never intended to. He'd grazed the man's thigh, where the bullet would pass right through him.

Now the trick was to get the man down the mountain and get Rachel safely locked away before the dude's buddies showed up.

"You shot me!" the man screamed. "You could have killed me."

"If I'd meant to kill you, you'd be dead." He glanced at Rachel. "You know how to shoot a gun?"

Her eyes widened. "You want me to shoot him?"

Any other time, he would have laughed at her deer-in-the-headlights look. "No, but his friends might be around. We're both going to have to be ready for anything. Have you ever handled one before?"

"I've shot blanks at bad guys in a movie."

"Good enough. If you see any of his friends, you don't hesitate to shoot." He gave her his gun and kept the man's.

"Um, okay."

"I mean it, Rachel. You don't hesitate. It could mean saving my life, Bella's, or your own."

She swallowed hard enough for him to see her throat flex. "I won't."

"Good." Because he needed to, he kissed her. Hard. "Stay next to me." He walked over to the man, who was still screaming his head off. "Get up."

"Go fuck yourself."

Dallas sighed. "I should just shoot you and leave you out here to rot. Get up or I let the dog gnaw on you." He had no intention of doing that, but the guy needed to believe he would.

Apparently, the threat of Bella going at it on him was enough motivation for the dude, and he stood. "Hands on your head, fingers clasped together, and spread your legs apart." He stuck the weapon in his waistband, then glanced at Rachel. "Keep the gun on him while I pat him down." The only thing on him was a phone, and Dallas took it. As much as he'd like to send it to Carter, it was evidence and would have to be turned over to the police.

"Let's go," he told Rachel. "And stay alert." He stayed behind Robert's man, who was barely limping, silently daring him to run. He didn't. Maybe that was because Bella growled at him until they got back on the trail. "Sit on your hands," he said to the man when they stopped.

Keeping Robert's man in his sights, he stepped next to Rachel. "You okay?" She nodded, but he could tell she was close to a meltdown. Dealing with movie bad guys was a lot different from dealing with real life ones.

What he wanted to do was pick her up, take her somewhere safe where people trying to kill her would never find her, and hold her until she gave him that special smile again. But she was close to losing it, and any tenderness he showed her would send her over the edge. So he kept the command in his voice. "Get Jack on the phone for me."

"Okay." She seemed relieved to have something to do besides holding a gun.

"Whiskey, how close to the cabin are you?" he said when she handed him her phone.

"Five minutes. SITREP."

"Rachel and I are unharmed. We're on the trail behind the cabin with one slightly wounded tango in custody. I don't know if he's alone. Can you clear the cabin, make sure there's not a surprise waiting for us inside?"

"Copy that. I'll buzz you with an all clear."

Their prisoner was trying to crawl away, and Dallas rolled his eyes. He stomped his foot down on the man's back. "What's your name?"

"Fuck off."

"Your mama didn't like you very much if that's what she named you."

Rachel snorted. "Robert called him Ebers. I assume that's his last name."

"Ebers, my man, you're not going anywhere but straight to jail. You try to sneak off again, I'm gonna let my dog have you, and I won't call her off this time." Bella looked up at him as if to say, "Yes, please, can I have him?"

"Do you think any more of Robert's men are around here somewhere?" Rachel said.

"I can't imagine he got sent here alone, but if there are more, they're keeping awfully quiet." Although Noah's friend had said he only saw one man following them. Maybe this one was supposed to just scout them out and wait for reinforcements. Dallas was sure the man had called his boss to let him know he'd found Rachel.

"We're going to wait here until we hear from Jack. Keep your eyes and ears open." He was proud of her. She hadn't panicked, and she'd followed his orders without question. His biggest regret was that they wouldn't be able to stay in the cabin now. That was their own little world, and now it was gone.

Bella was on her belly, inches away from Ebers, keeping guard on him. Dallas was sure she was hoping he'd try to escape so she could bite him again. Both his girls had surprised him today, Rachel with her composure, and Bella with her bravery.

"You still doing okay, sugar?"

Rachel shrugged. "I'm okay." Not really. There was a man sprawled at her feet who would have either killed her or taken her to Robert. There might or might not be more of Robert's men watching them at this very moment. She scanned the woods surrounding them. Was

Robert himself out there somewhere with a gun pointed at her? She backed up to the tree behind her, pressing her body against it.

The only reason…well, two reasons that she wasn't having a panic attack was first because Bella would alert them if anyone else was around. Right? She hoped to hell that was right. And second, she trusted Dallas with her life. He was a badass SEAL, trained for situations like this. He'd keep her safe.

She stared at the gun in her hand. Okay, three reasons. She had a weapon, and as much as she wished there wasn't a reason she was holding a gun, she knew how to shoot. But if it came down to it, could she kill someone? Her legs decided they no longer wanted to hold her up, and she slid down the tree. The bark scraped her back between her sports bra and the waist of her running shorts, and she wished she hadn't done that.

Dallas kneeled in front of her and put his hands on her knee. "You're not so okay, are you?"

She shook her head. "Not really. How did I end up here?" She glanced around them. "Wondering if someone out there has a gun pointed at my head." A shudder traveled down her spine. "Or yours."

"If there was anyone around, Bella would let us know. We're okay for now." His phone buzzed, and he stood as he answered. After listening, he said, "That was Jack, and they've cleared the cabin. He's headed this way."

She pushed up, then held the gun out with the barrel pointed down. "Can you take this now?" She hoped she never had to hold a gun again, even while filming a movie.

Jack appeared on the trail with Noah, his detective

friend, and four men dressed in what looked like SWAT gear. Jack came right over to her. "You doing okay, Rach?"

"I've had better days."

He squeezed her upper arm. "I imagine so." Two of the SWAT guys hauled Robert's man up and headed down the mountain with him. Jack introduced Deke to Dallas, then said, "Take Deke and his two guys to where you found... Did he tell you his name?"

Dallas shook his head. "The only words we got out of him were fuck you, but Rachel recognized him." He handed Deke Ebers's gun and phone. "These were all he had on him."

"Robert called him Ebers," she said.

"We'll try to get him to talk," Deke said. "But he'll probably clam up and demand a lawyer. Did he shoot at you?"

"No." Dallas glanced down at Bella. She had moved to his side now that her bad guy was gone. "He shot at my dog, though."

"We'll go for attempted murder, but that probably won't stick if he gets a good attorney, unless you're willing to say he shot at you or Rachel."

Rachel was of a mind to swear he'd shot at them. She'd about had enough of Robert and this madness.

"I'd love to say that, but by the time we caught up with Bella, she had him on the ground," Dallas said.

At hearing her name, Bella gazed up at him with ad-oration in her eyes. When they got back to the cabin, Rachel was going to give her an entire bag of treats.

Jack squatted in front of Bella. "Aren't you a good girl and so brave." He scratched around her ears, and her eyes practically rolled back in her head. "You sure look better than when I found you." He stood and turned to Dallas. "Anyway, take Deke and his guys to where you found your man. They want to look around and see if there are any signs of others in the area. Noah and I'll go back to the cabin with Rachel and Bella."

Bella had other ideas. When Dallas headed toward the woods with Deke and his men, she stayed right by his side.

"She has a crush on him," Rachel said.

Noah grinned. "I don't think she's the only one."

Was she that obvious? By the warmth in her cheeks, she was blushing. She turned away and headed for the cabin. Jack and Noah flanked her, both of them scanning their surroundings as they walked down. Both also had a gun held down at their side, a stark reminder that danger lurked. Not that she needed a reminder.

"I guess we can't stay in the cabin." Dried leaves crunched under her running shoes as she stepped on them, a sound she normally liked. Now, she wished she could be as quiet as a mouse.

"No, it's not safe now," Jack said.

She was afraid, and it was a feeling she didn't like. What if Bella hadn't been with them? Would they have been oblivious that they were being watched? Would Robert's man have shot her as they passed by? Was Robert himself nearby?

Dallas hadn't promised he wouldn't let anything happen to her, and she was glad for that. It would have been a promise he might not be able to keep. But she didn't doubt he would do everything possible to keep her safe. Probably even take a bullet for her if it came to that. Hell, the same probably went for the two men escorting her down the mountain.

Where would they go now that the cabin wasn't safe? Would Dallas stay with her? Now that Robert had found her, this should be over in a day, a few days at the most. She wanted to spend the time she had left here with Dallas, but that would put him in danger, and she'd never forgive herself if something happened to him.

She should have never come here.

By the time Dallas returned to the cabin with Deke, Rachel had them both packed up and ready to leave. Jack wanted them gone from the cabin immediately. He still hadn't said where they'd go, and she hadn't asked. Her nerves were stretched to their limit, and she was afraid that if he said Dallas wouldn't be staying with her, she'd burst into tears.

Dallas walked in and went straight to her. He wrapped his arms around her and held her tight. "You okay?"

She nodded against his chest. "Yeah, I'm good." Now that he was here.

Bella followed him in and went straight to her kitten. She sniffed Blue from one end to the other, making sure he was okay, then she set about giving him a bath.

Jack opened the door. "We need to roll."

"I packed your stuff for you," she told Dallas.

"Thanks." He kept one arm around her as he slid the strap of his duffel bag over his shoulder, then grabbed the handle of her suitcase. "Bella, let's go for a ride."

She picked up Blue by his neck and headed for the door.

"That's the damnedest thing I've ever seen," Noah said. He grasped the handle of Dallas's suitcase.

Rachel broke away from Dallas and lifted the box

with Bella and Blue's food and toys. As she followed Dallas and Noah out, she glanced back. This cabin had become a refuge, a place where she'd spent time with a cowboy, had made love to him on a bed with a handmade quilt. She wasn't ready for her time with him to be over.

When she faced forward, Dallas was standing in the doorway, looking at her with soft eyes, as if he knew and understood her sadness at having to leave their sanctuary.

"We still have some time left," he softly said as she passed him.

She gave him a smile she didn't really feel. A few days at the most now that Robert's men, and probably Robert, were here. He'd either be captured soon, or she'd be dead. Those were the only two possible outcomes.

Jack and Deke stood in the yard near the cars, both with their weapons out and their alert gazes scanning around them. She couldn't wait for this to be over and hopefully still be alive. If she never saw another gun for the rest of her life, she'd be happy.

"We're headed for our building site," Jack told Dallas. "Deke's going in front of you. Noah and I will follow to make sure no one's tailing you."

Her stomach took a sickening roll at the reminder of the danger they were in being out in the open. Maybe she could pretend it was just another movie.

This ain't no movie, Rach. People are trying to kill you. For real.

"Shut up, stupid voice in my head."

"Pardon?" Dallas opened the back door of the Jeep for Bella—still carrying Blue—to jump in. He tossed her suitcase and his duffel bag in, then took the box from her and slid it next to the suitcase.

"Just talking to myself."

He took his suitcase from Noah and set it on the floor. After closing the door, he put his hands on her shoulders and stared into her eyes. "I promise I'll protect you, Rachel. I won't let him hurt you."

You can't promise that. She didn't say it, though, only nodded and got in the Jeep.

Chapter Twenty

The trip to Jack's site was uneventful, and Dallas pulled up next to Jack's car in front of the only completed cabin. Deke had waved and kept going when they reached the entrance. Jack had stopped at the under-construction lodge and let Noah out. Dallas assumed Noah's car was around somewhere, and he'd head to his downtown loft.

"I guess this is your new home," he said after turning off the ignition.

"Okay."

His wildcat had turned into a scaredy cat, and he didn't like that at all. Not that he blamed her for being frightened when a ruthless man was doing his best to kill her. But he wanted her fighting spirit back. From the time they'd left the other cabin, she'd gone quiet, only giving him one-word answers when he'd tried to get her to talk.

"Are you staying here, too?"

"Do you want me to?" Was she tired of him? Not that he'd leave her alone and unprotected, but he'd sleep on the couch or floor if need be. He'd slept in much worse places.

"Please. Jack doesn't like you being with me, so I

thought maybe you were dropping me off here and you were going to stay somewhere else."

"What makes you think that? Has he said something to you?" It was true, but he hadn't thought Jack had voiced his opinion to her.

"No, but I feel his disapproval."

He kept forgetting that she was an empath. "He's afraid I'm going to hurt you." There was no danger of that. They both knew this was a sort of time-out and they would be returning to their lives soon.

"Hurt me?" She frowned. "You'd never hurt me."

"Not physically. He's afraid I'm going to break your heart or something like that." He smiled when she rolled her eyes.

"My heart is my business, not his."

He glanced out the window. Jack was standing on the porch of the cabin with his arms crossed over his chest. "He's giving us the stink eye, so we should probably get the Jeep unloaded."

"I have this childish urge to stick my tongue out at him."

"Go for it."

She grinned, then did just that, making him laugh. When Jack scowled, they grinned at each other.

"Let's get unloaded and settled in, then I'll show you around." He opened the back door, and Bella jumped out with Blue in her mouth. The cat never seemed to mind hanging by his neck. "Why don't you get Bella and her baby inside, and I'll get our stuff."

Rachel came around the Jeep. "Okay. Come on, Bella Boo. Let's go see our new house." The dog followed her up the steps and into the house.

"Deke headed downtown to interrogate Hargrove's man?" Dallas asked Jack.

Jack nodded. "He'll call if he gets any info from him, but Ebers will probably lawyer up. If we're lucky, his prints will be in the system and we'll at least learn who he is."

"Sure wish we had about five minutes with him before the police got him."

"Yeah, me, too."

Noah pulled up in a silver SUV. After parking it, he walked up and handed Dallas a set of keys. "Your new ride. There's an old barn on the property, and we'll hide the Jeep in there."

"Good idea." By now, Hargrove probably had a description of the Jeep.

"Peyton will be here shortly with groceries," Jack said. "If you or Rachel need anything else, let me know and one of us will get it to you. She shouldn't go anywhere, even in her disguise."

"Agree." He didn't want her anywhere Hargrove could find her.

Rachel came out and stopped next to him. "You agree to what?"

"That you're not leaving this property until Hargrove is behind bars." Or dead.

She stared at the mountains, and he wondered what she was seeing because it wasn't the beautiful view. As if making up her mind about something, she nodded, then slid her gaze over each of their faces, starting with Noah and ending with him.

Whatever was going through her mind, he didn't like that determined look in her eyes.

Keeping her attention on him, she said, "Robert

could spend weeks sneaking around, looking for me, watching me. I'm tired of it, and I'm done with hiding."

"Meaning?" As soon as he asked the question, he knew the answer. "No, not going to happen."

She narrowed her eyes, and he narrowed his right back. If she thought she could intimidate him, she better think again. He'd survived the worst anyone could throw at him, and one woman who barely reached his chin didn't stand a chance.

"What's not going to happen?" Noah said.

He kept his gaze on her. "Rachel wants to use herself as bait."

"No," Jack barked.

"No way," Noah said.

She scowled at each of them. "My life. My choice." She let out a long breath. "Okay, guys, I get that you all are hardwired to protect, but just think about it for a minute. This could go on for who knows how long, and we all have lives to get back to." She waved a hand at Jack. "Nichole isn't even living in your own house with you because you're afraid Robert could get to her."

"She's safe where she is," Jack said.

"The point is, she shouldn't have to be hiding out. I shouldn't have to. From what I know of SEALs, you guys know how to plan an operation and successfully carry it out. Am I wrong?"

That was a trap, and from Jack's grunt and Noah's silence, they knew it, too.

"Never thought I'd see the day three of the baddest guys on the planet turned chicken."

She was entirely too clever. Not one person—man or woman—had dared to call him and his SEAL brothers cowards until this one. She stared back at them with an innocence that he didn't trust for one minute.

Jack leaned toward her. "You want to repeat that, little girl?"

Noah snorted.

She lifted her chin. "Repeat what, the part about you all being chickens? Sure, I'll say it again." She poked Jack in the chest. "Chicken." Her finger landed on Noah. "Chicken."

When she swept her hand toward him, Dallas stepped forward, ramming his chest into her finger, and putting his face inches from hers. "Call me a chicken all day long, but I'm not putting you out there as bait." The idea was too ridiculous to even consider.

"I'm not talking about sticking me in the middle of the road and telling Robert to come get me. In a movie I stunt doubled in, the FBI agents tricked a serial killer by making him think his next victim was alone in her house. Unfortunately for him, there was an agent in every closet and behind every door. We can come up with something like that." She put her hand on his chest. "I trust all three of you to keep me safe."

"Not gonna happen."

"It's not a bad idea," Jack said.

Dallas turned on him. "Have you lost your mind? You know as well as I do that there are no guarantees of a successful operation. Sometimes things go south no matter how well you plan." He could attest to that. Had the scars to prove it. "I won't risk her getting hurt. We'll find another way."

Her eyes softened and she flattened her palm over her heart. "You won't let that happen." She patted her chest. "I know that to the depth of my soul."

"Rachel, please—"

She put her fingers over his lips. "We all know he's not going to stop until he finds me. Who's to say that won't be when I'm alone or that he won't find us while we're sleeping? Isn't it better to control how he finds me?"

"She's got a point," Noah said.

Jack nodded. "How about this? We talk to Deke, get him onboard."

"That's a bad idea. You know the cops will take over, and none of them have the training we do." Dallas couldn't imagine why Jack thought that was a good idea.

"Deke's former Delta Force, and some would argue that those dudes are the baddest."

Noah grunted. "That's a lie."

"Well, we know that, but the point is, he'd be a positive addition to the team," Jack said. "We just have to convince him not to include the police in our plans. He might not be willing since that could get him in trouble with his department, but if he signs on, I'd be a lot more comfortable with four of us."

"And if he doesn't?" Dallas couldn't imagine him risking his job.

"Then we go ahead with the three of us."

"I still don't like it." Seemed like he was outvoted, though. His phone chimed, and he eyed the screen. "It's TG." He put it on speaker.

"Yo, I'm here with Rachel, Noah, and Jack."

"Hey, darlin'."

"Hi, Carter. How are you?"

Dallas resisted the urge to take TG off speaker when she smiled at his phone.

"Better now that I hear your sweet voice. Whiskey, Double D, you boys helping Ghost keep our girl safe?"

"Affirmative," they both chimed.

"Good. Means I won't have to come down there and put a hurt on ya. Getting down to business, Hargrove chartered a private plane two days ago. Destination, Asheville. Him and four passengers. Took time to find the intel because it was a private charter, but the good news, I got photos of all of them. Sending them to your phone now."

"We caught one of them today." While the photos were downloading, he told TG what had happened. "Now Rachel wants us to use her as bait." There was no way TG would go for that.

"Worth considering. She couldn't have better protection than the three of you."

Dallas scowled when Rachel gave him a smug smile.

"Whatever you come up with, I can give you support from here."

"That would be great," Jack said. "Let us put our heads together and come up with a mission plan, then get back to you and see what you can contribute."

"Copy that. When this is over, darlin', you come see me so we can celebrate. Bring that crazy grandmother of yours and we'll party down."

"It's a date." Rachel fought back a laugh when Dallas actually growled.

"You got something in your throat, Manning?" Noah said after Dallas disconnected, amusement in his voice.

"Shut it, Alba."

Noah laughed. She glanced at Jack and by the frown on his face, he clearly wasn't amused. Seriously, he needed to stop acting like an overbearing big brother.

Never having had a brother, she thought it was kind of nice that he was looking out for her, but he didn't seem to understand that she had her eyes wide open where Dallas was concerned.

Her time with Dallas was a diversion, nothing more. She would go home to LA, and he would go home to Montana when all this was over. And if the thought of never seeing him again after that hurt her heart, that was her problem. She'd get over it. Eventually. Hopefully.

"So, what's the plan, guys?"

"The plan is for these two to go away so we can get settled in," Dallas said.

"But I thought we'd plan our mission." Now that she had their agreement, she was ready to get things in motion.

Jack eyed the car approaching the cabin. "There's Peyton with your groceries, and Noah's ride home. I'm going to the police station to talk to Deke. We'll meet back here first thing in the morning. Be thinking about how we're going to pull this off without putting Rachel in danger. Oh, and forward those photos to me so I can pass them on to Deke."

"Will do," Dallas said. "Call me if he learns anything from Hargrove's man."

Jack gave him a two-finger salute, then headed for his car. He stopped. "Almost forgot. Nichole said she'd call you tonight, Rachel."

"Am I going to be an auntie?"

"She made me promise not to say anything."

Oh, he was grinning like a loon. The feeling she'd had was confirmed. She was going to be an auntie.

"I think the answer is yes," Dallas said as Jack got in his car.

She laughed. "I think you're right."

"You boys get the groceries," Peyton said as she walked up the steps. "But first, lay one on me, my sexy man." She stopped in front of Noah and puckered her lips.

"My pleasure, princess."

Rachel really liked Peyton. She was sassy, funny, and sweet. It was impossible not to feel the deep love she and Noah had for each other, even if you weren't an empath. Since she was, the love pouring off both of them was overwhelming.

It was the same with Jack and Nichole. They were soulmates. Being around them when they were together made her long for someone in her life who made her feel like that, who loved her the way these two men did her friends.

Dallas brushed his fingers over her arm as he passed her to get the groceries. Her eyes traveled over him as he walked away from her. His body was a work of art. Being a SEAL was no doubt one reason he was in such good shape but growing up on a working ranch sure hadn't hurt.

It wasn't just his perfectly cut body that drew her to him. Yeah, she could see herself years and years from now still getting hot when she roamed her hands over his arms, chest, and anywhere else her hands landed on. What if he was her soulmate and she walked away? No, she'd know that, wouldn't she? She'd feel it.

"You're going to set him on fire if you keep looking at him like that," Peyton said.

"Busted," Rachel muttered.

Peyton laughed. "Not that I blame you. They are easy on the eyes."

"Truth." She glanced at Noah. "Have you set a date for your wedding?"

"Sometime next year. Right now, Noah and Jack are really busy getting the new center built and up and running. Who knows, we might sneak away one weekend and get married by an Elvis impersonator in Vegas."

"And Noah could sing his vows to you instead of saying them."

"I'd actually love that."

The guys jogged up the steps with bags of groceries in their arms. Rachel opened the door and followed them in. "Just set everything on the counter. I'll get it all put away."

"I didn't know what y'all liked, so I just got a bunch of everything," Peyton said. "There's ice cream in there you might want to get in the freezer." Bella walked into the kitchen, carrying Blue. Peyton's eyes widened. "Oh my gosh, would you look at that." She kneeled in front of Bella. "Who's this?"

"That's Bella and her kitten, Blue," Dallas said. "She found him in a cave and decided he belonged to her."

Peyton laughed. "That's the cutest thing ever." She lifted her gaze to Noah. "Lucky—"

"No, Lucky does not need a kitten." Noah held out his hand and helped her up. "We need to go, princess."

"Yeah, Dad's probably wondering where we are." She clapped her hands. "Y'all should come to dinner with us."

Rachel had no desire to be out in public while Robert was nosing around. "Thanks, but we need to get settled in here, and I want to get these groceries put away. Next time, okay?"

"I'll hide the Jeep on our way out," Noah said. "See you both in the morning."

"They're great people," Rachel said after they left. She peeked in the first bag, looking for the ice cream.

Dallas stepped behind her, put his hands on her hips, and nuzzled her neck. "You're great people."

She leaned her head against his chest. "You got something on your mind, cowboy?"

"I do."

"And what would that be?"

"You. Specifically, you under me."

"I like the sound of that." She looked in the next bag. "Ah, there you are." There were four flavors of ice cream. She took two out and held them up to him. "Help me get the cold stuff in the fridge, then I'm all yours."

"Actually, I want to do a walk-around, do a little scouting."

She hated these reminders of the danger hovering over them, but it was good thinking. "Okay, you do that while I get us settled in."

"I won't be long." He bent his head and kissed her, then snapped his fingers. "Come, Bella." He smiled as he shook his head. "No, leave Blue here."

Once they were gone, Rachel put the cold stuff away, then started on the rest of the groceries. She still had on her running shorts, and Blue jumped up and caught the bottom of her shorts. "Hey, you little stinker. Your claws are sharp." His back claws dug into her leg as he tried to climb up.

She pried his claws out of the material and brought him up in front of her face. "Where do you think you're going?" He meowed, and she set him on her shoulder. He seemed happy there, playing with her hair as she put the groceries away. She tried not to think about how much she was going to miss him and the rest of her rag-tag crew when she left.

She moved their suitcases to the main bedroom. The cabin was new and still faintly smelled of paint. The bed was king-size and had a quilt like the one in their other cabin. There were two doors in the room, one she assumed was a closet and the other the bathroom. She dropped Blue on the bed and gave him a toy to play with.

She was trying to decide whether to live out of her suitcase or put her things away when Dallas and Bella returned. "Everything okay?"

"For now. I'd really like a gate at the entrance. I'll call Jack in a while and see if he can make that happen." He walked to one of the closed doors and opened it. "Awesome." He crooked his finger, and like a woman bewitched, she went to him.

He reached into the large shower and turned on the water, then said, "Strip," in a bossy voice that made her want to obey his every command.

"You want me to take a shower?" They had been out running earlier and still had on their exercise clothes. She really was stinky.

"*We.* We're going to take a shower." He pulled his long-sleeve Henley over his head.

"We?" she squeaked. "I've never taken a shower with a man."

His grin was positively wicked. "Then you're in for a treat." He slid a finger inside her sports bra and tugged. "Take it off."

The things this man was teaching her! She let her inner wildcat come out, the one she'd never known before him that was inside her, just waiting to make itself known.

"You take it off."

The way his lips curved up was positively wicked. "You okay with a fireball burning us up? Because that's where we're headed if I play your game."

"So okay," she said, or maybe gushed. "Do your worst."

He laughed. "Oh, I plan to." He divested her of her sports bra before she knew what was happening. She loved his laugh and that happy gleam in his eyes. That first day, when she'd talked to him on the porch early the next morning, his eyes had been haunted. That had been the reason she hadn't insisted he find someplace else to stay.

"Damn," he said as his gaze landed on her breasts and stayed there. "Beautiful. Just fucking beautiful."

No man had ever looked at her the way he did, as if he wanted to devour her. He slid his hand behind her neck and lowered his mouth to hers. "Just a little taste," he murmured against her lips.

While he kissed her, he dropped his hands to the waist of her shorts and unzipped them. He dipped a finger inside the elastic of her panties and at his touch on her skin, she moaned. He was ruining her for any other man.

"Another minute and I'll have you on the floor." He stepped back. "Shorts off and in the shower with you."

She wanted more and leaned toward him.

He chuckled. "In the shower with you. I'll be back in a sec."

The shower in this cabin was twice the size of their previous one and would easily fit two people. Excited about this new adventure, she hurriedly stripped and stepped inside the stall. Two bottles of bodywash—a vanilla-scented one and a sandalwood one—shampoo, and conditioner were on a shelf, and she picked up the vanilla bodywash, uncapped it, and sniffed.

A hand reached over her shoulder and took the bottle from her. "Allow me."

Chapter Twenty-One

Dallas set the condom on the shelf, then poured a generous amount of the bodywash into the palm of his hand. He put his mouth next to Rachel's ear. "I'll tell you a secret. Shower sex is a first for me, too."

She tilted her head and looked up at him. "We're having shower sex?"

"Oh, yeah."

"And you've never done this before?"

"Never." He'd enlisted in the Navy as soon as he'd gotten his degree in farm and ranch management. College had been something he'd wanted to get through as fast as possible, so he'd doubled up on his classes, leaving little time for parties, girls, and shower sex.

He spread the bodywash over her shoulders, down her arms, then back up. "Lean back on me." She did, and he slid his hands down her sides, then up to her breasts. She pressed her backside into him, snuggling her bottom against his erection.

"Stop wiggling." This wasn't going to last if she kept doing that. He scraped his teeth down the side of her neck, then nipped her earlobe before sucking it into his mouth.

"Dallas."

"You like that, yeah?" Damn but he loved that raspy way she said his name. He poured more bodywash on his hands, then trailed his hand down her stomach. Her skin was wet and slick. He brushed his fingers over her sex, smiling when she responded with a breathy moan.

She slapped a hand over his and pushed. "Please."

"Please what? Tell me what you want." He nuzzled his nose against her neck. She smelled like vanilla, good enough to eat.

"Make me come, Dallas."

"Thought you'd never ask."

"Turn around." When she did, he dropped to his knees. He put his hands on her upper thighs and pulled her to him. She exhaled a long sigh when he slid his tongue through her folds. He wanted to hear her make those breathy noises all night long. Her hands landed on the top of his head, and she curled her fingers around his hair.

As warm water rained down on them, he pleasured her while trying not to think about their time together nearing its end. Could he walk away from her when this nasty business with Hargrove was over and she could go home? And her returning to her life and some other man's tongue being where his was?

Hell no!

Not happening. He wasn't going to give her up.

Later, they'd talk about how to make a relationship work. If he had to spend a few weekends in LA each month, he could bear it for her. Between movies, she could spend time in Montana. But for now, he only wanted to hear those noises she made when he sent her flying. So he let his tongue do what it wanted, and that was to drink her up.

"Dallas." The fingers that had seconds ago been curling around his hair now dug into his scalp. "Oh God, Dallas."

The taste of her on his tongue when she came was fast becoming a craving he wasn't sure he could live without. Not for the first time, he wished they'd met under normal circumstances. He wanted to take her out on dates, romance her, see where a relationship with her would go. But they didn't have that option, and in a few days, he would only have his memories of her if she wasn't agreeable to a long-distance relationship.

As he stood, he let his hands slide up her hips and up her sides to her face. He cupped her cheeks and brought his mouth to hers. While he kissed her, her hands were busy exploring him, and when they crept down his stomach, he caught them before they went any lower.

"You touch me right now, and it's going to be over." She had no idea what she did to him. He backed her up to the shower wall, then grabbed the condom, tore it open, and rolled it on. "Wrap your legs around me."

He slid into her wet heat and was positive he'd found heaven. She wrapped her arms around his neck and tightened her legs around his waist. "Yeah, like that."

"I wish you could know how good you feel inside me."

"Trust me, it feels damn good for me, too." When she sucked his bottom lip into her mouth, then bit down, his every nerve ending was electrified. She caught his rhythm, and their dance was one performed by couples through the ages, but it had never been like this for him before, as if they were made for each other.

"Look at me," he said when her eyes slid closed. "I want to see your eyes when you come for me."

She opened them, and as their gazes locked and held, he almost forgot how to breathe. His hips moved faster, harder, and when she cried his name out as convulsions shook her body, he couldn't hold back any longer. An explosion rocked through him and he thought his heart might beat itself right out of his chest. Was he having a heart attack? If so, what a way to go.

"Fuck me," he gasped as he buried his face against her neck.

She laughed. "I think I just did."

"And spectacularly so."

"You might have to come visit me once in a while for shower sex."

"I can't think of a better booty call." If she was thinking that, maybe they could make something work between them. For the first time since he'd started to want more than a fling with her, hope that there really could be more blossomed.

He turned off the water, and then carried her out of the shower. He wrapped a towel around her, then turned away to get rid of the condom. Would she really be open to some kind of relationship they could make work?

"You're beautiful, you know that, right?"

"Take off your rose-colored glasses." He faced her. "The men who captured me made sure that isn't true."

She put her fingertips on the worst scar on his chest, then moved to another one and another one. "I don't own a pair of rose-colored glasses. When I look at you, I see a beautiful man. These scars are a testament to what you endured. They're proof that you're strong and brave. Do they bother you? Is that why you always wear a long-sleeve shirt?"

The warmth from her fingers lingered on the places

she touched. She flattened her palm over his heart, and he put his hand over hers. "No, they don't bother me because there's nothing I can do about them, so what good does it do me to get all depressed about them? I wear a long-sleeve shirt in public because they bother everyone else."

"They don't bother me. I look at you, and I think, my God, he's beautiful."

"Rachel." He didn't have the words to tell her what was in his heart. Wasn't sure that even if he did, she'd want to hear them. All he could do was show her. He lifted her in his arms, carried her to the bed, and tried to show her what she meant to him.

Jack and Noah showed up early the next morning, and the four of them sat around the kitchen table with cups of coffee. After Rachel had fallen asleep, Dallas had spent most of the night thinking and planning how to keep Rachel out of the operation.

"Hargrove's man isn't talking, but Deke got an ID on him," Jack said. "His name's Calvin Ebers, and his first stint in prison was when he was nineteen for drug trafficking. He's done time for assault with a deadly weapon and carjacking among other things. Not a man you can turn your back on. We have to assume Hargrove's other men won't hesitate to put a bullet through any one of us given the chance."

Dallas wasn't surprised that Hargrove would surround himself with thugs. "Deke a part of this operation or not?"

"Not, but he's going to look the other way. He's not real happy about that, but he knows we have a better chance of catching Hargrove than the police do. He's distributed the photos TG sent us to all the cops, so they're all on the lookout for Hargrove and his men."

"I thought about this last night." Dallas glanced at Rachel. He guessed she wasn't going to like what he had to say. "Hargrove knows about the cabin, so that's where we need to stage the operation. We'll use me as bait."

"What?" Rachel grabbed his hand. "No. No way."

"Hear me out." He put his other hand over hers. "I'm sure the cabin's being watched, and I'll make a show of moving back in. When Hargrove can't find you, he'll come for me, thinking he can make me tell him where you are."

"It's too dangerous."

"Jack and Noah will have my six," Dallas said. She shook her head again. "Hey, it's okay. We're damn good at what we do. Hargrove won't even know they're there."

"Will you promise me one thing?"

"If I can."

"Promise me if it becomes a choice of you or him, you won't let it be you."

"It won't be him," Jack said. "We'll make sure of it."

Noah slapped his hand on the table. "Trust me, Rachel, Hargrove's messing with the wrong people."

"See?" Dallas said. "All's going to be good."

Rachel wanted to believe them, but Robert wouldn't hesitate to play dirty. A part of her wanted to insist Dallas take her with him, but that would just make her stupid. She didn't have the kind of skills these guys had. She would not only be in the way, but she would be a distraction.

"I have…" Jack glanced at her. "Ah, all the stuff we need in my car. Noah and I will head out now." He turned to Dallas. "We'll have to hide the car and walk in without being seen, so give us a thirty-minute head start."

"Copy that," Dallas said.

By *stuff*, she assumed he meant weapons. She hated the thought of them having to arm themselves up with God knew what, but if stuff included grenades and missiles, or whatever they needed to stay safe, she was all for it.

"Please be careful," she told the men when they stood to leave.

"Always." Jack stopped in front of her. "We got this, okay?"

"What he said," Noah said.

Dallas walked out with them, and she went to the window. They congregated by the trunk of Jack's car, and Jack handed a box to Dallas. She didn't doubt there were guns in that box, and she hoped to hell there was also a bulletproof vest.

They talked for a few minutes, then Jack and Noah got in the car and left. Dallas took the box to the SUV and put it on the back seat. He shut the door, then lifted his gaze to the window and stared at her.

After a moment, he strode back, never taking his eyes off her. His expression was one she'd never seen before. Focused and intent were the words that came to mind. *He has his warrior face on.* She backed away from the window.

Because of her, this man was going into battle. Because of her, he was risking his life. She couldn't let him put himself in danger. How could she live with herself if something happened to him? And it wasn't just him. Jack and Noah were involved now. What if they were hurt or worse? How could she face Nichole and Peyton?

"Call them back," she said when Dallas walked in. "I can't let you all risk yourselves like this."

He came right up to her and put his hands on her face, cradling her cheeks. "It's going to be okay, Rachel. We know what we're doing."

"How do you know he'll show up today?"

"Just a hunch. He wants this over as much as you do because he thinks he can go right back to his life once he takes care of you. We're not going to let that happen."

"Robert's a snake. He won't play fair."

"We know how to play dirty and won't hesitate to do what we have to." He kissed her. "It's time for you to feel safe." He kissed her again. "Nothing's going to happen to us, I promise."

This time when he kissed her, he lingered. His tongue tangled with hers, and his spicy scent surrounded her. He tasted like coffee and mint toothpaste. She fisted her hands in his shirt. Maybe she could hold on to him, keep him from leaving.

As if he understood what was going through her mind, he wrapped his hands around hers and gently pried them away. "I have to go, sugar." He kissed her one last time, then stepped away.

"I'm going to be worried sick. Will you call me as soon as it's over?"

"Yes. Stay inside and lock up behind me." He paused at the door. "We'll go out tonight and celebrate."

"Like a real date?"

"Yeah, like that." He winked, and then he was gone.

She slid the deadbolt closed, leaned back against the door, closed her eyes, and said a prayer that her three protectors would return safely home. Bella whined, and Rachel opened her eyes to see her and Blue looking up at her. Bella had a worried expression, and she looked at the door and whined again.

Rachel dropped to the floor and wrapped her arms around Bella. "He'll be back. He promised." Besides, they had a date tonight, and she was going to hold him to that.

To try and keep her mind off worrying about the guys, she decided to inventory the clothes she'd brought, see what kind of outfit she could put together for their date. She wished she could go shopping and find something sexy. A pretty sundress would be nice, but she'd have to make do with what she had, and there wasn't much in her suitcase.

"What do you guys think of this?" She held up a sleeveless pale blue blouse. It was the nicest one she had. Bella and Blue were on the bed, Bella seemingly interested in her choices and Blue more interested in catching Bella's tail.

"I think it will work." Paired with her black skinny jeans, her black half boots, the black belt with a silver buckle, and the silver bangle bracelets and hoops she'd bought for her college girl disguise, she'd do.

Once her date night outfit was decided on, she looked around. What could she do now to keep from worrying about her guys? She stretched out on the bed and played with the kitten for a while. Dallas would be at the cabin now, and she tried not to think about the danger he and the guys were in. She must have dozed off because she jerked up, disoriented when Bella barked, then shot off the bed and raced out of the room. Blue jumped inside the suitcase and disappeared under the clothes.

Right, she was at the new cabin. "You gotta go out, Bella Boo, just say so." She picked up her phone from the bed so she wouldn't miss a call from Dallas and followed the dog to the back door. She almost opened it but stopped and went to the kitchen window. There was no one and nothing suspicious in sight. As soon as she opened the door, Bella took off.

"Guess you really had to go, huh?" Bella never went far, and would bark when she wanted back in. After locking back up, she decided to make a cup of tea while she waited for Bella to return.

She set her phone on the counter, then found the cabinet with the cups in it. She was filling one with water to heat in the microwave when the front door crashed open. Robert stormed in and the cup fell out of her hands and shattered on the floor.

How was he here? She was stuck in one of those nightmares where your feet refused to move even though the monster was coming for you. Bella raced in behind him, growling and snapping at his legs. Robert tried to kick her, but she backed away.

Rachel shook off her stupor when Robert pointed a gun at Bella. "No! Don't hurt her." Broken china crunched under her sandals as she stepped forward. "Bella, come." Still growling, Bella backed toward her, never taking her eyes from the bad man.

When Bella's rear end bumped her legs, Rachel grabbed her collar. "You should leave. The guys are going to be back any minute."

Robert laughed. "They're busy looking for me."

"How'd you find me?" She needed to keep him talking while she tried to think of how to escape. If he didn't have a gun, she'd run or try to fight him, but if she tried anything, he'd shoot her. Which was what he planned to do anyway, so maybe she should try to get out the back door.

"My man put a tracker on the Jeep."

She glanced around. "Where are your men?" Were they outside, waiting to help him haul off her body?

"They're off playing war games with your toy soldiers." He smirked. "They actually begged me to let them show those boys what real soldiers can do."

"They're not soldiers." At his confused look, she said, "They're Navy, sailors, not soldiers." She didn't know if he was aware they were SEALs, and she wasn't going to enlighten him.

"Well, my men will be disappointed. They were looking forward to a challenge. But never mind that." His gaze roamed over her. "I was just going to put a bullet in your heart, but I've decided you owe me."

She took a step back. "I don't owe you anything." She wasn't sure what he believed she owed him, but she had a suspicion. Just the thought of him touching her sent her stomach into a sickening roll. Robert was a good-looking man, a walking cliché for tall, dark, and handsome. But the evil pouring off him had always given her the creeps.

If she could get close enough to the door, she'd make a run for it. If she could take him by surprise, she might have a chance to escape before he shot her.

"Think again, doll. Because of you, I have cops looking for me."

"You made that happen when you shot Henri." She took another step back, bringing Bella with her.

"With you gone, there won't be a witness, so no proof. Problem solved." When she inched back some more, he pointed the gun at Bella. "One more step, doll, and I'll shoot the dog."

"You won't get away with this." Brave words, but she was very much afraid he would.

He laughed again. "Oh, I think I will." He put his hand on his belt buckle. "On your knees."

"No." Was she having a heart attack? It was beating so hard and fast that her chest hurt.

"On your knees, doll. Now."

If she got out of this…no, *when* she did, the first man who called her doll was going to get punched in the nose.

"Do it, or I'll shoot the dog."

"You're a sick bastard." She couldn't do what he was asking. She just couldn't. "Let me put her in the bedroom. She won't like you touching me."

"Go, but you try anything, you'll both be dead."

If only she could get to a knife, but they were in a drawer, and she'd never get one before he shot her. He followed her down the hallway to the main bedroom, and after she pushed Bella inside, she pulled the door closed before Bella could get back out. When her hand was on the doorknob, she noticed the paracord bracelet on her wrist. She had a weapon! It wouldn't be as effective as a knife or gun, but it was better than nothing.

As she headed back to the living room, he walked behind her. She slipped the small blade from its slot. Careful not to cut herself, she gripped the flat end between her fingers.

Robert grabbed her hair, jerking her back against him. "In here." He pushed her into the bedroom.

If she let him keep her in this room, he would rape her and then kill her. She'd rather die fighting than let him put his hands on her. It was time to act. When he stood next to one of the twin beds, no longer blocking the doorway, she waited even though her mind was screaming at her to run. One thing she'd learned performing stunts in movies, timing was everything.

"On your knees, doll." One of his hands went to his belt buckle, and he lowered the hand holding the gun to his side.

And action! She was trained to become the person in a role at those words, and hearing them in her head, she became a woman fighting for her life and determined to win. Letting him see her fear and revulsion— emotions he fed off—she stepped forward until she was close enough to touch him. As she dipped her knees to fool him into believing she was falling to the floor, she raised her hand with the blade held tight in her fingers and dug it into his arm, just below his elbow, and dragged it down to his wrist.

"Fucking bitch," he yelled, the gun dropping to the floor as he brought his bleeding arm up.

She ran. Right out the door he'd kicked in. She made it outside, but she didn't know where to go. There wasn't another building or a place to hide that she could see in front of her, so she raced around the side of the cabin. As she passed the main bedroom window, she heard Bella barking up a storm.

Seeing woods behind the cabin, she headed for them. Her sandals were slowing her down, so she kicked them off. A few yards from the edge of the woods, a bullet flew past her head, and she stumbled, falling to the ground. She glanced behind her, and seeing Robert running after her, she scrambled up and zigzagged her way to the trees as another bullet came so close to her neck that she felt the air it displaced.

When she reached the woods, she kept going, even though her lungs were bursting. She wished her heart would stop pounding, as if it needed to beat that hard while it still could.

Chapter Twenty-Two

"Testing," Dallas said. He didn't know how or where Jack had gotten hold of comms, but he appreciated the hell out of his friend's resourcefulness.

"Whiskey here."

"Double D here."

"Seen any sign of Hargrove or his men?" He walked into the cabin. This place was filled with memories of a wildcat, and he chuckled, still amused that she'd tried to crack his head open.

"Negative," Jack said. "We have eyes on you. I'm to the west of the cabin. Double D's to the east."

Since the front of the cabin was cleared and only had a patch of grass before the drop-off, they'd agreed that the attack would come from the woods.

There were so many memories in this cabin that he'd never forget. Maybe Jack would let him buy it. His intention had been to clear the rooms, but as he walked down the hall, he went past the smaller bedroom, drawn to the spot where he'd first met the woman he was falling in love with.

An inexcusable lapse when the cold iron of a gun barrel pressed to the back of his head. A mistake he never should have made, but it wasn't as big of a mistake as the man holding the gun had just made.

"I'd pull the trigger right now if my boss didn't want you to suffer," said the man who was about to learn a lesson.

"Do you know why you shouldn't get close enough to me to dig your gun into my head?" Dallas said conversationally. Jack and Noah would hear that he had company, but they wouldn't move from their location, knowing he wasn't going to die at the hands of this idiot.

"Shut up," the man said as he pushed the gun harder against Dallas's head.

Dallas sighed. He hated stupid people with guns they should never have in their hands. The trick was to first get his head away, and he jerked it to the side, away from the gun's barrel. As he did that, he spun, wrapped a hand over the man's on the gun and pushed the barrel to the side. With his other arm and using all his strength, he thrust his elbow up into the man's throat while at the same time kicked his kneecap hard with the heel of his boot.

As soon as the man's fingers loosened on the trigger, Dallas relieved him of the gun. The man grabbed his throat as his knee gave out, and he fell to the floor.

"Word of advice. Never get close enough to an adversary for him to turn the tables on you. Like taking candy from a baby," he said to the dude looking up at him, wondering how he was flat ass on his back. "You picked the wrong person to play with. Where's your boss?"

The man spit at him.

"Wrong answer, asshole. I'm good with you dying

today, so if you want to see tomorrow, tell me where your fucking boss is."

"Have a tango in my sights," Jack said into Dallas's earpiece. "Going after him."

"One moving in from my side," Noah responded. "Sounds like an elephant tromping through the forest. Time to party."

Dallas chuckled. This really was a party compared to life in the sandbox. That these men coming after them thought they were hot shit was a joke. He pressed his gun into the man's ear. "You have three seconds to tell me where your boss is before I pull the trigger." As tempted as he was to do it, he wouldn't. But the bastard didn't need to know that.

"Go ahead. If you don't kill me, he will when he finds out you're not dead. About now, I'd say he's putting a bullet through Rachel Denning's heart."

Dallas's world stopped on its axis. The man had to be pulling his chain. "You're lying. He doesn't know where she is."

"Ebers put a tracker on the Jeep before you caught him. When the police come, make sure you tell them I'm cooperating."

"Ghost, he's messing with you," Jack said, having heard the conversation over their comms.

"What if he's not?" Dallas took a few seconds he didn't have to bind the man's hands and ankles together with zip ties. "I'm outta here. Come get him."

Not getting Rachel back wasn't an option. And when he did, they were going to talk about where they went from here, because not having her in his life wasn't an option either. As he raced to the SUV, he tried calling her, but got her voice mail. He tore off the comms and tossed them on the passenger seat, and as he sped back to their new cabin, he prayed he'd be in time. He had to be in time.

The twenty-minute drive from the cabin only took him fourteen minutes to return. Dirt and gravel flew up behind the SUV as he sped toward the cabin. A black Mercedes was parked in front, the nose only a few feet from the porch. He stopped directly behind it to prevent Hargrove from using the car to get away.

Dallas pocketed the SUV keys as he raced up the steps. The front door was open, and he growled at seeing the splintered wood where it had been kicked in. Holding his gun in front of him, he entered the cabin.

The only sound was Bella's barking. The living room, dining room, and kitchen were all in sight, and nothing looked out of place…except, was that blood on the floor? If that was Rachel's blood, Robert Hargrove was a dead man.

He eased down the hallway, following the blood trail, his heart erratically beating in his chest at the thought of what he might find. Since his car was still here, Hargrove hadn't left, but Dallas didn't sense him or Rachel in the house.

The blood led him to the first bedroom, and he eased around the corner. The room was empty, but there was a pool of blood next to one of the twin beds. Was that Rachel's? He couldn't think how it could be Hargrove's. It took every ounce of his training and discipline to stay calm. Losing his shit wouldn't help her.

"Where are you, Rachel?" he murmured. He cleared the closet, then the next bedroom and second bathroom. That only left the main bedroom, where it sounded like Bella was trying to dig her way through the wall.

When he eased the door open, she blew by him, running toward the front door. "Bella, come!" She skidded to a halt, looked at him, then the door, then barked. He got the message. She wanted him to follow her. First, he had to clear the main bedroom. "Come, Bella." She whined but came to him.

"Rachel?" he said. "If you're hiding, it's safe to come out." Nothing. He cleared the room and bathroom anyway, and as he was walking out of the room, he noted the wall next to the bedroom door. Bella had been maybe one more dig from breaking free.

She sure wasn't the same dog as the one that had tried to climb into her own skin the first time he'd talked to her. Her leash was on the kitchen counter, and when he walked over to get it, he saw Rachel's phone on the counter. His heart sank. Without it, she couldn't call for help.

"I sure wish you could talk," he said as he clipped the leash to Bella's collar. When they got outside, Bella put her nose to the ground, went back and forth at the bottom of the stops for a few seconds, then raced for the corner of the house, pulling him with her when she reached the end of her leash.

At the back of the cabin, with her nose still to the ground, she headed for the woods. Because he had to think positive if he didn't want to lose his mind, it had to mean Rachel had managed somehow to escape if Bella was leading him toward the trees. When she started running, he picked up his speed to keep up with her.

"Good, Bella. Let's find our girl."

"I'm going to kill you, bitch," Robert yelled.

Going to have to catch me first. Rachel dodged

around trees, changing directions every few minutes, hoping to lose him. She'd never been more grateful that running was a part of her training regimen.

She ignored her pounding heart and tender feet. None of those mattered more than getting away from him. She'd hoped he would decide she wasn't worth chasing, that he'd be better off leaving and trying again another day.

No such luck. He was chasing her. She willed herself to run faster. The sound of gunfire filled the air a millisecond before a bullet whizzed by her ear. Again! The bullet hit the tree in front of her, and the bark exploded from the impact, a piece hitting her cheek. She stumbled. *Damn, that hurt.*

He was too close. She darted to the right, then a few minutes later to the left. She had to lose him. The sound of his footsteps faded, but she didn't celebrate. He wouldn't give up until he found her.

She slid down, planting her butt on the ground behind a boulder and tried to catch her breath without wheezing and giving away her position. If only she had her phone so she could call Dallas. He and the guys were at the other cabin, waiting for Robert to show up, having no idea that he had found her.

A baseball-size rock poked into her leg, and she pushed it aside. At this point, Robert probably wouldn't bother raping her before just shooting her. Not being raped would be a blessing if he did manage to kill her, but she had no intention of dying.

Think, Rachel. Realizing she still had the blade in her hand, she slid it back in its slot as she tried to come up with a plan to save herself.

"Where are you, bitch?" he yelled.

She squeezed her eyes shut.

"Come out now, and I won't torture you."

Yeah, right. She was already lost and didn't know which way the cabin was. If she ran deeper into the woods, she could become lost forever, wandering around until she died of thirst or a bear ate her. The guys didn't even know she was missing, and even if they did, they didn't know where she was. The only way out of this was to go on the attack. To surprise him. She looked at her paracord bracelet, then at the rock she'd tossed aside as an idea formed. It could work.

She scanned the area around her, her gaze landing on two trees about four feet apart. Pushing up, she grabbed the rock before running to the trees. This had to work, she thought as she unraveled the paracord. She wrapped the line about two feet from the ground around the first tree, then hurried to the second one and tied the ends of the paracord together.

Timing was going to be everything, and as she positioned herself a few feet behind the cord next to the boulder, she squeezed her hand around the rock and tried to calm her breathing.

"Where the hell are you?" Robert called out. "The longer I have to chase you, the worse it's going to be for you." He was close now.

She blew out a long breath, then called on all her acting skills. "Oomph." She dropped to her knees. "Damn, that hurt," she cried out, revealing her location.

As soon as Robert appeared, she kept her body behind the boulder as she peeked around it. "Please. You don't have to do this." His eyes, so full of evil, stayed on her face as he stepped toward her. She'd counted on that, on him not looking down.

"By the time I'm done with you, doll, you're going to beg me to kill you." He had his gun down at his side as he started for her, and she kept her eyes on it. If he lifted it and pointed it her, she'd start running again. When he was only feet from her trip line, she ducked behind the rock, hoping he'd think she'd taken off.

"Fucking bitch!"

She peeked around the boulder. Yes, he was chasing her.

"Aghh."

The second she heard him crash to the ground, she stepped around the boulder, took aim, and threw the rock as hard as she could, hitting him in the head. Who knew having to learn to throw a spear accurately in one of her movies would pay off in a way she'd never expected? Go her!

Before he had a chance to recover, she raced to the gun he'd dropped and picked it up. He wasn't moving, but she wasn't about to check for a pulse. Not taking her eyes off him, she backed up until she was out of his reach.

Now what? She couldn't leave him out here and chance he'd get away again. If she knew for sure he was out cold, she'd tie him up with her paracord line, but that would mean getting close to him. What if he was faking it?

"I should just shoot you and be done with it," she said. He groaned. Okay, not dead. That was too bad, but she couldn't bring herself to shoot him even though he deserved it.

Robert groaned again, then rolled over. When he saw her, he sat up. "Your death is going to be slow and painful."

She held the gun in front of her with both hands the way she'd learned to do when handling a weapon in the movies. "Shut up, or I swear, I'll shoot you."

He laughed. "You don't have it in you to kill someone, doll."

"Maybe not, but I do," Dallas said, walking into view, his gun aimed at Robert.

Chapter Twenty-Three

"You okay, sugar?" Dallas was asking her that question entirely too often because of this bastard. He called on every bit of his discipline to keep from shooting Hargrove and then scooping Rachel up in his arms, never letting her go. Keeping his weapon trained on Hargrove, he stepped next to her.

Bella had led him straight to them, and when he'd heard their voices before getting eyes on them, he'd had to force himself to not rush in and reveal his presence. If Hargrove knew he was here, Dallas didn't want to think what the man would do. Well, he knew what Hargrove would have done. He'd have killed her.

When she'd goaded Hargrove into chasing her, his heart had about stopped. From his vantage point, he couldn't see the trip line she'd rigged, and he'd taken aim, ready to take Hargrove down. Before he could fire, the man had fallen on his face. Then Rachel had bashed him in the head with a perfectly aimed rock. He chuckled. His girl had a thing about braining people.

"No, I'm not okay. Take this, please."

She held the gun out, and he took it from her shaking hand. "You're amazing, you know that, right?"

"Not going to argue that, but I'm done with being amazing, okay?"

She would always be amazing to him. He stuck the gun she gave him into his waistband but kept his pointed at Hargrove, then wrapped an arm around her and tucked her against his side. "I don't think she likes him," he said, lifting his chin toward Bella, who was busy growling at Hargrove.

"Smart dog. So, what do we do with him?"

He glanced down at her, noticing for the first time the cut and purple bruise on her swollen cheek. "What's this? He do that do you?"

"Yeah, when he tried to shoot me but hit the tree in front of me instead. A piece of bark got me."

"Can I kill him?"

She leaned her head against his chest. "Tempting, but I don't think you'd look good in orange."

Hargrove groaned as he pushed to his feet. He gave Bella a wary look, then his eyes slid to Rachel. Dallas wanted to kill the bastard if for no other reason than the way he looked at her.

His gaze landed on Dallas. "A million dollars if you let me walk away."

Dallas snorted. "You're going to walk all right, but it's going to be straight to prison." Between his trust fund, his investments, his share in the ranch, and his bank account, he was worth considerably more than a measly million. But even if he didn't have a penny to his name, he wouldn't touch the man's money. He'd just as soon send Hargrove to hell.

"Two million."

"Not interested. Start walking. If you try to run,

I'll shoot you, then let Bella have at you." He took Rachel's hand.

They'd only taken a few steps when she grunted. "Sorry. My feet are a little sore."

He glanced down at her bare feet. "Where are your shoes?"

"I couldn't run in sandals." She lifted a foot, showing him the bottom. The sole was torn up and bleeding.

"Are you sure I can't kill him?"

"Still tempting, but no."

"You're no fun." He turned. "Climb on my back."

"I can walk, just not fast."

She wasn't walking out of here on those feet. "On my back, sugar." She sighed as if he was being unreasonable but slid her arms over his neck. "Wrap your legs around my waist."

When they came around the corner of the cabin, Jack was leaning against the hood of his car, next to Deke. A dark blue car was parked behind Jack's that he pegged as a typical detective's vehicle. As they walked toward the men, a police cruiser pulled up and parked.

He poked Hargrove in the back with the barrel of his gun. "I do believe your chariot has arrived."

Hargrove came to a sudden stop, turned, and glared past him at Rachel. "You should sleep with one eye open, bitch, because the day will come when you'll be sorry you interfered in my business."

Blood red rage tinged Dallas's vision. He pried Rachel's legs from around his waist and pulled her hands away from his neck, easing her down, then let his fist fly, sending the bastard to the ground.

He put his booted foot on Hargrove's chest and pressed hard as he leaned over the man's face. "You fucking come near her, you send anyone else to do your dirty work, it will be the last thing on this earth that you do." He dug the heel of his boot into Hargrove's chest. "If you're wondering if that's a threat or a promise, it's both."

"He's assaulting me." Hargrove looked over at Jack and Deke. "You saw that. I want him arrested."

Jack and Deke eyed each other. "What's he talking about? I didn't see anything," Jack said.

Deke shrugged. "Beats me." He glanced at the uniformed officer who'd come to stand next to them. "You see an assault happen here, Mike?"

With a puzzled expression on his face, the officer said, "Huh?" Then he looked at Rachel and winked.

Her giggle was a mighty fine thing to hear. He walked away from Hargrove. "He's all yours."

Rachel decided she was a bad, bad person for taking pleasure in watching Dallas punch Robert. But whatever. It was peanuts compared to what Robert planned to do to her.

The police officer and Deke got Robert up, handcuffed him, put him in the back of the cruiser, and then the officer got in the car and drove away. Bella circled her, sniffing her, and Rachel kneeled. She laughed as she wrapped her arms around the dog and buried her face in Bella's fur.

"You okay, Rachel?" Jack said, stepping in front of her.

"No, she is not," Dallas answered for her. "Her jaw is purple, and her feet are ripped to shreds."

"I'll live." She stood and fluttered her fingers at Deke as he joined them. "Hi, Deke. Fancy meeting you here."

He smiled. "Let's try not to make it a habit."

She was all for that.

Dallas glanced at her. "I'd really like to get her feet taken care of, and her jaw has to be hurting."

"Take pictures of her face and feet," Deke said. "We're going to need a statement. Can you come down to the station later today?"

"You bet. Whatever it takes to make sure Robert stays in jail." For his entire life, she prayed.

"Great. Jack's got my number. Just give me a call when you're headed my way. I'm really glad Dallas got to you before Hargrove had a chance to hurt you worse than he did."

Dallas grinned at her. "I had nothing to do with it, man. By the time I found her, she had Hargrove knocked out on the ground, his gun in her hand."

A warm feeling traveled through her at the pride for her she heard in his voice.

Both Jack and Deke raised their eyebrows. "I gotta hear this story," Jack said.

"Well, it started...oomph," she muttered when Dallas scooped her up.

"If you're going to tell us what happened, you're going to do it sitting down." He carried her to the porch and lowered her to a rocking chair. "Now you can talk." He leaned back against the porch rail, Jack and Deke doing the same.

"Okay, it started with Robert kicking the front door of your cabin in." All three men eyed the splintered door with identical scowls on their faces, and that made her grin. Now that it was over, she was feeling pretty pleased with herself. By the time she finished her story, all three of them were wide-eyed and slack-jawed.

"Badass," Deke said.

Jack shook his head. "Remind me never to mess with you."

Dallas laughed. "Yeah, don't piss off a wildcat. Right now, though, she needs a little doctoring. We'll call when she's ready to come make her statement."

"Now that Hargrove and his men are in custody, I'm going to get my wife and bring her home," Jack said. "Why don't y'all plan on coming over after you finish with the police? We'll throw some burgers on the grill." He glanced at Deke. "You and Heather should come over, too."

"We will if she's up to it. I'll let you know."

"His wife is due any day now," Jack told Dallas.

"Overdue, actually, and she's past ready for that little boy to show his self," Deke said as the two of them headed for their vehicles. "I'll send someone to get Hargrove's car."

Jack lifted a hand and waved. "And I'll call Noah and tell him to get the cabin door replaced."

"You good with dinner at Jack's?" Dallas said, picking her up after they drove away.

"What are you doing? I can walk."

"And I can make sure you don't have to. I promised you a date tonight, so if you want to go out, just us, I'll tell Jack we have other plans. Or after what you went through today, would you rather stay at the cabin tonight? I'll cook for you."

"I'm good with dinner at Jack's, but maybe we don't hang around after we eat." She actually would prefer to stay in with him, especially since she'd be leaving soon, but she also wanted to see Nichole.

"That works. You really were amazing today, but don't ever scare me like that again."

"I'll try not to. How did you know to come look for me?"

"Hargrove's man told me Ebers put a tracker on the Jeep. That meant he knew we'd moved to this cabin. All I could think was, what if I didn't find you before…" He shook his head as if he couldn't finish that thought, then stared down at her, his emotions fully open to her for the first time since she'd met him.

Did he even realize he was letting her see the depth of his fear when he didn't know what Robert might have done to her? She put her hand on his cheek. "Hey, I'm safe, and it's over. He'll rot in prison, and that will be the worst punishment for a man like him." She sure hoped that would be the outcome. "You can put me down now."

The ghost of a smile appeared as he stared down at her. "I could, but I won't." He carried her straight to the bathroom and lowered her to the counter.

"First, I have to do this." His mouth crashed down on hers, his hands landed on her hips, and he pushed his body between her legs.

He kissed her as if he was a starving man, and she was the meal that would sustain his life. He wasn't gentle, and she didn't want gentle. After almost dying, she needed his raw hunger. He made her feel alive. His tongue tangled with hers…no, they fought, their two tongues. A feverish battle of wills.

She put her hands on his jeans and fumbled for the button. "Need you," she murmured against his mouth.

"Let me take care of your feet first."

"Later. I need you now, Dallas, so much." She needed

him to make her forget, to erase the image of Robert telling her to get on her knees.

A growl deep from his throat was her only answer. He broke the kiss, yanked his shirt over his head, and then her shirt and bra were next to go. Their jeans, his boxer briefs, and her panties quickly followed.

"Wow. You're good at that clothes removal stuff. You learn that in SEAL school or from cowboying?"

He laughed. "It's all about motivation, sugar, and you have me very motivated." His expression sobered. "Are you sure about this? After what you've been—"

She put her fingers over his lips. "Make me forget."

"Thinking of him having his hands on you isn't something I want to remember either."

"Let's forget together then." He picked up the condom, and she took it from him. "Let me."

"With pleasure."

It was hot the way he watched her put the condom on him, and as he slid inside her, his eyes never left hers, and in their depths, she saw desire and something else. She wanted to believe it was love she saw, or at least, the beginning of love.

He wrapped his hand around her neck. "I can't go easy, Rachel. Not now."

"I don't want easy. Not today." She needed that raw hunger she'd seen on his face when he'd torn off their clothes. At hearing her answer, he seemed to surrender to whatever this thing between them was.

That thrilled her because he'd been closed off to her particular talent until recently. It had to mean that he was healing, that he was done with hiding. She didn't think he even knew he'd closed himself off from the world, from his friends and family. There was nothing more she wanted than to see him happy. She wanted that more than she wanted her own happiness.

Was that love?

His mouth came down on hers, his tongue found hers, he dug his fingers into the skin of her hips, and then he plunged deep inside her. As his thrusts grew faster, harder, she wrapped her legs around his waist, and her arms around his neck. He made a strangled noise when she clenched her core muscles around him.

"Aah. Good, Rachel. Feels so damn good."

She did it again, and he went wild. Pleasure grew inside her, building until she couldn't contain it anymore, and she screamed his name. His body stilled, a great shudder traveled through him, then he buried his face against her neck, and wrapped his arms around her, holding her tight.

"Wow," she said between gasps for breath. She rested her head on his chest and listened to the pounding of his heart.

He chuckled, his lips vibrating on her skin. "Yeah, wow."

Would he miss her when she left, and how long would it take her to stop missing him? She'd admitted to herself that this was a man she could love, but she was afraid her heart had taken that as a green light to belong to him. What if she never stopped missing him?

"You okay?" He leaned away and ran a critical gaze over her. "Oh, hell. I'm sorry." He gently rested the tips of his fingers on her jaw. "You're hurt, and I'm a selfish bastard. I shouldn't have kissed you."

"I wanted you to. Needed you to." Her jaw was throbbing, but she'd forgotten about it until now.

His gaze lowered to her feet, and he scowled. She

leaned over and peered down. Drops of blood were on the floor from her cut feet.

"I'm sorry," he said again as he stepped away.

"Please don't be. Honestly, I didn't even feel them." She did now. They were throbbing along with her jaw.

"Are you sure?" His eyes searched hers. "I should have taken care of you before taking what I wanted."

"Dallas, you did take care of me." She reached for his hand. "You gave me what I wanted and needed." This man...did he have any idea how big his heart was?

"Okay." He swiped a hand through his hair as he scanned the room. "I'm sure Jack put a first aid kit somewhere." He opened the cabinet under the counter, closed it, tried the linen closet, and when he didn't see one there, he pointed at her. "Don't move."

She sighed at his retreating backside. *You have a sexy as all get-out butt, Dallas Manning.* He sure did, but the scars on his back, arms, and legs brought tears to her eyes. Her feet and jaw were nothing compared to what was done to him. How had he endured that kind of pain and suffering without losing his mind?

And the scar on his face that had to have been made by a knife? She couldn't imagine how much it must have hurt. Strangely, although it was prominent, she hardly noticed it anymore.

There were so many things she wanted to know about him but was hesitant to ask. She didn't want to bring up bad memories with her questions. As far as she could tell, he wasn't suffering from PTSD. She'd never seen him jumpy or depressed. The one time she'd witnessed his nightmare, which she knew was of his time in captivity, he'd been fine the next morning. She wasn't even sure if he remembered having one.

He returned, holding a bag of frozen corn and a red box. "Found it." He set the box on the counter, then handed her the frozen corn. "Hold this to your cheek." He picked up his boxer briefs and slipped them on.

Well, that was disappointing. She much preferred him in all his naked glory. He reached for the first aid kit, stilled when his arm brushed her breast, then picked up her T-shirt. "Put this on. Your titties are too distracting."

She burst out laughing. He shrugged, his expression just too cute, that of a little boy caught with his hand in the cookie jar. She couldn't resist messing with him. She stretched her arms above her head, then shook like a wet dog, making her breasts jiggle. "Ah, that felt good."

"Rachel."

The way he growled her name sent real shivers through her. "Yes?" she innocently said as she blinked up at him.

He pushed the shirt into her hand. "On. Now."

She smirked. "Something bothering you, cowboy?"

Chapter Twenty-Four

Something was bothering Dallas all right. He'd had to have her and hadn't given a second thought as to what she'd been through or her jaw and torn-up feet. Never mind that she said she'd wanted that, too. He shouldn't have let his baser needs take control. She'd been through hell today, and he'd had every intention of bringing her back to the cabin and taking care of her.

She could have died at the hands of that bastard. The thought of a world without Rachel in it messed with his mind. He couldn't deny that he was falling for her, and that also messed with his mind. To hide what he feared was showing on his face—that he was falling for her and not knowing how she'd react to that—he dropped to his knees, bringing the first aid kit with him.

At least she'd put her shirt on, and he could concentrate on her feet instead of her breasts. Because hooyah, her breasts were magnificent, and he wasn't lying when he said they were a distraction.

The bottoms of her feet were a bloody mess. He closed his eyes and willed his rage down to a simmer. He really should have fucking killed Hargrove. He opened the first aid kit and took out a package of gauze, opened it, and then handed the gauze to her. "Wet this for me."

When she gave it back to him, he gently cleaned the bottoms of her feet, then picked out the small shards of rocks embedded in both of them. How had she kept running on these shredded feet? He looked up at her.

"Have I told you that you're badass?" And a very sexy one.

"I think it was Deke who told me that."

He grunted. He should have been the one to tell her how badass she was.

"Did they do this to you when you were captured?" She trailed the tip of her finger down the scar on his face.

"Uh-huh."

"They came so close to your eye."

Because they'd been aiming for his eye, but he wasn't going to share all the gory details with her. "You really tore your feet up." After cleaning them, he rubbed ointment on the soles. "You mind if I get a pair of socks out of your suitcase?"

"No."

"Be right back." He grabbed the thickest socks she had and put them on her when he returned to the bathroom. "I'll put some more salve on them before you go to bed." He took the bag of corn from her, cleaned the cut on her face, thankful it wasn't deep, then put ointment on it. He gave her back the frozen corn. "Keep this on your face for a while."

"Thank you."

He leaned back on his heels. "For what?" It still angered him that she'd had to save herself…hell, that he'd even left her alone so Hargrove could get to her.

"For taking care of me."

"When are you planning on going home?" He wanted to ask if she'd like to come to Montana after she finished filming her next movie, but he hesitated. She hadn't dropped any hints that she wanted to see him again after she went home. Maybe before he asked her that, he should feel her out, see if she was interested in trying for some kind of long-distance relationship.

"I need to go soon. In a few days, I guess."

That was disappointing. He was hoping she'd stay another week or two. He'd planned to talk to her later tonight about what she wanted where they were concerned, but he needed to know. "I was thinking maybe we could keep seeing each other. It won't be easy, but you could come to Montana between movies, and I could come see you sometimes."

"I'd like that. A lot."

"Yeah?" He was pretty sure his grin stretched from ear to ear. Also, he really liked how her eyes lit up when he'd asked.

"Yeah. I was afraid you were ready for me to get out of your hair."

"Not sure I'll ever be ready for that." He wished they weren't committed to going out tonight. They didn't have much time left, and he selfishly wanted her to himself. "Are you sure you're up for going over to Jack's tonight? Maybe you should keep off those feet."

"I'd like to go. I haven't gotten to spend much time with Nichole, and really, my feet are feeling better already. Besides, I have to go give Deke my statement, so we can do that on the way."

"Let's see how they feel when you walk on them."

He put his hands on her waist and lifted her, then eased her down on her feet.

"See, all better," she said, looking over her shoulder as she left the bathroom.

He was positive they hurt worse than she let on, and he'd make sure she stayed off them the rest of the day. "I guess we need to get dressed then."

As he had—much to her protests—at the police station, when they got to Jack and Nichole's, he carried her in. She'd tried to wear her running shoes, but they'd hurt her feet. They'd had a bit of an argument when she'd wanted to wear sandals and he'd been adamant that she was keeping the socks on. He'd won that one.

"I feel silly," she said as he rang the doorbell.

"What? Don't women think it's swoon-worthy when their man carries them? Besides, I like you in my arms."

She grinned at him. "So you're my man, huh?"

"I'd like to be."

Before she could respond to that, Jack opened the door. "What have we here?"

"Her feet are shredded from running barefoot in the woods. We're going to make her stay off them."

"Copy that. Nichole's out on the deck."

He followed Jack to the back, and as soon as they stepped out, Nichole jumped up. "Oh my God, Jack told me what happened. Are you okay?"

"I'm fine. My feet are a little messed up is all."

"Let me put her down, then you can maul her," he said when Nichole tried to hug Rachel. He lowered her to a chaise longue so she could stretch her legs out. She glanced up at him and smiled her special smile meant just for him, and damn if his heart didn't do a somersault. That had to be love. He'd had girlfriends off and on through the years and not a one of them made his heart bounce around with a special smile. Actually, he couldn't think of a single one who had a special smile just for him. He could see himself married to her.

Whoa there, Manning. Don't get ahead of yourself. He had some things he needed to settle before he took that step. He was still on medical leave with the Navy and needed to deal with that because he wasn't staying in. Then there was his future...or lack of one. Although he could afford to be a beach bum, probably for the rest of his existence, he needed a purpose. Before he could even think of getting married, he had to get his life in order. But— and this he was sure about—he didn't want her to be the one who got away.

Back to that special smile, her mouth deserved a kiss. And yeah, he was grabbing for any excuse to kiss her. He leaned down and brushed his lips over hers, and when she sighed, his heart tumbled again. It was time to retreat.

Jack hadn't come out with him, and that was a good excuse to leave. "I'm going to go find Jack and let you two have some girl time."

They were already talking a mile a minute by the time he walked inside. He found Jack in the kitchen making hamburger patties. "Need some help?"

"Grab us a beer from the fridge, then you can slice the onions and tomatoes."

"These some of Peyton's beers?" He really liked the ones he'd tried already.

"Yeah. I invited them over tonight, but they already had plans. Some kind of business dinner Peyton couldn't get out of. Deke and Heather passed on coming. Deke thinks she might have that baby tonight, so they wanted to stay close to home."

Dallas twisted the caps off the bottles, then put one on the counter next to Jack.

"Thanks. Now that you've spent time here, what do you think of Asheville?"

"I like it. The mountains are different from home. More trees and greener."

"Think you'd like living here?"

And there it was. The question he'd been expecting. "Maybe." He wasn't ready to commit, but unlike when he'd first had his suspicions about Jack's reason for inviting him here, then asking for input on equine therapy, he had an open mind.

Asheville was growing on him, and he'd been reading up on equine therapy. The more he learned about it, the more the idea settled in his mind that it was something he'd like and would get great satisfaction from. It sure beat being one of Phoenix's hired hands. But damn, Montana. He was a Montana boy, born and bred, and he'd never considered before now that Montana wouldn't be his home until the day he died.

Then there was his family. They expected him to come back to the ranch when his military days were over. His mother would not be at all happy if her baby boy permanently moved two thousand miles away. He had some thinking to do.

Jack washed his hands. "I don't think by now it will come as a surprise that I'm offering you a job."

"No surprise, but I need some time to think about it."

"Fair enough. How's Rachel doing?"

"Her jaw hurts and her feet are a mess, but other than that, surprisingly good." A lot of people, men included, would be traumatized by what she'd gone through, but she was a trooper. "Deke said the FBI showed up and took possession of Hargrove. The feds want him for illegal arms dealing, along with murder and some other things."

"Hope the bastard rots in prison." Jack glanced at him. "I guess Rachel will be leaving soon?"

"In a few days."

"That okay with you?"

He shrugged. "Don't have much choice in the matter. She lives in LA, and filming on her next movie starts soon." He finished slicing the onions, then started on the tomatoes. Being guys, they didn't talk about feelings, but Jack was one of his best friends, and maybe it would help get his head straight to talk about what was going on in his mind where Rachel was concerned. "Want to hear something weird?"

"Hit me up." Jack slid the tray of burgers into the refrigerator.

"After…" This wasn't easy to talk about, even with his best friend. "I can't stand for anyone to touch me now. Not sure why, other than there isn't a place on my body those bastards didn't hurt, so I don't like hands on me anymore. Feels like bugs are crawling under my skin when someone touches me. Except for Rachel. From day one, it didn't bother me for her to touch me. Oh, and for reasons I don't even want to try to figure out, I didn't cringe when Dirty Mary touched me."

Jack laughed. "You ask me, that there's the weird part. Dirty Mary, huh?"

"Yeah. Go figure." Finished with slicing the tomatoes, he added them and the onions to a platter that already had lettuce on it.

"I assume the girls are catching up on everything that's happened. Let's leave them be for a while. Grab your beer."

Dallas followed Jack to the living room. Jack sat in a chair and stretched out his legs. "Why do you suppose you can tolerate Rachel touching you when you can't handle it from anyone else?"

"I don't know." Dallas took a seat on the sofa, set his beer on a coaster, leaned his elbows on his knees, and stared down at the floor. He could shut this conversation down right now, or go all in. Decision made, he said, "How did you know you were in love with Nichole?"

"It's like that, huh?"

"Not sure, but maybe. I know that I want to figure out a way to keep seeing her, but there's no way I can be happy living in Hollywood." He lifted his gaze to Jack. "I need space."

"Okay, I have a question for you. Are you sure you're not thinking Rachel might be the one only because she can touch you without you feeling like bugs are crawling under your skin? Are you using her as a crutch?"

"I don't know." He was as positive as he could be that wasn't the case. But what if it was?

That's what you get for eavesdropping, Rach. You hear things you wished you hadn't. She'd come in to go to the bathroom and had stilled when she realized Dallas was talking about her. She hadn't been surprised when he'd said he couldn't live in Hollywood. He wasn't meant to be a city man, and that was okay. She was getting tired of the place and all the trappings herself. Montana sounded like a place she'd like to live someday if things worked out with them.

Then Jack had asked his question. "Are you using her as a crutch?"

"I don't know."

Her heart actually hurt at hearing Dallas's answer. What was she supposed to do? Hang around while he figured out the answer to that question? And while she was waiting, fall in love with him? She was already halfway there. If he decided he didn't want her, where did that leave her? Heartbroken, that was where.

She backed out of the kitchen on her sock-clad feet.

"That was fast," Rachel said when she came back outside.

"Um…" Stupid tears filled her eyes.

"Rach? What's wrong?"

She shook her head. "Not now, okay?" Nichole was her best friend, and they talked about everything, but if she told what she'd overheard, she'd start crying. The last thing she wanted was for Dallas to come out and see her bawling.

Nichole reached for her hand. "Okay for now, sweetie, but we're going to talk. Why don't we plan to have lunch tomorrow? I'll come pick you up."

"I'd like that."

"So tell me about your next movie. What's it about?"

"It's a murder mystery. The protagonist is an FBI profiler. The bad guy, a serial killer, murdered her sister years ago, but she doesn't know that. Now he's fixated on her."

"Sounds scary. What kind of stunts will you be doing?"

"Not sure yet. I have a meeting next week with the stunt coordinator to go over all of that." As they talked about movies and the latest Hollywood gossip, the feeling that she was ready to leave that life behind grew. But what would she do?

"I miss the mountains," she said as she took in the beautiful views surrounding them. Maybe she'd move home. The more she thought about it, the more the idea appealed. The question was, what would she do for a job?

"Does that mean you're ready to come home?"

She heard the hope in Nichole's voice. "I don't know. Maybe. Especially now that I'm going to be an auntie."

"You know I'd love nothing more than to have you here."

The guys walked out carrying platters of food. "The grill should be ready," Jack said.

Dallas set a plate of garnishes on the table, then sat in the chair next to her. "How are your feet feeling?"

"Fine."

"You grew up in Asheville. Do you miss it?"

"Sometimes." A lot lately. She wished he'd stop talking to her.

"Think you'd move back someday?"

Why did he keep asking her questions? "Probably." He was starting to look at her funny, no doubt puzzled by her one-word answers. Maybe he'd give up and stop talking to her.

"Jack's trying to talk me into heading up his therapy horse part of his foundation. I was hoping, since this is your home and your best friend lives here, that—"

"That what? I'd give up everything I've worked for and move back just because you're here?" Embarrassed that she'd lost it in front of Jack and Nichole, she snapped her mouth shut.

"What's going on, Rachel?"

"Um, Jack, come help me fix everyone's drinks," Nichole said.

"Good idea."

Rachel almost laughed at how fast he disappeared inside, but she didn't feel like laughing right now. She kept her gaze on the mountains, because if she looked at Dallas, she'd cry.

"Talk to me. I obviously did something wrong, but I can't fix it if I don't know what."

She swallowed past the lump in her throat, and willing herself not to cry, she faced him. "Tell me something. Are you thinking I might be *the one* because I'm the only woman who can touch you without you feeling like bugs are crawling under your skin? Are you using me as a crutch?"

His eyes widened. "You heard that?"

"I did. You don't know the answer, do you?" At his hesitation, and the confusion as to what he felt and wanted coming from him, she turned her eyes back to the view. She liked it better when she couldn't read him. "And if you're wrong, where does that leave me?" By his silence, he apparently didn't have an answer to that either. She swung her legs over the edge of the chaise longue.

"What are you doing? You shouldn't be walking on those feet," he said when she stood.

"I'm not yours to worry about." When he got up, she shook her head. "Stay here. I'm just going inside for a little while." She could tell by the expression on his face that he didn't like it, but he sat back in the chair.

"You okay?" Nichole said when she entered the kitchen.

"No. Will you take me back to the cabin?"

Jack glanced between them. "What's happening?"

"I heard you and Dallas talking when I came in to go to the bathroom. I didn't mean to eavesdrop, but—" she shrugged "—I did. He's a great guy, a wonderful one really, but I can't sit around waiting for him to figure out if the only reason he's with me is because he can tolerate me touching him."

"Shit," Jack said. "I'm sorry you heard that, but for what it's worth, I think he really does have feelings for you. Strong ones."

"And if the day comes when he realizes he doesn't and he leaves, taking my heart with him? Sorry, but that doesn't work for me."

"Come on. I'll take you back." Nichole stepped over and hugged her, then gave Jack a quick kiss. "Don't let Dallas follow her. She needs a little time to think."

"Might have to tackle him and tie him to a tree, but I'll try. Be careful." He pulled Rachel into a hug. "We're always here for you, you know that."

"I do, and thanks. Love you both."

"Wow," Nichole said when they were in her car, on the way to the cabin. "I didn't know that Dallas can't handle being touched. Well, except by you."

"If you could see all the scars on his body, you'd understand. I don't know how he survived what those people did to him."

"You're in love with him, aren't you?"

"I don't know. Maybe. I wish I wasn't."

"Well, the heart rarely listens to what our brain thinks is best for us."

"Stupid heart." When Nichole laughed, Rachel found herself laughing, too.

"You know, I think Jack's right, that Dallas really does have strong feelings for you."

"Maybe, but I meant it when I said I can't hang around only to end up with a broken heart…well, more broken than it already is." In fact, the thought of seeing Dallas when he returned to the cabin—no. She just couldn't. It would hurt too much. She pulled out her phone and logged into airline flight schedules. "I know I said we'd have lunch tomorrow, but there's a flight home later tonight, and I want to be on it. Problem is, my rental car's at the other cabin, so can you take me there?"

"Of course I will, but are you sure that's what you want to do? Maybe the two of you should have a long talk when he gets back to the cabin."

"Until he figures out if what's between us is real for him or not, there's nothing to talk about."

Nichole sighed. "Okay, but I'm not happy we didn't get to spend much time together while you were here."

"Yeah, me, too."

"You take care of our cowboy, okay, Bella Doo?" Rachel said, her voice cracking as tears fell down her cheeks. She was sitting on the bed she'd never share with Dallas again. She wouldn't be here to hold him when he had a nightmare.

"Promise you'll snuggle up to him when he has a nightmare." She smiled through her tears when Bella licked her face. "You're such a sweet girl." She picked up Blue and gave him a kiss on his little nose. He squirmed, trying to get away.

"I'm going to miss you both so much." She tried not to think about how much she was going to miss Dallas, but her heart was breaking. She picked up his pillow and brought it to her face, inhaling his spicy scent.

"Oh God, Bella, I'm smelling his pillow. I'm in love with him, aren't I?" She was a fool for thinking she could have some fun with him and then walk away unscathed. Would he miss his pillow if she took it with her? "I'm pathetic." She put the pillow back, but when she packed her suitcase, she picked up the T-shirt he'd worn last night and brought it to her face. It smelled like him, too. She put it in her suitcase. She really was pathetic.

When she gave the dog one last hug, Bella whined as if she knew goodbyes were being said. She loaded her suitcase in the car with tears still burning her eyes, fully intending to leave right then. She opened the door of the car and tried to get in, but she couldn't. Not without saying goodbye to him, too. She went back inside, found paper and a pen, and wrote him a note.

Now she could go.

Chapter Twenty-Five

Jack returned, and Dallas watched for Rachel to follow him out, but she didn't come. "Where are the girls?"

"Inside."

He stood, intending to go get her. He'd messed up, and they needed to talk.

"Sit. Rachel needs a little time, so leave them be."

"I need to talk to her."

"Unfortunately for you, she doesn't want to talk to you right now."

Was giving her time the wrong move, like too much time to think and she'd decide she didn't need his sorry ass in her life? He should go talk to her.

"Sit the hell down," Jack snapped.

Dallas gritted his teeth but dropped back on the seat. It was probably better he waited until they were back at the cabin anyway, where they could have a private conversation.

Jack pulled two beers from the ice bucket and handed Dallas one. "I'm not one to go around giving advice on love and stuff, but you probably need to take some time yourself to think about what you want before either one of you get any deeper. She's hurting, Dallas, and that makes me want to put a fist in your face."

"I don't want to hurt her." But he had, and it was killing him not to make it right. Why had he hesitated to answer her? He'd already admitted to himself that he was falling for her. He was, right? And there was the problem. He'd hesitated because he'd never lie to her.

"Just give it some time, both of you, while you figure out what she means to you. Now, enough of this girly talk. There's an equine therapy place for vets in Colorado that I've heard great things about. I talked to the owner and arranged for you to spend a week there."

"I can do that. It would give me a chance to check out their operation and decide if it's something I want to do." The more he read about equine therapy, the more it interested him.

"Good. I was thinking you could wrap up finding us the horses we need in the next day or two, then head over there."

"It's not a done deal though." It pretty much was, but Dallas didn't want to commit yet. For one thing, his family was expecting him to come home, and he needed to talk to them before making a final decision.

"Positive thinking." Jack stood and went to the grill. "These are done."

"I'll go get the girls."

"They said to eat without them."

Dallas narrowed his eyes. "What the hell's going on?" He strode inside the house. The girls were nowhere to be found. He marched back outside. "They're not in there."

"I know."

"The hell, Jack. Where is she?"

"She wanted to go back to the cabin, so Nichole took her." Jack grabbed his arm when he turned to leave.

"Calm down, okay? Remember we talked about giving her some time? Let's eat these burgers, then you can go to her."

"I'm not hungry." Not anymore.

"I am, so you can sit and watch me eat."

"Now I want to punch you in the face."

Jack laughed. "You can try."

He was not happy, but he managed to eat a burger. "Your dogs aren't around."

"They're in the bedroom. I'll let them out."

He was gone before Dallas could tell him not to bother, that he was leaving. A few minutes later, three dogs came tumbling out of the house. Being the well-behaved lady that she was, Dakota approached, then sat at his feet, waiting for permission to greet him. Rambo tried, but couldn't stop wiggling his butt at the sight of Dallas. Maggie May landed in his lap, her body quivering with excitement.

Jack sighed. "Can't teach that one a thing. Someone threw her out of a pickup, and I think she must have landed on her head. But she's sweet. Loves everybody."

Dallas gave her chin a good rub. "She still stealing stuff?"

"Anything and everything she can manage to sneak away."

"You're a funny girl, Maggie May." He leaned over and gave some attention to Rambo, and then Dakota. "What's your plan for Bella? We haven't spent much time on training her." He didn't like the idea of her going to someone who didn't understand her and what she'd been through.

"She hasn't been ready for training, not until she learns it's safe to trust again."

"I'm not an expert on dogs, but I think she's ready now. You have someone in mind to give her to?" And what would happen to Blue? Bella would be crushed if her kitten was taken away from her.

"Bella has always belonged to you," Jack said.

"Say what?"

"What I just said. Bella's yours. Always has been."

"You're a sly devil, brother." His happiness at hearing that surprised him. "What about while I'm gone?"

"We'll keep her at the kennels."

He hated having to send her back to a kennel, but he couldn't take her with him to Colorado or Montana. "You have to keep her kitten with her."

"Ah, no. Not at the kennels. That would drive the other dogs batshit crazy. I guess they'll have to stay here. Might have to keep them separated because of the cat." His gaze landed on Maggie May. "Although that one would probably love having a cat and will try to steal him away."

"I still haven't given you a final answer, yet you've got my life all organized."

"You'll be back."

"We'll see."

As Dallas drove back to the cabin, he was happy about a lot of things. Bella was his, and she and Blue would be taken care of until he returned. Yep, he was going to accept Jack's offer. The idea of working with horses and vets suffering from the atrocities of war excited him. He couldn't think of anything else that would give him so much satisfaction.

Although he'd meant to leave as soon as he ate the damn burger, Jack had reeled him in with his ideas of what he wanted for Operation Warriors Center. Dallas was in awe of his friend. Jack had started with Operation K-9 Brothers, simply training dogs to help veterans in need, and now he was building the foundation in ways that would help so many of their brothers and sisters.

He couldn't wait to talk about everything with Rachel.

The cabin was dark when he arrived. Had she already gone to bed? He walked inside and flipped the light switch on. Bella was there to greet him. Blue hopped across the floor with his back arched and his fur standing straight up as he eyed Bella's wagging tail.

Dallas laughed at the silly cat. Yes, he was happy. This beautiful dog that came with a crazy cat was his. He was excited about his new job, and he was sure—ninety-nine percent sure anyway—that he wasn't using Rachel as a crutch. He was falling in love with her. He was sure of it.

Apparently, she was asleep. Would she let him curl up behind her? He walked into the main bedroom, his heart sinking a little when she wasn't in the bed they'd shared. He headed to the other bedroom. She wasn't in there either, or the third one. His heart fell to his stomach.

He returned to their bedroom to see if her clothes were in the closet. A piece of paper on the pillow of his side of the bed caught his attention.

That white paper with blue ink words resting on his pillow shattered every bit of that happiness he'd walked into the cabin with. She was gone. He didn't have to read the words to know that, but his heavy steps took him to the note.

He picked up the paper, squeezed his eyes shut for a moment, then read her words.

Dallas,
I almost left without saying goodbye, but I couldn't without telling you some things. Maybe you don't want to hear this, but I love you. I do. The problem is, I don't want to, not if you can never love me back the way I need you to.

I can't be your crutch because I'm the only woman you can stand to touch you. I can't be your safety net. All I can ever be is the woman you love without reason. If I can be that for you, come find me. If you can't look me in the eyes and say that I'm that woman, forget you ever knew me.

Please take the time you need to discover what's in your heart. My wish for you is that you find happiness, even if that's not with me.
Rachel

Bella whined and nudged his leg. "Why did you let her go?"

If he left now, could he catch up with her before her flight departed? He read the letter again, then dropped it on the bed. She'd asked him to take time to discover what was in his heart, and for her, he would do that.

Chapter Twenty-Six

"It's been three weeks, and not a word from him," Rachel said. She heard Nichole's sigh over the phone. "I need to forget about him." Easier said than done. She knew, because she'd tried. She refused to ask if Nichole or Jack had talked to Dallas, but was he okay? Then she got mad at herself for worrying about him.

"All I know is that he spent time at an equine therapy for vets place, then went home to Montana," Nichole said. "Jack's been in touch with him, but my husband is infuriatingly mum on what they're talking about."

"You know what, I don't want to talk about him anymore." She was past tired of crying over a SEAL cowboy.

"Okay, let's forget about him. What's the latest Hollywood gossip? Who's secretly screwing who?"

Rachel laughed, and it felt really good to laugh. She told Nichole about a famous married actor who was cheating on his wife.

"No way! They look so happy."

"Well, that's Hollywood for you. Honestly, when I moved here and managed to get my foot in the door, I was in awe. I thought I'd found my place in the world. But the shine has worn off. I'm tired, Nick, of the fake smiles and the air kisses. The glitter isn't so shiny any-more."

"What do you want to do then?"

And wasn't that the million-dollar question? "I don't know." She just knew that after this movie was in the can, she was done.

"Why don't you come home?"

"And do what?" With Nichole being pregnant now, she'd love to be home. "How are you feeling? Any morning sickness?"

"No, not so far, and I can't tell you how happy that makes me."

"Any cravings yet?"

Nichole laughed. "Yeah, popcorn dipped in honey. I don't know why. One night Jack made a bowl of pop-corn, and I kept thinking how good that would be with honey. Now I have to have that every night."

"Okay, that's weird."

"Tell me about it. Jack just got home, so I'm going to let you go. I wish you were here, Rach, so I could give you a hug."

"Same, bestie. Same."

This movie was killing her. Some of the stunts were over-the-top, and they had required long meetings with her stunt coordinator, the director, and the famous ac-tress playing the part of the FBI profiler. The actress was a diva, but Rachel had worked with divas before, and refused to let the woman mess with her head when she ordered Rachel to make her look good. Never mind that she'd worked with Shayla on two other films and had made the woman look like a badass. She was so done with these people.

As often happened making a movie, everything ran past schedule. It was late when she got home, and she hadn't had dinner. Her stomach was eating itself. She stuck her head in her refrigerator to see what she had that could be eaten straight out of a carton while she listened to her messages.

One was from her grandmother asking when she could go back to the dude ranch with the hot cowboys. Dallas's family's dude ranch. Which made her think of Dallas, and she wasn't so fond of her grandmother for that. She'd call June later.

The next message was from Jack, asking her to call him when she got a minute. That was unexpected. She only ever had phone calls from his wife, never him. If he hadn't sounded so casual and added when she got a minute, she would have panicked, thinking something had happened to Nichole. She closed the refrigerator door, more curious as to why he was calling than her growling stomach.

"It's Rachel," she said when he answered. "What's up?"

"Wanted to offer you a job."

She wasn't expecting that. "Doing what?"

"You know I'm expanding Operation K-9 Brothers. The new foundation will be called Operation Warriors Center. You saw the cabins and lodge we're building. The intention is for vets who need our help adjusting to civilian life to have the opportunity to stay for a week or two with their families. Like I told you when you were here, I want to offer them a variety of activities. Things like rock wall climbing, trail hiking, overnight camping, stuff for their kids to do, and whatever else we can think of, and I need someone to head that up. Nichole told me you were getting disillusioned out there in La-La Land, and I think you'd be perfect for what I have in mind."

She was stunned. Even better than a job she thought she'd love, she could go home. There was just one problem. "It's really tempting, Jack, but there's one issue."

"Dallas?"

"Yeah. Is he coming to work for you? If so, I don't think—"

"Before you say no, take a few days and think it over. Don't let a dumb cowboy who can't get his head out of his ass keep you from something you want. Besides, things usually have a way of working out."

"Okay, I'll think about it." After she finished talking to him, she couldn't help wondering if he knew something she didn't. No, if he did, surely he would have said something. His offer did excite her. It would give her tremendous satisfaction to help people while doing things she loved.

She could climb a rock wall like a monkey, and hiking was one of her favorite activities. Ideas were already popping into her head. She could organize Saturday night talent contests, there were all kinds of fun field games kids would love, and... She laughed. Her mind was going a mile a minute. It beat crying over a cowboy, that was for sure.

The cowboy in question was the complication. Could she handle seeing Dallas every day? What if he showed up someday with a girlfriend? That would kill her. She'd probably have big boobies—fake ones, of course—and fat Botox lips. Okay, she was being ridiculous, but she wasn't feeling charitable toward him at the moment.

Was she willing to turn down a job she really wanted

because of him? She'd do as Jack asked and take some time to think about it. In the meantime, her stomach was demanding to be fed.

Dallas's honorable discharge from the Navy was official. It happened much sooner than he'd planned, but after what he'd gone through, it was time. He'd ended up spending two weeks in Colorado and was now sold on equine therapy. He couldn't wait to get the program up and running for Operation Warriors Center.

He'd be in Asheville right now if he hadn't felt the need to spend time with his family. Tomorrow, he was leaving. Since he was taking Lego with him and also wanted his truck in Asheville, he was driving. His father and siblings were supporting his decision, but his mother was not happy.

"Asheville is two thousand and ninety miles from here," his mother said, coming into the kitchen. "That's entirely too far away from your family."

"Google is not your friend, Mom." It was going to be a helluva drive towing a horse trailer. Not willing to risk leaving Lego unattended, he was planning to spend his nights sleeping in his truck in Walmart parking lots or at rest stops. He'd slept in worse places on deployments.

"Your family needs you here. The ranch needs you."

She wasn't going to give up, but he got it. She wanted her children near her where she could make sure they were safe and happy. When Shiloh had enlisted in the Coast Guard, then he in the Navy, she'd about had a meltdown.

"The ranch doesn't need me."

"How can you say that?" She refilled his coffee,

poured herself a cup, and then sat across from him. "Phoenix would love to have you work with him."

"*For* him, you mean." He reached across the table and put his hand over hers. "I promise I'll come back a couple of times a year, and you know you can visit whenever you want. I'm excited about this, Mom. What we're creating is going to help a lot of people who are important to me. Some of these men and women are struggling to fit back into civilian life. They're lost, and some decide they can't face another day."

Tears filled her eyes. "Approximately six thousand veterans a year make that decision. I know because I googled it. When you first came home after your ordeal, I was terrified you were going to be one of them."

Ah hell, she was killing him. "I'd never do that to you. That's a promise. I'm okay, really. The thing is, if I can help save one of those lives, how can I not be a part of what Jack is doing?" He'd told his family over dinner his first night home about his experience in Colorado and how amazing equine therapy was.

"I've never seen you so excited about something, son," his father had said. "I think it's going to be good for you."

He wasn't wrong.

"Well, I guess I better start planning a vacation." She pushed her chair back, then stood. "You make sure you find a house that's big enough for your family when we come."

"All of you at the same time?" Heaven help him.

That night, and as he did every night before going to sleep, and even though he had it memorized, he read Rachel's letter. He lingered over his favorite words. She loved him. It had been the hardest thing he'd ever done, but he hadn't tried to call her. When he talked to her, it would be in person. God, he missed her.

The next morning, he loaded Lego in the trailer. "We're going on an adventure, buddy." Lego snorted, telling Dallas he wasn't quite believing it if it involved a horse trailer. Once he had Lego loaded and settled, he walked over to his family. Every single one of them were there to see him off except for Shiloh. She'd called him last night, and they'd had a long talk. She thought what he was doing was awesome and promised to come see him and the operation when she could get leave.

"Take your time and drive safe." His father hugged him. "I love you, son."

Denver, Austin, and Phoenix took their turns giving him a hug and pats on the back.

"I just want you to be happy," Cheyenne said as she wrapped her arms around him.

"That's the intention."

"If you see June Denning, tell her she's welcome back anytime. She was a hoot."

"I will." He was sorry he'd missed meeting Rachel's grandmother.

His mother cried. "Are you sure this is what you want to do?"

"I'm sure. I love you, Mama mine," he whispered in her ear as she hugged him.

"You call every night when you stop so I know you weren't in an accident and laid up in a hospital somewhere. Google says there are four thousand incidents a year involving horse trailers. You better not become a statistic."

He glanced at his father and siblings. "Someone needs to put a child lock on her Google access."

"I did," Austin muttered. "She figured out how to unlock it."

When his mother wouldn't let go, he pried her arms from him. "I'm not going to be a statistic, but I'll call you every night when I stop." He kissed her cheek. "I love you."

After another round of hugs and goodbyes, he was finally on his way. Fifteen minutes later but still on Manning land, he stopped on the last rise before reaching the highway and got out of the truck.

He'd never told his family about his problem with being touched, and knowing they'd all want to give him a hug, he'd steeled himself not to cringe. Funny thing, though. He hadn't minded at all, and that was a welcome surprise. He still didn't like the idea of strangers touching him, but he was making progress. That was good. Damn good.

Except for his years in the Navy, he'd spent his life on this ranch, and as he turned in a circle, taking in the incredible views and his family's land, there was an ache in his heart that he was leaving. Grazing cattle dotted the landscape as far as he could see, in the far distance Phoenix's horses romped in their pastures, and over a hill and not visible was Cheyenne's dude ranch.

He loved this place to the bottom of his soul, but there was nothing here for him. Whether he was leaving for good or not, he didn't know, but he was excited about his future. Lego stuck his head out the trailer's open window and nickered.

"Ready to get going, huh?" He pulled a mint from his pocket. The mustang lipped the mint from his palm. "Let's get this show on the road." He scratched his horse's muzzle, then got back in the truck and drove away.

* * *

Five long and exhausting days later, Dallas pulled to a stop in front of the second cabin he'd shared with Rachel. Jack was letting him stay here until he found a place to live. He stared at the cabin for a minute, remembering the night he'd raced back here to find her gone. That had gutted him, and he never wanted to feel that kind of hurt again.

"As soon as I get things settled here, wildcat, I'm coming for you."

He called Jack to let him know he'd arrived, then unloaded Lego. After tying the halter line to the trailer, he carried his suitcases into the cabin. That done, he went back outside. "You ready to see your new home, buddy?" Lego nudged his pocket, wanting another mint. Dallas gave him one, then untied him and walked him over to the barn. He'd unload his saddles and tack later.

Knowing Dallas was bringing his horse with him, Jack and Noah had put a rush on getting the barn's foundation, walls, and roof finished to the specifications Dallas had given them before he left for Colorado. He walked his horse inside and looked around.

Only one stall was finished, and it had a gold plaque with Lego's name on it on the door. Dallas laughed as he led Lego to it. "Guess this is your new home. What do you think?" Lego stuck his head over the top of the door as if inspecting his new digs. Because the mustang had spent five days in a trailer except for the times he'd been walked, Dallas didn't want to coop the horse up yet. He took him out to the enclosed pasture, unhooked the line from the halter, and slapped Lego's rear end. "Go explore."

For a few minutes, he watched Lego, appreciating the beauty of a galloping horse. Gray with a black face, black mane, legs, and tail, Lego was a striking horse. There was a water trough near the gate, but it was empty. Dallas grinned at seeing the old-fashioned pump next to it. After filling the trough, he whistled. Lego spun around and raced to him.

Dallas flicked his hand through the water. "Thirsty?" Lego lowered his head and lapped up water. Hearing a vehicle approaching, Dallas recognized Jack's truck. "You hang out here for a bit while I talk to Jack."

"How was the trip?" Jack asked, coming up next to him.

"Long." He lifted a chin toward the barn. "I didn't expect you'd get this much done by the time I got back."

"Noah pushed the men hard to get the walls and roof up so he could have a stall ready for your horse." He eyed Lego. "I don't know anything about horses, but that one's a beauty."

"Yeah, he is. I've had him since he was weaned from his mama. My brother took care of him while I was away." There was something he'd thought about on the long drive from Butte. "Noah mentioned that he invested in the foundation."

"He did."

"I want to too." He wanted to feel like he was a true partner, not just an employee.

"Money's always welcome. How much you thinking?"

"How much you need?" When Jack raised his brows, Dallas couldn't stop his grin. "Let's just say whatever the amount is, you'd be hard pressed to scare me away."

"You telling me all those times you let me buy you a beer you were a rich-ass dude?"

"Something like that."

"Hmph. When you get settled, we'll sit down and talk numbers. We have sponsors, and I work every day to line up more, but we have big plans for this place. Even with the sponsors and what Noah and I have invested, money's tight."

"I can help ease the load." Considerably.

"Welcome aboard then." He raised his fist, and Dallas bumped his against Jack's. "I offered Rachel a job, by the way."

That got his attention. "Doing what, and did she accept?"

When Jack told him what he had in mind for Rachel, Dallas agreed that the job description was perfect for her. But would she walk away from making movies?

"She hasn't accepted yet. From what she told Nichole, she's not happy anymore out there in La-La Land and is ready for a change. She's interested in the job, but her reluctance is because of you."

Yeah, she wouldn't want to be around him if they weren't together. "Maybe I can overcome that reluctance."

"I'm counting on it."

Chapter Twenty-Seven

The stunt scheduled for today called for her to fall off a Jet Ski while being chased by the bad guy. After changing into a yellow bikini that matched the one the actress wore in the scene, Rachel went to the portable cabana where makeup was housed. Once a blond wig was secured to her own hair and makeup applied that made her look like Shayla, she headed to the Jet Skis parked near the ocean's edge.

She'd practiced the stunt over the past few days, and the biggest trick when she fell off was keeping her boobs inside her bathing suit top when she hit the water. Shayla had nixed Rachel's suggestion that a one piece would be more suitable for this scene.

There would be four boats with camera crews surrounding her and Jensen, the stunt double for the villain. They'd get film from the front, back, and sides. There would also be underwater cameramen waiting to film her when she fell off at the predetermined spot. The scene took place on the FBI profiler's day off, and to work off the stress of her job, she liked to take her Jet Ski out in the ocean.

Rachel walked into the water and mounted her Jet Ski as the grip held it for her, while another grip did the same for Jensen. Shayla had already shot her scene on the Jet Ski, up to the point where the serial killer appeared and the chase began.

"Catch me if you can," she yelled to Jensen over the sound of the waves, laughing as she took off. Once they were past the breakers, Jensen floated in place while she kept going. The director was in the boat in front of her, and because of the loud surf, the boats' motors, and the whine of the Jet Ski, they were using flags. As soon as she saw the green flag, signaling "Action", she became Glennis, the profiler out for a stress-relieving jaunt on her Jet Ski.

I should do this more often, Glennis thought, as she crested another swell. *When her fellow agents caught the son of a bitch serial killer targeting young girls, all blond like her sister had been, she was going to take a week off and spend every day on the ocean, the only place lately that gave her peace.*

A military helicopter flew over, and she watched it, looking over her shoulder as it passed her. Her gaze fell to another Jet Ski behind her, coming up fast. There was something about the way the rider was focused on her that set off alarm bells.

Her mind flashed to the warning this morning in her personal email. The sender had claimed to know she was profiling him...and yes, it was a man. She knew that because she was damn good at her job. With each profile she did, an image would form of what their unsub looked like, and her fellow agents claimed it was spooky how spot-on she usually was. In the email, he'd told her he was coming for her, and she knew, just knew, the man who'd killed seven—that they knew of—women was making good on his threat.

*She was a profiler, not a trained agent, and her heart
took a dive to her stomach as she wondered if this was
the day she was going to die. She glanced back again.
He was gaining on her. Nope, not dying today. She
twisted the throttle to full open. What should she do?
Get to the beach where there were people. He'd have
to back off then.*

*That would have worked if she hadn't stalled the Jet
Ski by accidently hitting the kill switch. By the time she
got it started again, he was close, too close, only a few
feet behind her and not slowing down. She turned the
throttle to the max, but she was too late. He rammed the
back of her Jet Ski, sending her flying into the water.
He circled around and aimed for her, trying to run over
her. She inhaled air into her lungs, then dived, kicking her feet hard.*

As choreographed, his Jet Ski barely missed hitting
her head. She came up behind him, and when she saw
the red flag on the lead boat, signaling filming had
stopped, she swam in place until Jensen returned and
stopped.

"Every time we do that one, I'm afraid I'm going to
bash your head in when I ride over you," he said after
she climbed on the back of his Jet Ski.

That comment sent her straight to thinking of a cowboy she'd been doing her best to forget.

Late the next afternoon, Bran, the stunt coordinator, told
her there was a change in the schedule. "Put the bikini
back on, then meet me by the Jet Skis."

"A retake? I thought we were good to go." Oh, well,
it wasn't the first time she'd thought a scene was in
the can, then had to do it again. She looked around.

"Where's Jensen and the makeup people?" The camera crew was set up, and the director was talking to her assistant, but Jensen was nowhere in sight.

"Just get the bathing suit on, Rachel."

Weird. She changed, then walked down to where Bran was standing by the Jet Skis. There was still no sign of Jensen, nor were there grips waiting to help get the skis in the ocean. And why didn't she need the wig and makeup?

"Okay, now what?"

"They want you to walk along the shoreline."

"And do what?"

He shrugged. "Just walk."

"That's not a stunt." There was something about the way his eyes darted around that made her suspicious. "What's going on?"

"We have a new investor, and he wants this scene changed. Money talks, so just walk, okay?"

"Whatever." If they wanted to pay her to walk, she'd walk. Seemed stupid, though.

"Not that way. The other way," he said when she started off down the beach.

She scowled, not liking the weirdness going on here. She turned around. "This is me walking the other way. Is there any particular way I'm supposed to walk for this stunt that's not a stunt?"

"Walk however you want."

So, she walked. In the direction they wanted her to. For no reason she could figure. No wonder she was tired of this life. Jack's job offer was an answer to her prayers. Well, it would be if she wouldn't have to see a certain cowboy every day. She didn't know if she could handle that.

How long was she supposed to walk? Until she disappeared over the horizon? She'd be good with that. Irritated with this stupid stunt and with being pretty sure Bran was hiding something, she lifted her feet high and stomped through the waves.

What in the world was that noise? It sounded like the pounding of horse hooves on the sand. There wasn't a horse anywhere in the script. She probably wasn't supposed to turn around, but she did anyway. The setting sun was in her eyes, making her squint. All she could make out was a huge black horse with a rider wearing a black cowboy hat racing at her.

The fool was going to run the horse right over her. If this was the new stunt, they damn well should have told her she really was going to die today. She glanced over at the cameras trained on her as they rolled, then to Bran—who was grinning at her—then to the director, who had a look of pure delight on her face.

"What's happening?" she screamed as the black-hatted rider reached her, and then she looked into the eyes of her SEAL cowboy. She laughed as he leaned over and scooped her up.

Laughing with her, Dallas dropped Rachel in front of him. "I caught myself a wildcat."

"Oh my God, how are you here?" She pressed her hand over her heart.

"I came for you." He pulled Raven—the horse he'd borrowed from someone Phoenix knew in LA—to a stop. "I love you," he blurted out.

"You do?"

"Absolutely, and I'm sorry I made you doubt that." He pressed his forehead against hers. "We'll talk about everything when we're not sitting on a horse with all those people watching us, but I need you to know one thing right now. I love you with everything I am, and then some."

She threw her arms around his neck. "That was the best stunt ever. Does this mean you'll be my cowboy and only my cowboy? That if I come to work for Jack, I'll never have to see you with some fake-boobies girlfriend?"

He snorted. "No fake-boobies girlfriend for me. If I can't have you, I'll just go and die a lonely old man when my time comes."

"You can have me," she said right before she slammed her lips against his.

"And that's a wrap, people!" the director yelled as Dallas rode into the sunset with his girl.

Epilogue

Jack stood on the wraparound porch of the center's lodge, his gaze sweeping over the grounds. Eight years ago, he'd had a dream to build a place where his brothers and sisters in arms and their families could come, a safe place where they could put aside their troubles for a week or two. Where they could meet others suffering the same and know they weren't alone. Where the only thing they needed to worry about was having fun.

It wasn't all fun. He'd brought Noah's head doc onboard, and she worked with the vets in group and single sessions while they were here. When needed, she counseled their families. Those who were here to get a dog were required to attend daily training sessions with the dog they'd go home with, and they had to keep their dog's kennel clean. Those who signed up for equine therapy had to clean stalls and groom horses. What continued to amaze him was how their guests stepped up and helped out when they saw something needing doing. It shouldn't though. These people wanted to feel useful.

The dogs, keeping their sponsors happy, and administrative duties were his responsibility. Dallas's equine therapy was a favorite of their guests, and his wife, Rachel, had proven to be one of his best hires. Their guests loved her, and she was always coming up with fun ideas to keep them entertained. The children especially loved acting in her plays.

Noah had taken over everything else, including building maintenance, anything to do with the lodge and cabins, the shooting range, and ran their landscape crew with the precision of a general. The grounds were beautiful. Jack didn't know what he'd do without him. Without any of them, actually.

"Daddy, watch!" yelled Jordan, his seven-year-old son.

"Wow, good job, buddy." He swallowed his laugh when Maggie May fell over backward. He assumed his son was trying to teach her to sit. Jordan had decided that Maggie May was his dog, and he was determined to teach her tricks. The dog was dumber than a brick, but neither Jordan nor Maggie May seemed to care. All that mattered was the two of them loved each other to distraction.

"Where's Cammie?"

"She's riding a pony. She's not really 'cause Mommy's holding her on the pony, but Mommy said we're letting her think she is."

"I see." His three-year-old daughter was as stubborn as they came. Cameron also thought she could do everything by herself.

The shouts from the kids playing T-ball caught his attention. He chuckled at seeing Rambo with their ball in his mouth. The kids were having more fun chasing him than actually playing. Deke, the game umpire, and Heather, the cheerleader for their son's team, were ignoring the kids in favor of kissing. Jack wished Nichole would find him. He'd like to be kissing her right now.

He lowered his hand to the top of Dakota's head. "You doing okay, girl?" She leaned against his leg. She was getting old, and he was going to cry like a baby when he lost her. But this wasn't a day to think about that.

Twice a year, in the spring and fall, they held a week-long open house. Many of their alumni returned for the festivities. Locals were welcome, Operation Warriors Center sponsors showed up, and best of all, friends and family came. It was a lot of work to organize what always ended up being controlled chaos, but those two weeks were his favorite. This week was their fall event, so the activities had been geared toward winter games.

"Your Grammie and Dirty Mary are telling my brothers dirty jokes," Dallas said as he walked up with Noah. Bella was glued to Dallas's leg. She wasn't fond of open house days. Too many strange people, too much noise, and she didn't like being away from her cat. She also didn't like being away from Dallas, so it was always a dilemma whether to come with him or stay home. Since Dallas always gave her a choice, she'd obviously decided to stick with him today. On non-open house days, it was quieter, and many times her cat would come with them. Blue loved the barn and horses, especially Dallas's horse, Lego.

Noah snorted. "Dirty Mary's also asking which one of them wants to date a cougar. She told them that once they got it on with a cougar, they'd be ruined for anyone else."

"They seem to be enjoying themselves," he said as he watched Dallas's brothers laughing their asses off.

Dallas chuckled. "Yeah, they love Dirty Mary."

A very pregnant Rachel, Nichole carrying a sleeping

Cammie, and Peyton joined them, each wife snuggling against her husband's side. Jack eased his daughter away from Nichole and held Cammie to his chest, inhaling her little-girl smell. She was growing up too fast. Before he knew it, he'd have to get the shotgun out to scare off a bunch of teenage boys. Yeah, he hadn't forgotten the things that ran through a boy's dirty little mind. Cammie could have supervised dates when she turned eighteen…maybe.

"Oh." Rachel took Dallas's hand and put it on her stomach. "Your daughter's been playing kick Mommy's tummy all day."

The expression on Dallas's face as he felt his baby kicking was pure happiness. This was their first, so it was all new to them, and even though he'd experienced it twice, Jack had the sudden desire to see Nichole with a rounded belly again. He glanced down at his wife, and his breath caught at the longing he saw in her eyes. She'd said only two, but from the way she was looking at Rachel's stomach, maybe he could talk her into one more. They could start trying tonight.

"You want to feel?" Rachel asked Peyton.

Peyton's eyes widened, and she actually took a step away. "No, that might be contagious."

"You're silly," Rachel said, laughing. "Being pregnant is not contagious."

Noah and Peyton didn't want kids, saying all they needed was each other. Jack thought they didn't know what they were missing, but he respected their decision.

"Where's Lucky?" he said, realizing he hadn't seen their dog for a while.

"He decided he wanted to hang with TG and June

for a while," Noah said. "Might be because that's where the food is. That dog loves to eat."

TG and June had become close friends over the years. TG's mother had walked out on him and his dad when he was a baby, and Jack thought June had become a kind of mother figure to the man. Not surprising, June and Dirty Mary had an ongoing game of trying to be the most outrageous. They were highly entertaining.

He eyed his brothers. "Remember that night in Kandahar when we were hunkered down trying to stay warm and we made predictions about what we'd be doing when we returned to civilian life?" He glanced at each of the wives, then his gaze slid over the grounds and what they'd accomplished. "None of us predicted this. That we'd each have a beautiful wife and a place we created that's helping so many of our people."

"Hooyah," Dallas said, holding up his fist.

Jack and Noah bumped their fists to his, the three of them saying "Hooyah" together.

Life was good, damn good.

* * * * *

Acknowledgments

This is my twentieth book and twenty times now that I've written an acknowledgment. I stared at a blank page trying to think of a new, clever beginning, one I've not written before. Then I realized I don't have to be clever; I just need to extend my heartfelt thank-you to the people in my life who are there for me. Some I know personally, and some I've never met but are no less important.

So, let's get to it.

To the fans of my books…without you I wouldn't be writing this because there wouldn't be any books from me without you. Thank you for your support, for your reviews, and for your emails telling me how much you love a book or character. I'll even thank you for your impatience for the next book. Some of us are friends on various social media sites, and on my bucket list is that someday I get to meet you.

And then there are Sandra's Rowdies, my Facebook reader group. OMG, you guys… I don't even know how to tell you how much you mean to me. You have earned the name Rowdies, so be proud of it. I swear, y'all make me laugh so hard. Rowdies Rule! I seriously love you!

I've met a lot of authors and many of those amazing

people are friends, but to Jenny Holiday, Miranda Liasson, and AE Jones, I love to the bottom of my heart how we are there for each other during the ups and downs. Our emails, phone calls, Zoom chats, and FaceTimes mean everything to me. Love you all!

I want to say a very special thank you to Kerri Buckley and Deborah Nemeth. Thank you both so much for making my Carina Press experience just awesome. I hope for many more years of working together.

Courtney Miller-Callihan, author agent extraordinaire, what an amazing journey we've had. Let's keep it going, okay?

To my family, I love you bunches! Thank you for believing in me.

About the Author

Bestselling, award-winning author Sandra Owens lives in the beautiful Blue Ridge Mountains of North Carolina. Her family and friends often question her sanity but have ceased being surprised by what she might get up to next. She's jumped out of a plane, flown in an aerobatic plane while the pilot performed death-defying stunts, gotten into laser gun fights in Air Combat, and ridden a Harley motorcycle for years. She regrets nothing.

Sandra is a Romance Writers of America Honor Roll member and a 2013 Golden Heart Finalist for her contemporary romance *Crazy for Her*. In addition to her contemporary romance and romantic suspense novels, she writes Regency stories. Her books have won many awards including The Readers' Choice and The Golden Quill.

To find out about other books by Sandra Owens or to be alerted to cover reveals, new releases, and other fun stuff, sign up for her newsletter at bit.ly/2FVUPKS.

Join Sandra's Facebook Reader Group… Sandra's Rowdies: facebook.com/groups/1827166257533001/

Website: sandra-owens.com
Connect with Sandra:
Facebook: bit.ly/2ruKKPl
Twitter: twitter.com/SandyOwens1

Discovering that her fiancé is only marrying her to gain control of her family's brewery, Peyton Sutton's "I do" turns into a hard pass, but he won't take no for an answer. The last thing Navy SEAL Noah Alba expects to find while on leave in the Blue Ridge Mountains is a runaway bride in need of a bodyguard. Peyton can't outrun her ex, Noah can't outrun his past, and protecting her is no way to avoid a simmering attraction...

Keep reading for an excerpt from book two in the Operation K-9 Brothers series,
Keeping Guard *by Sandra Owens!*

Chapter One

"He's a stray someone tied to our gate a few nights ago."

Noah Alba, Double D—or sometimes just DD— to his SEAL teammates, stared at the fifty pounds of wiggling animal. "Are you sure it's actually a dog?"

The thing looked more like something put together all wrong. Wiry fur stuck up and out at odd angles and had to be about a dozen different colors. There was more fur on his furiously wagging tail than on its body. The oddest parts of the animal were the two different colored eyes, one blue and one brown. There was intelligence in those odd eyes, though, an alertness that Noah liked.

His friend and former teammate laughed. "Actually, no."

A year ago, Jack Daniels—Whiskey to the team— and his dog had come home to Asheville, North Carolina. When he learned that his arm and shoulder were permanently damaged, he'd started Operation K-9 Brothers to train therapy dogs to be companions to their military brothers and sisters who were suffering from PTSD.

Noah was both proud and impressed with what his friend had accomplished, but the last thing he wanted was to be around people and dogs. Former teammate included. The only reason he didn't do a vanishing act was because his commander had ordered him here. If he left, he'd be AWOL. He'd fucked up his life enough without getting charged with a serious crime.

"He's yours to work with while you're here," Jack said.

"Oh, hell no." The last dog he'd been around was dead because of him.

Jack put his hand on Noah's shoulder. "Yes, and that's an order, DD."

Noah pressed his lips together to keep from telling him what he could do with his order and the dog. What had his commander been thinking by sending him here, and not only that, but also ordering him to report directly to Whiskey? Hell, Jack wasn't even in the Navy anymore.

"You'll work with me every day on training him while you're here. You also need to give him a name."

The ever-simmering rage inside him burned hotter. "You're making a mistake trusting me with a dog."

"I disagree."

Noah slipped his hand into the pocket of his jeans, his fingers wrapping around the pair of dice he always carried. They'd belonged to his father, a reminder of everything he refused to be. All he had to do to remind himself that he was not his father was to touch the pair of dice. Throughout his life, he'd touched them thousands of times, and it always worked, always led him to find the calm in his soul that made him not his father. To be the kind of man his mother would have been proud of.

For the first time since he was a boy, his rage didn't go from boiling over back to simmering when he touched them. "I need to go somewhere for a while."

"Take the dog with you."

Noah hated the knowing look in Jack's eyes, like his friend knew he was losing it and understood. Maybe he did. Jack had appeared three nights ago at their home base in Virginia Beach, announcing that he was taking Noah home with him. Noah had told him to go to hell.

"You have two choices," Jack had answered. "Come with me or tell our commander you refused to obey an order. Makes no never mind to me which you pick."

Noah knew his friend and teammate was there to save him, and that made him antsy. He didn't want to need saving, had never expected to be the one his SEAL brothers had to worry about. He had his shit together. Nothing could be as bad as what his boy-self had survived, right? Or so he'd thought until his mistake caused the team's dog and their translator to be blown up.

Noah took the dog with him…as far as his temporary apartment. The ants weren't just crawling under his skin, they were biting. He couldn't be near a dog right now. Every time he looked at the thing, he saw his team's dog.

After giving the dog time to do his business, Noah took him inside. "Here's the thing, dog. I don't own this place, so don't chew on the furniture or pee on the floor." Unable to think of anything else the dog needed to know, he left the creature to his own devices.

He ended up on the Blue Ridge Parkway, his rental car pointed in the direction of the waterfall Jack had taken him to yesterday. After hiking down to the bottom of the falls, Jack had said, "This is a good place to come when you feel like you're about to lose your shit."

He'd glanced around. "If you let it, you can find a few moments of peace here."

"Speaking from experience?" Noah had asked.

"I've spent quiet time here, especially after I first came home." He smiled. "Before I met Nichole."

That was another thing. Jack had gone and fallen in love. Noah never thought he'd see Whiskey look at a woman with sappy eyes. Nichole was great, and she'd even seemed disappointed when Noah said he was going to find an apartment to rent while he was here.

He didn't think Jack was happy about that, either—he'd prefer to have him where he could keep an eye on him. Understandable, since Noah had been falling down drunk when Jack arrived to collect him.

After Noah swore there'd be no repeat performance—all the booze he'd poured down his throat hadn't wiped his memory clean, anyway—Jack helped him find a lease-by-the-month place. He'd moved in right away, grateful that he hadn't had to sit around with Jack and Nichole last night and pretend he was enjoying himself.

If Noah had to be around people twenty-four-seven, he was going to climb out of his skin.

Peyton Sutton wasn't supposed to hear her fiancé telling his best man that he was only marrying her because her father had promised him a share of her family's brewery. The share that was supposed to be hers.

The rat bastard. She'd only overheard the conversation because she'd gotten last-minute cold feet and wanted to talk to Dalton, needed him to assure her that they were both ready for a lifelong commitment. Turned out he was more committed to her father than to her.

After she graduated from college, her father had dangled a carrot in front of her. Do this and a share in the company will be yours one day. Do that and the entire company will be yours one day. She'd jumped through hoops doing this and that, trying to please him. Like saying yes when Dalton asked her to marry him. Dalton was Elk Antler Brewery's chief financial officer, the son her father had always wanted, and marrying Dalton would make Gerald Sutton happy with her.

Well, to hell with both of them.

She gathered up the skirts of the princess wedding gown she'd grown to hate. She was done with trying to please her father.

From the time he'd let her hang out at Elk Antler Brewery, she'd been fascinated by the process of making beer. She'd been thirteen the first time he'd brought her there, pointing at the corner where she could do her homework. It was supposed to be punishment for not getting a perfect score on her math test.

That day had been far from punishment and set the course of her life. She spent her afternoons at the downtown brewery, supposedly doing her homework, but anytime her father was in a meeting or out of the building, she was learning how to make beer instead. Her father's brewmaster had taken a liking to her, and over the years he'd shared his knowledge, his love of brewing, and his recipes. She could step into his shoes and no one would notice.

She'd returned home with degrees in business and marketing and went to work for her father. Pleasing him was impossible—even with bringing in more business with tours and events—but she'd kept trying anyway.

Until today.

She was over it. He'd made her a promise that he obviously had no intention of keeping. The long hours she'd put in, the heart she put into the brewery, the jumping through hoops for him apparently meant nothing.

"Where is she?"

Peyton stilled at hearing her father's voice. If he found her, he'd convince her to go through with the wedding.

With the voluminous skirts of the gown gathered up, she headed in the opposite direction. She didn't have a plan since it hadn't for a minute occurred to her that she'd sneak out on her own wedding.

Three hundred and twenty-nine guests were seated in the country club ballroom waiting for her to walk down the aisle in a matter of minutes. They were sure going to be in for a surprise when the bride didn't appear. Avoiding the ballroom, she scooted into the banquet hall. The staff setting up for the reception all stopped what they were doing to stare at her. She nodded at the bartender, snatched two bottles of champagne, and almost laughed at his wide eyes.

"You never saw me," she tossed over her shoulder as she headed for the door leading to the parking lot. She should be in tears, crushed, heartbroken…blah, blah, blah. Weirdly, what she felt was free.

Outside, she paused for a moment, and as she breathed in the pine-scented mountain air, the heavy weight that had settled on her shoulders ever since Dalton had put an engagement ring on her finger lifted, carried away by the breeze. As much as she wanted to luxuriate in the feeling of freedom, she needed to go before someone found her. But where to?

Her car wasn't here since she'd arrived with her father in the limo he'd rented. She spied Dalton's silver

Mercedes parked near the main entrance and headed for it. Wasn't her fault he'd once shown her where he'd hidden a spare key remote.

She cringed at the Just Married someone had written on the rear window with white shoe polish. Couldn't be helped. She needed a getaway car, and Dalton's was her only choice. After retrieving the key, she unlocked the door, got in, put the champagne bottles on the passenger seat, and then spent minutes she didn't have getting the skirts of the stupid gown inside so she could close the door.

The next time she planned to get married, she was wearing one of those slip wedding dresses. Much easier to escape in if need be. She glanced in the rearview mirror, saw her father and Dalton walk out of the building, and hauled ass.

With no direction in mind, she drove around, and at the entrance to the Blue Ridge Parkway, turned on her blinker. What she really wanted to do was go home, get out of this ridiculous dress, put on her jammies, and then plow her way through the champagne.

Or go to the brewery and make beer. Getting lost in recipes, that was her peace place. Where all her troubles floated away. But she couldn't do either of those things. Home and the brewery were the first places her father and Dalton would look.

She needed to find somewhere she could think, make a plan for where she'd go from here. After her stunt today, she doubted her father would welcome her back to the place she loved above all else. Oh, he probably would if she went back and married Dalton, but that was so not happening.

Peyton blinked away the tears that threatened at the

thought of never setting food in Elk Antler Brewery again, tears from losing something she loved…and that was not Dalton. Not good to bawl her eyes out while driving. Along with a place to consider her future, she needed somewhere she could have a good cry in private.

After driving along the Parkway for a while, she saw a sign announcing a waterfall. No other cars were in sight in the parking lot, and she decided it was the perfect place.

She parked in the lot, grabbed the two bottles of champagne, then headed for the trail. She stopped and eyed the steep path down. No way was she going to manage that wearing white satin heels without falling and breaking her neck. She kicked them off. The sheer white stockings the bridal shop consultant said she had to wear soon followed. They were her first ever stockings, and she hated them as much as the dress.

Even barefoot, going down was tricky in a gown consisting of more material than all the clothes in her closet put together. A squirrel clinging upside down to a tall pine tree chattered at her as she passed. "Yeah, yeah, I'm not having a good day, either."

She almost slipped when she stepped on a mossy rock, and, forgetting she had a champagne bottle in her hand, she grabbed hold of a rhododendron branch. The bottle rolled and bounced down the trail. Thankfully, it didn't break. She needed that champagne.

"Well, that wasn't a piece of cake," she muttered after finally making it to the waterfall with both bottles intact. Speaking of cake, she should have snatched some of her wedding cake while she was at it since she hadn't eaten anything all day because her stomach had been in knots.

The dress her father had paid a small fortune for was torn and dirt streaked. He wasn't going to be happy about that, but she wasn't happy with him, either, so they were even. She headed for a boulder with a flat surface. She tried to climb up it, but that proved impossible when wearing a million yards of…whatever the dress was made of. Fashion and fabrics weren't her thing. Clothes were a necessity, something she had to put on before she could appear in public. And right now, there was no public, and she wanted on top of that boulder. She deserved to be up there after knowing her actions would cost her the only thing that mattered to her.

So…it was a struggle, but she finally got the hated gown off. Irritated with the stupid thing, she tossed it to the side with more force than she'd intended.

It tumbled down the embankment, landing in the waterfall pool.

"Oops." Who knew a dress that heavy could travel so far?

Free of the gown, she climbed up to the top of the boulder, giving thanks that it wasn't winter, when she'd be freezing her bottom off wearing only a sexy white corset that she *had* wanted to wear. She'd imagined that Dalton would finally look at her with desire in his eyes when he saw her in it, spicing up their sex life.

Although brewing beer and creating events that brought beer lovers to Elk Antler Brewery was her jam—or had been—she wanted to experience how it felt to be truly wanted by someone.

She was, as far as she'd gathered, the result of a one-night stand between her parents. The mother she only vaguely remembered had dropped her off at her father's when Peyton was four years old, then had disappeared from her life. Her father had kept her, but she'd never been sure he'd been happy to have her. That uncertainty was the reason she'd spent her life until now trying to please him…so he wouldn't give her away like her mother had.

All good reasons why the champagne should go straight down her throat. She managed to pop the cork on one of the bottles. The cork shot up before arcing and falling into the pool to join her wedding gown.

"Cheers to me." She lifted the bottle to her mouth as tears rolled down her cheeks for what she'd lost today.

Don't miss Keeping Guard *by Sandra Owens, book two in the Operation K-9 Brothers series, available now.*

www.CarinaPress.com

Also available from Sandra Owens
Just Jenny
Winner of the Readers' Choice Award

The small mountain town of Blue Ridge Valley is the home of three best friends, Jenny, Autumn, and Savannah. Each woman believes she has her life perfectly planned, but there is a saying in the mountains… If everything is coming your way, you're in the wrong lane.

Jenny Nance has a plan—save enough money to tour the world. The desire to traipse the globe is a dream she once shared with her twin sister. Jenny made a deathbed promise to her sister that she would go to all the places they had fantasized visiting together. Nothing will entice her to break her vow to Natalie, not even the sexy new Blue Ridge Valley police chief… No matter how attracted she is to him.

Dylan Conrad left the Chicago Police Department to accept the position as Chief of Police in Blue Ridge Valley. Burned out and haunted by a tragedy of his own, he needs to get away from the memories tormenting him. He's hoping to find peace in the small mountain town, but the quirky residents, an infamous moonshiner, an errant prized bull, and a feisty redhead by the name of Jenny weren't quite what he had in mind.

Love Harlequin romance?

DISCOVER.

Be the first to find out about promotions, news and exclusive content!

Facebook.com/HarlequinBooks

Twitter.com/HarlequinBooks

Instagram.com/HarlequinBooks

Pinterest.com/HarlequinBooks

YouTube.com/HarlequinBooks

ReaderService.com

EXPLORE.

Sign up for the Harlequin e-newsletter and download a free book from any series at **TryHarlequin.com**

CONNECT.

Join our Harlequin community to share your thoughts and connect with other romance readers!
Facebook.com/groups/HarlequinConnection

HARLEQUIN

Heartfelt or thrilling, passionate or uplifting—Harlequin is more than just happily-ever-after.

With twelve different series to choose from and new books available every month, you are sure to find stories that will move you, uplift you, inspire and delight you.

SIGN UP FOR THE HARLEQUIN NEWSLETTER

Be the first to hear about great new reads and exciting offers!

Harlequin.com/newsletters